On A Cloudy Day

IMANI LEWIS

Dedicated to my mother for her never ending support, my brother for making sure I make a book that is good enough for me to read, and my wonderful fiancé for making sure this book got completed and that I never gave up even if I wanted to.

dream
/drēm/

noun

noun: **dream**; plural noun: **dreams**

a series of thoughts, images, and sensations
occurring in a person's mind during sleep.

a cherished aspiration, ambition, or ideal

verb

experience dreams during sleep.

PROLOGUE

Lifted.

Floating.

Ascending towards the sky.

I feel almost weightless as my body glides upwards. I look around me to try and figure out where I am but there's nothing. Darkness and what appear to be stars is all I see around me.

I try to reach my hand out to touch one, but I can't move. I look towards the force that's pulling me up, and I'm met with nothing but a bright light. It's like I'm being pulled into the sun, but the heat is subtle, and I can barely feel it.

My arms and legs are dangling at my sides, making my body form an upside-down U. My hair is flowing around my face as if it's in space defying gravity.

As I get closer to the star, I must squint to keep from going temporarily blind, but it doesn't help as I'm pulled into the stars embrace like a warm gentle hug. I close my eyes, succumbing to the feeling pulsating through me, like a crackling of energy zapping through my veins. I hear the star softly whisper my name, caressing my ear drums with its soft voice.

Jordan, it says once.

Jordan.

It sounds like it's coming from everywhere and nowhere at the same time.

Jordan! it says more harshly, and I snap my eyes open as the star I'm floating in starts to shake.

Pieces of its barrier begin to break off like puzzles, giving me a peak of the starry abyss I traveled through to get here. Panic starts to flicker in my lower stomach as I watch the gentle euphoria I bathed in, dim its light and come crashing down.

JORDAN

"JORDAN!" I shoot out of my sleep and collide my head with something hard and huge. "Ow! What the hell !?" I hear someone say in the fuzzy space beside me.

I rub my forehead, then eyes, as I try to gain consciousness and clear the sleep out of my eyes. Focusing on my surroundings, I see that I'm in my childhood bedroom. I take in my Tame Impala poster over my desk next to the dry erase board emphasizing the importance of today's date.

MOVE IN DAY.

"Really Jordan? I wake you up early like you asked, and you thank me by trying to crack my skull open?"

I look to my right and see Rylie lying on the floor massaging the spot where my forehead collided with hers. I try to stifle my laughter while looking at my best friend, but it overtakes me and I plop back on my bed, almost coughing up a lung. I peak over at her and notice her frown was replaced with a smile and she starts laughing too.

"I see you managed to successfully wake the hibernating bear," I hear my stepdad Benny, short for Benjamin, call on the other side of the door. I roll my eyes gently as my laughter starts to die down.

Don't get me wrong, I love Benny, but sometimes I think he forgets that I'm 20 and not 2. Or maybe, he's trying to make up for the time he wasn't in my life from the ages of newborn to 10. Either way, his intentions are pure, so I let it slide and humor him sometimes.

I pull the covers up over my head trying to see if I can disappear back into my peaceful slumber by shutting reality out.

"Don't make me bring Ben in here to sing his wake-up song to you," Rylie says to my right. I guess my experiment didn't work.

I groan loudly and finally raise back up and eventually out of my bed. I stretch as I watch Ry grab a few unfolded boxes from my closet. "Hurry up and get your moving clothes and attitude together, we need to beat this move in day traffic."

"Why are you so gung-ho about moving? Last week you almost cried about having to leave your hamster for another year," I snort as I make my way to the same closet she pulled boxes from to find my go-to chill outfit.

"Well, last week Theodore didn't shit in my hand as I tried to tell him I loved him. Besides, my mom started getting on my nerves about the whole 'hurry up and secure an internship' fiasco and I am in desperate need of release from her overbearing grasps."

I change into some Nike workout leggings and a cream-colored oversized hoodie that had the initials CAU on the front. Slipping my feet into some white, black and red Air Max 95s, I grab the last of the boxes from the closet and toss them into the pile Rylie created in the middle of my room.

"You know your mom just wants the best for you. She's trying to make sure you're set in life," I shrug as I move towards my desk and start to pack up my essentials. She groans, "why do you sound just like her?"

"We might've had a few secret meetings behind your back," I say playfully winking at her, "Now start packing. I know you didn't wake me up just to watch."

"Ah, my plan is foiled." We both laugh and start to work on packing up my room.

About 3 hours later, we finish putting everything I need into boxes and head downstairs. I see my mom working on breakfast for all of us in the beautiful open spaced kitchen.

Our kitchen is something you'd see on HGTV and is used as inspiration when you want to renovate your house. We have a huge island in the middle with white quartz countertops and cream-colored cabinets. Along the front side of the island we had 4 barstools and placemats we only set out as decoration. Our dishwasher was next to our stove and blended in with the cabinets, so you couldn't even tell it was a dishwasher. Our refrigerator was the same way and had so much space, you could fit two dead bodies in there. You know, if you wanted to at least.

My mom was at the stove flipping pancakes and adding them to the leaning tower of cakes on the plate to the right of her. Benny oversaw the fruit cutting for our homemade fruit cups. I think he chooses this job just so he can slip and eat some of the fruit as he cuts. I wouldn't even put it past him if that was the case. I also know that he sneaks my little brother, Jamie, some grapes to keep him sedated and from jumping all over the counters. He was only two, but this little boy was a firecracker. He was also the love of my life and takes up all the space in my heart currently. Not like anyone else would ever be able to anyway.

"Morning Mom," I say as I kiss her cheek. She smiles and scrunches up her nose in response. My mom was so cute with her little antics and sweet spirit. It hurts me whenever I see her hurting or in pain, both physically and emotionally.

"Morning my Jor. Morning to you too Ryles," she says air kissing towards Rylie and quickly turning back to the pancake tower to concentrate as she tries to add another pancake to the top.

I saunter over to Jamie and play peek-a-boo with him behind Benny's back. He was sitting on the counter next to Ben, with his little feet hanging off the side of the island. He laughs a hearty laugh that melts my insides even more than he already did.

"Morning Buu," I say as I stop playing peek-a-boo and walk up to poke his belly.

He got the nickname Buu because when he was a baby, he was so chubby with a lot of rolls that he reminded me of a milk chocolate colored Majin Buu.

"Jo-Jor! Jo-Jor!" I smile at his nickname for me and kiss his forehead. "Yuckie!" he says as he tries to wipe my kiss off.

"Uh-uh Buu, my love is forever. Sorry," I poke his nose then go take a seat on one of the barstools.

Rylie has already made herself comfortable on her unassigned-assigned barstool seat that's been "hers" since she and I have been friends.

That's about 18 years.

Now, she's munching on some bacon from the bacon platter my mom laid out on the island, next to the scrambled egg platter and syrup cup.

"Okay girls, after breakfast we're heading straight to the school. Move in starts at 8, so we only have 30 minutes to get it movin'," Ben says this as he gyrates his hips and I cringe so hard it hurts.

"Uncle Ben please stop," Ry says as she puts her head into her hands from secondhand embarrassment.

Once they finish preparing breakfast, we all move to the dining table in the dining room to the left of the kitchen. We eat as we talk about the long day we have ahead of us. My mom jokes about Jamie being old enough to help carry the boxes up to my dorm, and Benny countered by saying Jamie could drive the car there and do all the work while we go to the movies.

After Rylie finishes her third helping, we decide to just drag her away from the food because we were going to be late. She snuck a couple more pieces of bacon and reluctantly followed behind us. We got to the school and sure enough, it was packed.

This was my third year in college, and I attended Clark Atlanta University. It was one of the big three alongside Spelman and Morehouse. My mom was a Spelman Alumni and when I told her which college I chose; she was excited for me to experience the culture. My stepdad Ben, however, was from Florida, so he went to the University of Miami and still wasn't used to the downtown Atlanta college life.

As we arrive to the school, we see police officers directing traffic and a whole bunch of golf carts that the housing employees use to get around during this hectic time. First order of business was to figure out which room me and Rylie would be in this year.

We packed up her room a couple of days ago and already loaded it into my mom's Audi SUV. She stayed the night at my place the rest of the time. We roomed together the past couple of years and stayed in a traditionally styled dorm room. It was a great experience, but we both needed more space, so we applied for an apartment style this year. We applied last year too, but they gave them all to the upperclassmen.

I was driving my mom's car and my mom, Benny, and Jamie were in Ben's car following behind me. I finally pull into the housing office parking lot after waiting in a little traffic from all the families in attendance and new freshman.

"Maybe I'll finally find a man this year, cross fingers," Rylie says as she looks out the window at the new students she doesn't recognize. I shake my head at her, "You don't need a man when you have me," I chuckle as I put the car in park towards the back of the lot.

"Last time I checked, you couldn't make the inside of my thighs quiver, and If you could, I would've been elevated this relationship years ago."

"I could easily do that with a little help from some toy- "

"OKAY! This conversation is over," Rylie sing-songs while opening her car door and hopping out.

"Alright Jo-bear, Ry-Tie, you ready to get this show on the road?" Ben walks from his parking spot a couple cars away and meets us at mom's Audi.

"Uncle Ben, we're on school grounds, I am now a stranger to you," Rylie says as she puts on her shades. Ben laughs and starts walking towards the housing building. He notices my curious look as I search behind him for my mom and Jamie.

"Jamie fell asleep and your mom didn't want to wake him because he, quote 'looks too adorable right now' unquote, so she'll join us for the fun part." I'm not at all disappointed by this because I knew Jamie would become agitated from standing still in a line for too long and would want to explore. He's just like me in that aspect, wanting to dabble in any and everything that seems interesting; ready to discover a world anew. Let's just hope he isn't *fully* like me and has an idea of what he wants to do with his life.

"Uncle Ben, nobody verbally says quote like that anymore," Rylie says shaking her head and laughing. As we enter the housing line, Ben cocks his head at her seeming genuinely confused and says, "I'm sorry stranger, do I know you?"

"Ha Ha," she retorts sarcastically and lightly punches his arm. We move forward in line and we're almost to the front desk.

"I hope they gave us the apartment style we requested," I turn my head toward Ry.

"If they don't want a call from an angry black woman they better had," she scrunches her eyebrows together trying to look intimidating.

I gasp suddenly. "What if we have suite style? How would we fit your inflated ego?" I place my hand over my mouth. After a beat, I bust out laughing and she rolls her eyes.

"I don't have time for you guys today. I don't want to embarrass myself in front of my unknown future husband."

We get to the desk and find out we got granted the last available apartment unit and we almost scream from excitement. We get the keys and they tell us the move-in instructions, but I'm too busy planning out the many ways I'm going to rearrange my room this school year.

Back at Bens Audi coupe (yea this family lives for the Audi brand), we meet up with my Mom and relay the information to her. Next thing I know, we're at the Heritage Building unloading the truck into our apartment. We're on the second floor so it's not that bad of a move.

Some of the housing employees help us move in, and I learned from the disaster that was move in day last year, that the earlier you are, the more people that are here to help and the faster the job gets done. This is because everyone is pumped up on adrenaline, and the caffeine they consumed that morning in preparation for today.

Two guys named Zavier and Jodie help us move in, and I can tell Rylie already has her eyes set on at least one of them. I, on the other hand, am trying to get my hands on the nearest home goods so I can decorate our living space and cover up the ugliness of the pre-given furniture in the apartment. Jamie is in our living area playing his educational games on his iPad, while my mom unpacks me and Rylie's boxes and takes them to our respective rooms.

Before I know it, we've unpacked everything and took a trip to Home Goods, Target, Hobby Lobby and Walmart.

"Wow, we did a good job," My Mom says as she places both hands on her hip and glances around.

"Goo-Job!" Jamie says as he jumps up excited trying to give me a high five.

"Yes Buu, Good Job," I say high fiving him.

"Well I'm pooped," Rylie says plopping down on the couch in the living area.

"Want to go out to eat to celebrate?" Ben asks us after placing the last Gatorade we bought in the fridge.

"No thanks Uncle Ben, we're going to order some pizza like last year. You know, tradition and all that good stuff," Rylie says waving her hand in the air.

"Pizza! Pizza!" Jamie says as his eyes almost bulge out of his sockets.

"Welp, looks like we have to order pizza tonight now too," my mom chuckles as she looks at Jamie with adoration in her eyes. I look around the room and smile at my unconventional family. Rylie's parents are a part of that family too, but they had to go to a wedding in New York and couldn't make it to the move in day. Rylie was excited to find that out because she did not want her mom in here questioning everyone about on campus job opportunities, the curfew policy, and asking students if they needed an extra study buddy.

Rylie's mom was a lot to handle, which is why I'm surprised her and my mom became best friends in the first place. My mom is the calm serene breeze and Rylie's mom is the storm that comes to blow your house into a dimension with little singing dwarfs. Her Dad is like my mom, chill and laid back, but he also is hilarious and knows how to have fun. Oh, and he's a sucker when it comes to his "little girl Ry Ry". Rylie claims she's annoyed by this nickname, but I know deep down she loves it.

My other best friend, Camille, and her grandmother were also missing. This was because Camille always worked nonstop and barely even had time for herself.

"Okay girls, we'll leave you to it. Come give me a hug," my mom says smiling with her eyes gleaming and I can already see the tears forming.

Me and Ry give my mom a hug and as she hugs us, she says, "I am so proud of you guys, and I know you're destined to do great things, so I am never worried about you. Though I am worried about the actual journey you'll take and the ups and downs I can't prevent. Just never forget to breathe okay?" I feel the tears from her eyes start to run down the side of my face and I pull back to look at her.

"I love you mom."

I wasn't a crier, in fact, I felt like crying didn't do anything but make me look weak and affected. I rarely cried in public or even private.

I hear Rylie trying to suppress a sob, so I pull her away from my mom and try to get her to gather herself. "Okay, I'll call your mom when I get in the car Rylie, to let her know how the move in day went. Make sure you text her too because you know how worrisome she can be."

"I know Auntie, I will. I love you too," Ry says wiping her eyes.

"Alright love bugs bring it in," Ben says as he gathers everyone into another hug. "You get in here too booger!" he says too a trouble making Jamie, already trying to get into some cabinets.

Jamie runs over and crashes into my leg and I laugh as we're all connected in a big group hug. After a few seconds we reluctantly let go and my family leaves.

"Then there was two," I say as I turn from the closed front door of our apartment, "Please tell me you already started up your Papa John's app. I'm in need of some greasy fattening food right now."

"One Alfredo Spinach for you and one Buffalo Chicken for me," Rylie says towards me, but her face is looking down at her phone screen. I can't hide the huge smile on my face as I think about the amazingness I'm about to gobble down in about 50 minutes.

"Have I ever told you I loved you?" I ask her, plotting down on the couch next to her.

"Only like a gazillion times, but it doesn't hurt to say it one more," she winks at me.

For the next couple hours, we eat our pizza while binge watching The Office for the 100th time because how can you ever get tired of The Office?

I look over at the clock and notice it's 2:00am and turn to a snoring Rylie. She's sprawled out, with the blanket hanging off the lower half of her body. She's laying on the couch next to the accent chair I moved too when the pizza arrived.

I turn off the TV and pull her blanket up to cover her whole body, then throw away all the trash we have on the coffee table. I put our leftovers in the fridge then go to my room so I can crash.

As I snuggle into my bed, I give a relaxed sigh and silent prayer that this school year flies by smoothly as I slowly ease into that peaceful abyss that is sleep.

MALAKAI

Still.

Motionless.

Quiet.

I raise my head from my hands as I take in my surroundings.

It's a blanket of white cushion looking fluff. It's almost like I'm sitting on a cloud.

It's so warm here.

I look to where I'm sitting and notice I'm on a stone bench, kind of like one you would see in the Hercules or the 300 movie. I'm wearing the clothes I must've fell asleep in and my skin is glowing just a bit, like it's concealing some type of cosmic energy.

Where am I?

I look around more and notice that the white cotton candy looking fluff goes on forever like it has no end. Didn't I have this dream before? Yes. I've had a similar dream, but I wasn't sitting on a bench in them with my arms resting on my knees, and it didn't start off with my head in my hands.

In the other dream I was in this cloud looking world, but I was walking like I knew where I was going. Like I had a set destination. Is there anyone else here? Should I try to call out? Why can't I stand up? Why can I only move my arms?

I start to panic but that quickly fades when I notice a small glowing blip in the distance ahead of me. It seems to be growing bigger. What is that?

As it grows larger and larger, I realize that it's floating closer to me. It sort of resembles that glowing bubble Glinda in the Wizard of Oz floated down in to meet Dorothy.

How am I still thinking of movie references in my dreams? And why is this blip getting closer? It's starting to get hot in here. I should shade my eyes. I place my arm over my eyes when the blip comes to a stop. I'm squinting because the light is so bright, it's like I'm looking directly at the sun.

Malakai.

Did it just say my name?

Malakai.

Okay clearly, I'm going crazy.

It calls my name again, but in a slow mesmerizing way that has me lowering my arm and staring at it in awe. I feel as though I'm in a trance. I reach my arm out to touch it, curiosity getting the best of me. I don't even know why I'm trying to touch it. You can't touch light, let alone a star, and this blip had to be a star with the way it was blinding me. But still, my arm moved towards it.

Mesmerized.

Malakai.

Closer.

Mesmerized.

Malakai.

Almost there.

When my fingers brush the light, it bursts, and consumes me.

Beep-Beep. Beep-Beep. Beep-Beep. My fingers brush against the alarm clock by my bedside, blindly trying to find the snooze button.

Once they succeed in their mission, my arm falls slack again off the side of my bed. "What the hell?" I say out loud but mostly to myself. I kept having weird dreams on random nights and could never decipher the meaning of them. My head throbbed, and I immediately knew that the effects of my insomnia would be a bitch today.

My phone rings which causes me to wince in pain at the loud noise directly by my ear on the pillow. I hurry up and answer it without looking at the screen.

"What?" I hiss out, not trying to sound annoyed but I can't help it.

"Looks like sleeping beauty's up from her beauty nap," I hear someone laugh on the other end of the phone.

"What do you want Sai?" I retort, not in the mood for his games right now.

"Well, since you're finally up with the rest of the population, me and Ant wanted to go throw the ball around at the field, and I'd figured I'd try to call. Ant said it was a lost cause, but I had faith. You down?"

I pinch the bridge of my nose and breathe out. "What time is it?"

"7:00am bro. We wanted an early start before the event tonight."

"I'll come, just give me a minute."

"Perfect, we're pulling into your driveway now, see you in 60 seconds." Click.

I pull a pillow over my face to block out the rising sun rays seeping through the blinds in my room. Even though I just woke up, I feel exhausted as hell like I hadn't slept in weeks. I reach over to my bedside table and feel around for a 5-hour energy. I usually keep them there for times like this, when I need an extra kick to get me through the day. I find it then bring it to my lips as I slowly remove the pillow and open my eyes, adjusting to the light.

After gulping down the 5 hour, I hear activity downstairs in my house, and I know that Ant and Sai let themselves in, like always. I throw the pillow back over my face, silently willing them to change their minds and go back to the car. Why did I agree to this?

I hear footsteps bounding up the stairs and audibly groan, knowing they're about to give me shit. They burst in my room and I brace myself for what's about to happen.

"Get your ass up Woods," I hear Saiyr say as he saunters over to my bed. I assume he saunters because I can't see him, but I hear his voice get closer with every word.

"You've got to stop doing this Kai," I hear Anthony say as he stands leaning on the door. Again, that was an assumption because I still haven't turned to look at them. I just know my friends well enough to know their every antic.

"You act like I can control what's happening to me," I say but my words sound muffled under the pillow. My comfort is yanked off my face by Saiyr, sucker punching me with the light. I rush to put my arm over my eyes. I have a vague sense of Deja-vu, but I can't grasp the image that flickers in my mind.

"Hurry up before the field gets packed Woods. We need to make sure that throwing arm of yours is good to go by the time the season starts," Ant says as he pushes off the door frame and heads to my closet.

He comes out a second later, tossing my gym bag onto the foot of my bed causing my cleats to hit my shin and a small burst of pain to shoot up my leg. This causes me to wake up fully.

"Alright alright, I'm getting up," I slowly rise and toss the blanket off me. I blink up at Anthony towering over me and look over to see Saiyr sitting at my desk, flipping through a magazine I had laying there.

I stand up and Ant takes a step back, patting my shoulder a little too firmly as if pushing me towards the bathroom.

"You're in dire need of a shower bro," Saiyr says covering his nose with his finger but not looking up from the magazine. I now see it's my OG Playboy edition from 1999 with Naomi Campbell on the front.

"And you're in dire need of a facial reconstruction but I don't say anything."

I walk into the bathroom and close the door, lowering the volume to his laughter. I lean over the sink and look at myself in the mirror. "Wow, you look like shit," I quietly say, and start the water so I can brush my teeth.

After doing my routine, I hop in the shower, even though I'm about to go sweat and have to do this all over again.

Once I'm dressed, I meet them downstairs in the kitchen and grab a granny smith apple from the fruit bowl in the middle of the breakfast table.

"You ready?" I ask lifting an eyebrow at them standing by the front door.

"Funny, get your ass in the car," Ant says.

After tossing the football around for a couple of hours, and going through a few drills, we lay out on the grass, exhausted, watching the clouds slide around in the sky.

"You figure out what you're going to say at the event tonight yet?" Anthony asks me, still entranced by the clouds. I let the question linger in the air for a little second before responding. "I kind of have a general idea, but I keep feeling like it's missing something."

Tonight, was my mom's book release party for her newest release titled *Where to Now*. It's one of the most highly anticipated releases of the year and is sure to become a New York Times Bestseller by the end of the week.

I'm supposed to be giving a little speech and introducing her to speak and answer questions to multiple execs and longtime fans who oversaw her popular fan pages. Pressure doesn't even begin to describe what I've been feeling lately, which probably explains why my insomnia has kicked back in at full force.

"I don't know why you didn't just ask me to write it for you. I'm a beast at coming up with shit to say on the spot," Saiyr says, and I can hear the smile in his voice.

"So, we're just going to act like your speech at the championship party last year was Oscar worthy?" I laugh in reply.

"That one doesn't count, I was drunk and barely coherent to what was actually happening."

"Who's to say you won't be a drunk fool tonight either," Anthony questions him.

"Wow, what do you take me for?" he gasps in mock horror, "I won't get drunk until the after party tonight, I mean I do have *some* morals Davidson."

We hear some giggles off to our right and I lift my head up a little to see what the commotion was.

"And here come the things that test those morals," Saiyr growls like a lion who's just found their prey.

"Calm your tits Jacobs, I'm sure they wouldn't want you drooling all over their polished shoes," I retort.

I recognized the girls that piled onto the field as the cheerleading team at my school. We were juniors at San Diego State University, so we played for the Aztecs. The cheerleaders weren't supposed to be practicing today, but I guess they felt they needed to make sure everyone was in sync and ready to go for the first game coming up soon.

One of them winks at me and I recognize her as this girl named Tracey that's in my literature research class. I roll my eyes and put my head back down on the grass.

"Alright boys, watch and learn." Saiyr stands up and brushes off his pants, then rubs at his hair to get the grass out. Me and Ant raise up to sit with our arms rested behind our backs, giving us a perfect view of the group of girls stretching each other out across the field in front of us.

He walks up to the new captain, Britney, then bows like she was the Queen of England or something. I shake my head at him and watch her laugh at what he's doing.

Sometimes I'm surprised at the number of girls he pulls with his corny pick-up lines. I always tell him they only put up with him because of his hazel colored eyes.

He kisses her hand and I swear I can see a blush on her face from here. The other cheerleader girls snicker to themselves, causing Anthony and I to look at each other with the "is he really pulling this off?" look.

She gives him her phone, I'm assuming to put his number in, because I see him start to make a phone call. He turns to look at us with a wicked grin and Britney's phone pressed to his ear. I hear his phone go off in the bag next to me and reluctantly go to answer it knowing he's about to make a show of this.

I look at his phone screen and see an unknown number on the caller ID. I answer and put it to my ear without saying anything, looking at him in his eyes.

"What was that you said about her not wanting me?" he winks at me.

"I'm sure she wouldn't after she finds out your dick is broken and can't get up even if held at gun point," I wink back, and he just laughs then hangs up.

He gives her back her phone then says something that makes her laugh. After he's done swooning her, he waves at the other cheerleaders, and starts walking back over to us.

"Take notes boys, I just got a date to the event tonight."

"You're bringing a random chick to Mrs. W's important event?" Anthony says standing up and collecting his bag from the grass beside him.

"She's not random bro, I know her." Saiyr grabs his bag and tosses It over his shoulder.

"Oh yea? What's her name?"

"Braylin, Bianca something, I forgot, but it doesn't matter." He repositions his bag so that it's draped across his chest like a crossbody. "Look, all she needs to know is my name so she can scream it all night tonight."

We all walk to Anthony's red convertible Mercedes C-class, and Saiyr hops in the back without waiting for the door to be unlocked.

"If you bust up my car, I'm busting your knee and you'll be out the whole season," Ant says to him as he slides in the driver's seat.

"Look at you boys, all spiffy and crisp looking. You ready for your speech son?" My dad says as we walk up to greet him on the curb. I had him meet us outside of the event venue at the valet booth.

Saiyr, Anthony and I, all got ready at Anthony's house after stopping by mine so I could shower again and grab my suit for tonight.

"Of course, Mr. C, our Malakai is always prepared," Saiyr winks at me while patting both of his hands on my shoulders while standing beside me. "If you'll excuse me, I see my lovely date for the evening inside looking delectable."

His eyes widen when he realizes who he's talking too, "I mean divine." He hurries inside before my dad can reply to his slip up.

"Remind me again why we're friends with him?" Anthony whispers in my ear. I give a slight chuckle, unable to fully laugh because my nerves are getting the best of me. "Mr. C, always a pleasure," Anthony nods at my dad then shakes his hand firmly and heads in.

"Those boys are something else, aren't they?" I just nod in response, unable to fully focus on the man in front of me. "What's going on with you son?"

I snap out of the momentary daydream I slipped into and just shake my head, "It's nothing dad, just nerves, that's all."

He gives me a once over then shakes his head. "Follow me."

He leads me inside the venue to a vacant room down a dimly lit hall. It was the venue owner's main office and was filled with multiple bookshelves of books and little historical trinkets.

"Alright, tell me what's going on." He leans against the desk in the middle of the room with his hands resting in his pants pockets.

I walk past him to look out the windows behind the desk. They were facing the parking lot out front and gave a perfect view of the people waiting for the valet to park their cars.

"It's just-," I begin to say then stop. Dad waits for me to continue, giving me the time I need to gather my thoughts. "I just want to say the perfect words and not mess up her big night, because it's really important to her. I want them all to know exactly how good of a person she is and how important her work is to the world."

I turn from the window and face him, hoping not to see a disappointing look in his eyes. I'm relieved when I see him smiling at me, then get a little annoyed.

"I'm serious dad, I know it might not be that big of a deal to some, but it's a big deal to me."

"I know son, it just warms my heart to see the love you have for your mom. I could only hope you feel the same way about me."

"Dad," I groan out, not really in a joking mood.

"Okay Okay," he puts his hands up in defense, "But seriously, don't think too much about it. Anything you say about your mom will come from the heart and will mean the world to her. It's clear as day what your mom means to you and that will be conveyed through your eyes. Don't sweat the words too much and just say exactly what's on your heart." He takes one hand out, waving it in the air dismissively like the answer to my problems were straightforward.

I shake my head and give him a half smile. "Why do you make everything sound so much simpler?"

He walks over and hooks his arm behind my neck like he was giving me a noogie. "Because I'm a cool dad."

I escape from his grasp and he lets out a soft laugh. "You're not that cool," I mumble as I straighten my suit jacket.

"You're right, but I do have an even cooler son who helps me to see the positive in every situation, even when he can't see it himself." He starts walking towards the door.

"Well, let me go make sure your mother isn't a nervous wreck like her son. I love you, you'll do amazing."

With that statement, he walks out the door and leaves me to stand and think more on what he said. After a few deep breathes and whispering encouraging movie quotes to myself, I head out towards the back of the building where the event is taking place.

As I walk in, I see it's packed with rows of seats, and cameras sit at the back of the room angled toward the elevated stage upfront. I spot Saiyr, Anthony and the cheerleading captain, Britney, sitting up front. They're engaged in what looks like an amusing debate, but I don't have time to stop and chat. I want to see my mom before everything starts, so I head towards the stairs that lead to the backstage.

Once I'm backstage, I see multiple people running back and forth preparing for the event.

It's set up to be like a recorded book club with a question and answer session, that'll go up on all streaming and social media platforms. I spot my mom sitting in a makeup chair while a makeup artist taps a brush into some powder then swipes it across her face.

My dad stands next to her, both parents engaged in their conversation, laughing and smiling about something.

Seeing them together always gets me excited about the idea of finding my wife one day. Too bad it's not going to be anytime soon. Girls these days only want to be with me because of my status and the fact that I might go pro one day, so I'm a walking money sign to them.

On top of that, I need to get my life in order before I allow someone into my life again.

I walk over to my parents and it's like my mom could sense my presence because she immediately looks in my direction.

"Malakai! You made it! I was afraid you'd gotten lost and couldn't find the building." The makeup artist stops applying the powder and my mom hops out the seat.

She gathers me into a big warm hug and kisses my cheek, then grabs a wipe from the makeup artists' station and wipes the lipstick stain that was left behind. "Hey Ma," I say giving a shy smile, "You ready for tonight?"

"I am now that you're here," she smiles and cups both of my cheeks in her hands.

"I'm proud of you Ma. You're dream of becoming a famous author came true."

"I couldn't have done it without you, you know that." She hugs me again then holds me out at arm's length, giving me a once over then a quizzical look. "Are you trying to steal all of my spotlight? The cameras are going to forget about me and put all their focus on you."

"I told him that when he tried the suit on at the tailors," my Dad said walking up and sliding his arm around my mom's waist.

I shake my head and before I can respond, someone who's working the event walks up and says, "Mrs. Woods, we go on in 5 minutes, if you could make your way towards the stage please," then runs off in the other direction.

"Well, that's my cue loves, see you on the other side," she kisses my dad then gives me one last hug before heading to the front of the stage and sitting on the red cushioned chair.

They had the stage set up like it was the Oprah Winfrey talk show and I admired the whole set up. My dad and I watch from backstage as they begin the countdown until the start of the event and yell action.

The crowd gives a round of applause and then the host begins her introduction. The event moves on smoothly and my mom answers questions from the audience, then reads an excerpt from her book which sparks a discussion with her and the host about the struggles of finding your purpose in the world today.

I paid attention for the most part, but as it got closer to the time for me to say my speech, my nerves shot up to an all-time high. "Now we have a special word from Mrs. Wood's son, Malakai Woods, quarterback of the San Diego state Aztecs!"

On cue I walk out to the front of the stage and wave to the crowd as I stand at the podium to the right of the couch set up. I hear Saiyr and Anthony barking like dogs and cheering me on. Once the applause dies down, I begin my speech.

"Good Evening everyone. I struggled so much with finding the right words to say about my mother tonight, not because I couldn't think of anything, but because I thought of everything." I look around the crowd and make eye contact with Saiyr and he shoots me a thumbs up.

"I thought of everything she's done for me over the years, and everything she means to me. I thought of how, when I was younger, she showed me that my words are powerful and will always make an impact no matter how little or unimportant *I* think they are."

I look at my mom and see her eyes start to glisten with unshed tears. "She showed me that no matter what obstacle is thrown in your path, you can always overcome it, not by merely stepping over, but she said I needed to bulldoze my way through it and make sure there's no life left in it."

My mom laughs along with the crowd. I look past her to where my dad is standing off to the side of the stage in perfect view of me.

"I know that with her words and her work, she has impacted and is able to impact so many lives, and help people through the rough times and remind them, 'it's okay to slow down and breathe, as long as with that next breath you come out more determined than before'. I love you mom and want you to know that you deserve this more than anyone."

Someone brings out a trophy and hands it to me. "I would like to present you with the Bailey's Women's Prize for Fiction." The audience erupts into applause and my mom's mouth drops open in shock.

She puts her hand to her chest and rises from her seat to come towards me. I hand her the award and kiss her cheek, "Surprise Mom."

"How'd you keep this from me?"

"They emailed Dad saying they wanted to honor you and dad asked if we could pull this little surprise on you and they were all for it." She turns towards dad across the stage and blows him a kiss and he winks in response.

"Congratulations Mom." I give her a hug then walk off the stage to sit next to Anthony in the front row.

"Another shot bartender!" Saiyr yells to a kid standing by the punch bowl at the party.

"It's your turn to carry him out to the car," Anthony says to me as we watch him standing on top of a coffee table dancing to the music blasting from the speakers.

He had a solo cup in his right hand, and his left hand was firmly secured on Britney's waist as she was bent over twerking on him. "How are they both even on that table right now?" I ask Anthony, genuinely confused.

"Hey Malakai," a voice says to me from behind. I turn around to see Tracey from the cheerleading team looking at me with heavy eyelids. Seems as though someone got some liquid courage to come talk to me.

"Wassup Tracey?"

It's sad to see how desperate females are for attention these days. I know she only wants me because I have a 6 pack and a guaranteed spot on any pro team of my choosing. She doesn't even know me other than the fact that I have a pretty face that is a blessing and a curse.

"Brit told me what you did for your mom, so freakin' sweet of you," she tries to add a sexy breathy tone to her voice, but ends up sounding like she's wheezing and trying to breathe through a bad lung.

"Yep," I reply but look around the room trying to figure when and where Anthony snuck off too. He must've left right when he heard her voice.

Bastard.

"So, listen, my parents are gone for the rest of the night," she shouts over the music and I look back at her, noticing that she's gotten a little closer. She is now so close, that her breasts are almost touching my stomach.

She was shorter than me, probably around 5'5 and I was a big 6'2 with muscles that'll give Michael B. Jordan a run for his money.

"If you want, you can come over and watch a little Netflix. Maybe chill after," she looks up at me while batting her eyelashes and I have to contain the laughter that's trying to escape my mouth.

"Listen, I'm not really interested. You're a cool girl though, I'm just not really feeling..." I move my hand back and forth between us, "This."

Her eyes go wide.

"Oh, did you think I wanted to have sex with you?" She tries to morph her face to reflect something that resembles disgust, but it just shows the sting of rejection. "I just wanted someone to hang out with after the party since I'll be bored. But clearly, all guys think about is the next vagina they can bury themselves into." She snorts while rolling her eyes dramatically.

She looks passed my shoulder at what I'm assuming is another prospect on her list then back at me. "You know what, never mind. If you'll excuse me." She grabs the cup out of a random guys hand next to us and downs its contents in one swift gulp. She shoves the drink into my chest, and I grab it so that it doesn't fall and get crushed by the dancing college students. She brushes past me, towards the direction of her new love interest.

Once she's gone, I blow out the breath I didn't realize I was holding and look to the kitchen, locking eyes with Anthony. He walks back over and places his hand on my shoulder.

"Sorry to leave you hangin' bro, but *that* was one train wreck I was looking to avoid." We both laugh and go back to enjoying the party, talking to our other friends and students that go to our school.

That night I get home at 3:00 am and try to go through the front door as quietly as possible, so I don't wake anyone up. I'm sure they already heard the alarm system beep, but I still wanted to be cautious.

My mom had a big night and she was tired at dinner when we went out to celebrate after the event. I head towards the stairs and walk up them slowly, so they don't creek under my weight.

Once safely in my room, I close the door behind me and plop on my bed. The only light on in here was coming from the lamp on my nightstand, which caused a nice subtle ambience to flood the room.

After a beat, I look to turn my nightstand light off and attempt to force myself to go to sleep. Now that I wasn't stressing as much anymore, maybe my body will start acting right again.

I notice a piece of paper on the nightstand and pick it up to read it.

PROUD OF YOU SON. YOU WILL DO AMAZING THINGS IN LIFE. (IF YOU COULD LEARN TO THROW A FOOTBALL RIGHT THAT IS) ;).

LOVE DAD.

Hearing my dad say things like this always had me feeling warm and happy on the inside, so why does reading it now make me feel uneasy?

I put the paper back down on the nightstand and turn off the light. Once I close my eyes, the feeling of sleep begins to creep up on me, and I'm grateful tonight I'll be able to get probably the best sleep I've had in a long time.

What is this soft feeling?

I open my eyes and see that I'm lying, stomach down, on what appears to be a huge white cotton ball.

What the hell?

I use my arm to raise myself up, then my legs to help me stand. I wobble a little but end up finding my footing. I have to squint my eyes a little to adjust to the brightness of the place I'm in. Once my eyes are adjusted, I take a look around and see nothing but a cloudy substance I'm standing on, and the sky looks like a never-ending sunset. Orange and purple colors are splashed across the sky like a Wassily Kandinsky painting.

The cloud mass goes on with no end in either direction I turn my head. I turn to look behind me and notice something in the distance.

Is that a person?

They appear to be sitting on a bench with their head in their hands. They look troubled.

I look down to see I'm wearing my oversized Michael Jackson Thriller shirt and my knee-high socks.

Aren't clouds supposed to be wet or something? Why do my feet feel like I'm wearing foot warmers?

I start to make my way towards the figure sitting on the bench and I am now able to make out that it's a man. Well not really a man per say, more like a young adult who has yet to experience the joys of middle age living.

(That's what Benny usually says to me and Rylie when we say we can't wait to graduate college and get in our careers).

When I get about 10 feet away from this person, I see that he is wearing black dress socks, dark grey tailored suit pants and a baby pink dress shirt with the all the buttons un-done, revealing a white wife beater underneath.

His hair is a nice low-cut fade, and his beard connects to said fade with a mustache to go with it, all low cut.

As if he senses my presence, he looks up and I stop dead in my tracks. My breath hitches as I am knocked slowly off balance by the face looking back at me. I can see now that his hair is a dark brown, almost black color, and his eyes are a tad shade lighter than his hair, but still brown. I glance over his body which is a nice athletic build with broad shoulders and his biceps slightly bulging out of his rolled-up dress sleeves. I see a glimpse of some tattoos, but don't focus on those too much because I'm just trying to drink all of him in.

My gaze slides back up to his face where I notice that he has his ears pierced. A small silver hoop in the right and a nice sized diamond stud in the left. His nice sized lips that contain just the right amount of juice, curve up into a cocky-ish mixed with boyish-charm grin, and flashes me his all too perfectly straight pearly whites.

My body wants to faint from the knockout that is this Adonis in front of me, but for some reason, my feet start to walk towards him. It's like there's some magnetic pull he has.

Usually when I dream about a guy, there's always one feature that is abnormally weird or ugly. Whether his nose takes up 90 percent of his face, his right leg is a baby leg and his left leg is a hulk leg, or something else of that nature.

When I get within breathing distance of this man, he raises up from the bench and towers over me. My God he's gorgeous.

Sorry God.

But thank you for giving me this man even if it's just for one night. I don't even let myself ogle over guys, but I am dreaming so I'll let it slide just this once.

"Finally, a decent man of my dreams," I say towards him, surprised I can even speak to such a beautiful man without giving myself a mental pep-talk about not sounding stupid.

He gives a slight chuckle and the sound was enough to make me want to throw my panties to the side. What the hell is wrong with me? I'm never like this, especially for a random guy I don't know. I'm starting to sound like Rylie.

"*Ah she speaks, they never speak,*" he says, letting his eyes lazily walk all over me, causing me to feel eerily naked.

They? Who's they?

"They?" I ask, curious as to how this dream man has a memory he can tap into. Do dream people have memories? I make a mental note to research it when I wake up.

"Yea, the other girls in my dreams. They usually just drop to their knees first, but lucky for you, I'm in the mood for conversation," he reaches up and grabs one of my curls, stretching it all the way out, revealing the severe shrinkage I deal with on the day to day.

"And besides, I've never had a girl as beautiful as you in my dreams before, so I'm willing to change directions and do something new." He releases my curl and I don't know if it's his cocky demeanor, demeaning comments, or the fact that he felt it was okay to touch me without asking, but I feel a flicker of heat start to rise in my face and it causes anger to simmer in my blood. Things like this is what causes me to hate the male species even more.

"First of all, I don't know what you think this is, but this is just a dream, and you're just a random figment of my imagination."

"Actually, the people that you see in your dreams are actually people you've seen somewhere out in the world."

I look up at him perplexed, "How do you know real world facts?" I shake my head, "Never mind, I have to remember that I'm actually talking to myself and that this interaction isn't in fact real." I take a step back from him and begin to pace.

"Actually, this is my dream and usually when there's a female in it, it's intended to be a wet one. I don't see anything getting wet yet, or even close to being damp." He goes back and plops down on the bench, "I'm not in the mood anyway to rock your world so I'll just sit here until I wake up, I guess."

He lies back on the bench so that his right leg is dangling off the side and his left arm is draped over his eyes.

"Clearly my brain is broken, and you are getting confused," I walk up and tower over him. You would think that I'd cast a shadow but seeing that there's no actual sun in this dream, there are no shadows or shade anywhere.

He looks as if he's exhausted and been through a lot which is not possible because he is just a blip in my brain.

"For the record, if I wanted to get with you, I would. This is a dream so really there are no consequences. But I don't want you in the slightest," I place my hands on my hip as I peer down at him and he snorts.

"Yeah right," he says, taking his arm away from over his eyes. "If you didn't want me, you wouldn't've had your mouth dangling open and a waterfall of drool spilling out at the sight of me."

"I was more so shocked at the fact that you had all your features in tack and wasn't some weird abnormal creature that I usually get."

Suddenly there's a subtle rumble in the distance. "What was that?" He asks me.

Rumble.

It grows a little louder. "I don't know," I look up from where he's lying down and turn to the direction of the rumbling, which is coming from somewhere to the right of the bench.

Rumble

It's a lot louder now and the cloud world we're in starts to crumble. The ground moving somewhere I can't see, and my skin starts to crawl.

I look to him with a slight sense of panic and he's already standing up from the bench. I look back to where the rumble was coming from and see that the sky is starting to turn from a warm sunny looking orange purple hue, to a now dark grey almost storm cloud looking color.

The white cloud ground is starting to rumble even harder like an earthquake and I can see some of the clouds starting to drop and fall, giving way to a black starry abyss below. I slowly step back until I'm standing next to the Adonis and quickly glance at his face.

His features do anything but settle the unnerved feeling I have inside because he looks scared himself.

"What's happening!?" I shout at him over the sound of the rumbling earthquake. "I was going to ask you that!" he shouts back, looking at me with such intensity that I have to look away.

RUMBLE.

A loud rumble roars overhead, causing a ringing in my ears and the earthquake shakes even harder. More and more clouds start to drop around us until there's only a singular *cloud, which is what the bench and me and the Adonis are standing on.*

I go to grab a hold of his hand to make sure we both make it out okay and before I can touch him, there's another loud rumble and I'm falling through the clouds to the dark starry abyss below. It's like time slowed down and I'm falling.

Falling.

Falling.

Falling....

JORDAN

"Alright, next week we'll have our first test, so make sure you study! See you next week!" I gather my binder and textbook from my desk and place it into my bookbag.

The last class of the day always drags, and I silently curse myself for putting the least interesting class I have, last on my schedule. As I put my airpods in and start to play my music, my phone vibrates with a text from Rylie.

Rylie:

Location?

Me:

Walking out of class. Meet me in the courtyard

Rylie:

Okay hand sign emoji

I walk out the double doors and see Rylie sitting on the round brick border by the big tree talking to someone. When I see who it is, I bust into a huge grin and pick up my pace a little.

"Camille!" I say when I get up to them and wrap my friend into a hug. We almost fall over at the force of my hug, but Camille does a good job of keeping us steady.

"Why is this my first time seeing you all semester?" She asks me before releasing me from her grasp.

"Well if you weren't busy working all the time, maybe I'd see you more," I retort back.

"Wow I missed you guys," she says looking back and forth between me and Rylie.

Rylie and I met Camille in high school our freshman year when she transferred over. We instantly clicked and have been inseparable ever since. Camille is one year older than us, so she became something like an older sister.

When circumstances in her life changed, she had to move into her grandmother's place and helped take care of the bills to release some of stress off her. This caused Cam to end up becoming a part time student and pick up extra shifts at the diner she works at. She got promoted to manager and now works even more, but she also makes a lot more so if anyone deserves it, it's her.

"We missed you more," Rylie says, standing up and pulling all of us into a group hug.

"Do you have to work today?" I ask Camille.

"Believe it or not, I have a day off, that's why I called Rylie 'cause I knew she didn't have class when I got out of mine."

"You know what this calls for?" Rylie asked.

"What? Ditching responsibilities and flying across the country to the beach?" Camille asks, with a gleam of hope in her eyes.

"Going to the library and finding a nice quiet place to curl up and read a book?" I ask, feeling my own excitement tremble in my fingertips.

"Nope," Rylie grabs our hands and leads us to our apartment, "SPA DAY!"

I finish applying the Aztec healing clay mask to Camille's face as we sing along to the Pocahontas movie on the television.

Usually during our spa days, we put on some feel-good music, like a Tibetan singing bowl but today felt like a Disney day. We always feel good watching Disney movies, so we put all of them in a list and had a Disney marathon.

Once our masks were dry and we could barely move our lips to sing along to the songs, we rinsed it off and cuddled up together on the couch. Since Camille was the only one in our group who was 21 already, she went out and bought wine before we started with the festivities, so now we were sipping on that.

"I forgot how badly I needed this," Camille sighs as she peers into her almost empty glass of wine.

"Girl what? You've been depriving yourself of the golden goodness that is Stella Rosa Peach?" Rylie says looking almost offended.

"Of course not, you know I like to indulge in my wines every now and then," she says laughing, "I meant hanging out with you guys. Doing things that make me happy."

I snuggle into her side and rest my head on her shoulder. "I wish you didn't have to overwork yourself as much as you do," I say into her shoulder.

"Me too, we need to fight the man," Rylie shouts like she's giving a powerful speech to a group of rally protestors.

"That all sounds nice and everything but that's just the card life dealt me," Camille shrugs, "just have to suck it up and keep it pushing."

We sit in silence for a minute and I guess this leaves Rylie antsy because she jumps up from the couch.

"I have an idea," she says, and I can see the wheels turning in her head at her sudden brilliant plan she just concocted.

"What is it?" I say yawning into my hand.

"Let's make you a tinder!" Camille laughs and I shake my head at the fact Rylie thinks finding Camille a man will solve all her problems.

"I'm talking about you, dimple," she quirks her eyebrow at me and now I'm furiously shaking my head at her in protest. "How did this even get turned on me?" I ask in horror.

"Oh, come on, it'll be fun!" She sits back down but now is sitting on the coffee table in front of me, so we are looking at each other in the eye.

"Besides, when's the last time you ever gave a guy the time of day?"

14 years ago.

"Why does that matter?" I say crossing my arms.

"I think it'll be fun to set up a profile for you and see all the guys you'll match with."

"Why are you even thinking about this right now?" I roll my eyes.

"I'm down!" I hear Camille say next to me and drop my mouth open, feeling betrayed. "You too!? What is this?"

She shrugs, "Ryles is right, it sounds like a hell of a lot of fun, and I love seeing you out of your comfort zone," she walks over and grabs Rylie's laptop from the kitchen table. Rylie moves back to the couch and sits to the left of me and Camille sits to the right of me, setting the laptop down in front of me.

"You know what? Camille switch with Jor so she doesn't see the profile until the end," Rylie says.

"Good Idea."

I reluctantly switch with Cam and lay back closing my eyes, trying to will this to be over. I appreciate Rylie for shifting the conversation off of Camille and trying to make it lighthearted but really it has me cringing and wanting to lock myself into my room.

Even though I know my friends' intentions are pure, I really wish they would just respect my wishes when I say I don't ever want to find love or be in love. I just feel like the concept of loving someone whole heartedly is a sham. I hate to say it, but I'm just patiently waiting for my mom to call me and say her, and Benny are getting a divorce because romantic love is only temporary and never lasts forever. Just look at the divorce rate skyrocketing these days.

I don't need a man to be happy, nor do I need a man to be successful and live life to the fullest. All I need is me, my family, and friends. I'll be perfectly fine and feel fulfilled in life. Well, as fulfilled as I'll ever be because I can never be fulfilled. My ability to be whole was snatched away from me years ago.

"This picture is perfect," I hear Rylie say and Cam mumbles in agreement. After a few more moments hearing Rylie and Cam "Ooh and Aah" over whatever it is they were seeing on the screen, Rylie sings "Done!" and I sigh, bracing myself for what's going to happen next.

They pass the laptop to me and I look at what they've deemed acceptable for a dating profile for me.

I look and see that they chose mostly pictures of me laughing and being caught off-guard, but showing me in my element when doing things I love. There were a couple selfies that they took from my Instagram of me making silly faces and one of me trying to do the serious model face but failing miserably. Under my picture, I see the bio that they wrote for me and bust out laughing.

HI, I'M JORDAN AND AS YOU CAN SEE, I SPEND MOST OF MY TIME LAUGHING AT NOTHING. MESSAGE ME IF YOU'RE LOOKING FOR A COOL DOWN TO EARTH GIRL TO HANGOUT WITH AND

ISN'T AFRAID TO TELL YOU WHEN YOU HAVE A BOOGER IN YOUR NOSE

They couldn't be serious.

"So, you think I guy would want to hit me up after reading this childish ass bio?" I look at them, genuinely curious.

"Jor, trust us. We've been in the dating game for a long time, we know what we're doing," Rylie says as she walks to the fridge to grab some more wine.

"And remind me when's the last time your flirting tactics actually worked?" I said grabbing my wine glass so she could add more to it. On cue, a message notification popped up on Rylie's laptop.

"Ooh look! a match already!" Cam says jumping up to see who it is that matched with me.

"Oh yea, I went ahead and swiped right on a couple of guys that seemed like good prospects for our Jordan," Rylie says, topping all three of us off and setting the bottle on the coffee table.

"Let's see who the prospects are," Camille says swiping through the matches I got already.

They were cute guys, I'll give them that, but my heart just wasn't in it, so they weren't really wowing me as much as they were the other girls.

"They're cute aren't they Jo?" Camille asks as she glances at me then at the computer screen filled with guy's pictures.

"They're okay," I reply absent mindedly, playing with some lint on the blanket I'm cuddled in.

"Okay?" Rylie shoots a look of shock at me, the wine glass in her right hand almost spilling over from the sudden jolt.

Looking at us, you would think we were a bunch of middle-aged women out in the corporate world, desperate to find love in a world full of lust crazed men. Or men afraid of commitment. I loathed those type of men so much that it burned through my entire being.

"Do you see these fine ass dudes on this computer?" Ry's voice says in the background. I'm pulled out of my thoughts, back to reality and the situation I'm in.

"If you like them so much, why don't you guys hit them up?" I yawn into my hand and nestle my head onto Camille's shoulder again. "Can we please go back to watching Disney princesses being fawned over by their overly obnoxious princes?"

I grab the remote to turn the volume of our movie marathon up. When I was younger, I was obsessed with Disney princesses and finding my beloved prince charming. Having the wedding of my dreams and singing in the forest with random talking animals was always on my bucket list. Funny how quickly life can snatch your bucket list and dump it in the grinder then toss it over a bridge into a never-ending river.

Am I being dramatic? Maybe a little.

Actually no.

My feelings are justified, and I won't ever let anyone downplay the severity of what happened to me. I'm not ever willing to forgive and I sure as hell will never forget.

"Fine fine, but we will revisit this right after," Rylie states closing the laptop and pushing all the way back onto the couch.

One hour later, Camille is snoring in my ear and Rylie's leg is twitching while being draped over my thigh.

I knew the effects of the wine would kick in sooner or later, I'm just thankful that it came sooner and before they decided to pull back up the tinder profile.

I slowly ease my way out from under Rylie's leg, and she moves to cradle a pillow in the fetal position, and I give a sigh of relief. Camille was barely laying on my shoulder, so when I moved, she still had support from the pillow behind her. How do I keep finding myself up alone at night with Rylie sleep and sound?

I place our glasses and put them in the sink, giving myself a mental note to wash them in the morning. Now that I think about it, Rylie probably falls asleep because she knows I'll be the one to make sure everything is clean. I make another mental note to ask her why she falls asleep so early.

Once the living area is as clean as it's going to get with two basically dead bodies on the couch, I make my way to my bathroom. During the last movie, Rylie downloaded Tinder on my phone without me noticing, so when I hear a notification pop up as I put my hair into a pineapple, I nearly jump scared out of my mind. I look down to see it says that I had yet another match that wanted to chat.

"What's up with this generation and relying on dating apps to meet their 'forever partner'" I do air quotes to myself and silently laugh as I remember Benny doing them during move in day.

I should call them.

I make another mental note. My mind is going to explode with all these mental notes.

I look back at the notification once my hair is done being put up so I can go to sleep tangle free. I grab the phone and unlock it as I turn off the light and walk to my room. I look at the picture of the match and recognize the face, but it takes me a little second to put the face with the memory.

It was Zavier, one of the guys from move in day that helped us move in. I look at the message and see that he sent a simple hand waving emoji with a smile next to it. I don't know if it's because I'm up alone and bored or if I'm curious to see what lame flirting techniques he was going to use and wanted a nice laugh.

I send an identical message back and plug my phone into the charger by my bedside. Within 30 seconds, my phone screen lights up with another reply.

Zavier:

I'm surprised to see you on this app

Surprised? What did he know about me? I'm slightly annoyed but I don't let it seep into the message I type out.

Me:

Surprised? Why?

Not even 20 seconds go by.

Zavier:

You just don't seem like the type to be on one of these dating apps

Me:

Maybe I was bored and wanted to explore my options

Zavier:

Like I said. You don't seem like the type

He was starting to get on my nerves with the assumptions on my character.

Me:

Did you message me just to say that or ….

Zavier:

Sorry lol, I'm messing this up already. Can we start over?

Me:

Just so you know, I'm not interested in dating or anything

Zavier:

That's okay, I'm fine with just being friends. I don't have enough of those

That makes me laugh and decide, 'What the heck', and entertain him further. After all, I was bored and somewhat alone, despite the hibernating bears in the room next to me.

We go on to talk about school and the classes we're taking and our schedules. He tells me that he wanted to talk to me when he saw me with my family but felt it wasn't appropriate. He then sends a text immediately after that saying not to worry because he honestly is perfectly fine with being just friends.

After about an hour or so of texting, he says he has to go to sleep to prepare for his 8 am in the morning and tells me not to be a stranger when I see him on campus. I reply back saying, "Who are you again?" and he replies with an, "Lmao good one. Have a good night Jordan," and I put the phone face down on my nightstand without giving a reply.

JORDAN

A week later, I wake up before my alarm clock sings its annoyingly hair-ripping melody in my ear.

Last night, just like the past few nights, I didn't dream. It was just a big black nothingness while I slept. I know they say that everyone dreams, you just forget them before you wake up, but that wasn't the case for me. I literally dreamt of black nothingness. Like nothing was there at all.

I've never experienced anything like it and definitely not for a week straight.

Letting go of these thoughts, I grab my phone from the nightstand to see what time it is, so I can mentally plan out how much time I have to just lay in bed before having to get up to start my day.

It reads 6:32am, which is perfect because that means I have a solid 40 minutes to myself before I hop in the shower. My eyes glide down towards the notifications I missed during my sleep and go through them one by one.

10 NEW NOTIFICATIONS FROM TINDER.

Delete.

ONE NEW NOTIFICATION FROM SUNTRUST.

Delete.

I knew I was still broke.

ONE NEW NOTIFICATION FROM UNKNOWN NUMBER.

Unknown number? Did Rylie give my number to some random guy again and he's just now trying to cash in? I open the message.

+1 (470) 209-5268

Is this Jordan?

I sigh in exasperation. "Rylie," I say under my breath, quietly scolding her. She needs to stop being so obsessed with me not wanting a boyfriend. It's not the end of the world if Jordan Jameson doesn't fall in love.

I delete the message and put on the audiobook I'm currently listening to, then immerse myself into the story. Closing my eyes, I let L.J. Shen whisk me off into the world of Todos Santos and escape my reality just for a little bit.

My real phone alarm goes off at 7:15 and I drag myself out of the bed, to go take a shower. I peak into the living room and see Rylie asleep at our kitchen table. She fell asleep studying last night for the test in her 11 am class. The joys of having classes that start later in the morning. I liked 8 am's because less people took them and that meant less people roaming the campus this early. This also meant less chances of having to stop and talk to a few people I know from my previous classes.

I don't really have people I hang out with outside of Camille and Rylie because I'm always busying myself with something.

I get out of the shower and throw on my favorite high wasted mom jeans that I thrifted at this thrift shop called Rag-O-Rama. I distressed them myself and paired the jeans with a nice spaghetti strapped yellow knit top. It was form fitting and showed off the little bit of definition I had in my obliques from going to the gym twice a month.

I throw on my white crocs with my rainbow, unicorn, cactus, peace sign, and pineapple charms. I untie the scarf from my hair and shake it out of its pineapple shape, picking the roots to give me more volume.

My hair was dyed a nice copper red, like the color SZA wore for her SXSW performance. My curl pattern is 4a and my skin tone is a lighter complexion. I move my septum piercing to where it's facing out and showing itself to the world.

I glance at my right wrist that sported the rose gold watch my mom bought me a couple of Christmases ago. The time read 7:48. I grab my bookbag and head to class.

Since it was early September, the weather in Atlanta was still warm and feeling like summer. It wouldn't start to get colder until mid-October early November. Then again, you never really know what you're going to get with Georgia because the weather is so bipolar here.

After my first class was done, I had a little break before my 11:30 started. I decided to go get myself some breakfast at Dunkin' Donuts since I had time to kill.

As I'm walking over, I decide to redownload twitter to my phone because I was bored. I wasn't big on social media and only used it when I wanted a laugh or felt like updating my pictures.

When I get to Dunkin' Donuts, I order a glazed donut with raspberry filling and an iced coffee with extra vanilla and cream. I had a serious sweet tooth; I couldn't help it. I sit down in the sparsely populated courtyard and decide to call my mom at her job.

Pausing the music playing in my airpods, I dial her office number. She works as a Public Relations and Fundraising Manager at a company called Ocultech. I know she helps companies with their image and setting up their fundraising events. That's pretty much all I know about what she does and where she works.

"Hey love," my mom says as she soon as she answers.

I smile at my mom's voice, "Hey Mom, how's work?"

"You know, same old stuff just a different day. How are your classes coming along? Do you like them?"

I proceed to tell her about my annoying monotoned 3:30 pm professor and how whenever he talks, he just sounds like the adults off Charlie Brown.

As I'm talking a text notification pops up on my phone and I see it's from the same unknow number as before. This guy is a persistent one I see. I pull down the notification to fully view what the message says.

+1 (470) 209-5268

If this is Jordan, I really need to speak with you

"The hell?" I realize I say this out loud because my mom says, "Excuse me?" and I quickly apologize.

"Just got a weird text, sorry."

"Who's it from?" she asks with a worried tone in her voice.

"I'm not sure, probably Rylie playing games with me, you know how she is." Another message pops up.

+1 (470) 209-5268

I know you see this message. Please.

I silently curse myself for leaving my read receipts on.

"Mom, I have to go, I'll call you back later on today okay?" I say and hang up the phone. I look around me, feeling the sudden urge that I'm being watched.

I grab my bag and hurry across the yard towards the building of my 11:30 class, where I know there will be a lot of people, just in case.

Once I get there, I laugh at myself and say that I'm being too paranoid and that it probably *is* just Rylie playing games with me. She's never up before the time she has to be, so she knew I wouldn't expect her if she were to text me something like that. I save the messages so I can show and confront her later.

"There's my girl!" Rylie shouts as I walk into our apartment after the excruciatingly long 3:30 class I just had. I don't even remember all he taught us because I zoned out for most of it.

I drop my bag over by my room door and go to sit at the kitchen table. Rylie was in the kitchen cooking up some ground chicken for our taco night. We don't eat beef or pork in this household. Nothing against dark meat eaters, just a preference.

"Don't there's my girl me, I know it was you," I say to her with an accusatory look.

"You know it was me what?" She replies genuinely confused, still focusing on pushing the ground chicken around in the pan.

"You know what," I say and pull out my phone so I can pull up the messages. I walk over to her and show her the screen, and she looks over it while still moving the chicken.

"Um Jor, I don't know who that is, but it definitely isn't me," she deadpans looking me straight into my eyes. I want to tell her she's lying and that she can drop the act, but deep down I know she's telling the truth. Besides, I can always tell when Ry is lying or up to something.

"Well, have you given my number out to any random guys you met?" I say going back to sit in my chair, trying to think about who in the world it could be texting me.

"I only did that once and told you I'd never do it again. Besides, that was like three years ago," she says sautéing the meat one last time, turning off the burner, and moving it to a green colored bowl.

I sit there thinking, and even though it's a long shot, I say, "Maybe my number got exposed on Tinder. You know hackers are really savvy these days."

I get up to grab the sour cream, cheese, lettuce, and tomatoes from the refrigerator.

"I doubt that's what happened because if that was the case, you would've got a hell of a lot more messages from different random numbers," Rylie says going to the cabinet and grabbing the tortillas.

"Why don't you ask them who they are? That's the easiest way to solve this mystery," she says shrugging like it's no big deal.

"I can't do that, what if they track my location?" I sit back down at the table.

"Honey, if they were going to track your location, they would've been did that because they already have your number and clearly know who you are," she turns and stops when she sees the look of horror on my face, and puts the tortillas down then walks over to sit across from me at the table.

"Do you want me to call the number? I can block my color ID."

"No that's okay, I'll text them back." I just stare at my phone for a couple minutes without moving.

"Okay Ms. Sloth, while you do that, I'll finish preparing dinner."

She goes back over to the stove and places the tortillas in a new frying pan to give them just the right amount of crisp, the only way I like to eat my tacos.

I let out a heavy breath and my fingers fly across the screen quickly typing out a reply and hitting send before I can turn back.

Me:

Who is this?

Why was I so scared? I knew the answer but then told myself there was no way it could be who I think it is.

There's just no way.

I walk to my room and throw my phone on to the bed then close the door. I was being a little dramatic, but I was doing everything I could to help decrease the amount of anxiety I had.

When I turn back to look at Rylie, she shakes her head as she places the finished tortillas on the counter next to the other ingredients.

"You are something else," she says smiling at me.

"Look who's talking," I say as a little of the anxiety eases up a bit.

We sit down and eat, and I appreciate Rylie for always being the friend to cheer everyone up and get them to forget all their problems. I could only hope I'm there for her just as much.

After dinner, Rylie says she has to go to sleep early to meet with her group mates early in the morning since "Prissy Ashley" (a girl she says that's in her group and claims she can't meet any other time) just had to only be available before the birds even came out to sing.

"Goodnight Ry," I wave to her, then look around and realize that she cleaned up this time. Wow cooked and cleaned. I need to marry her.

I walk back into my room and the anxiety hits me full force. My stomach starts turning and protesting and before I know it, I'm in the bathroom.

After spending a good amount of time in there, I finally come back out and stare at the phone lying face down in the middle of my bed.

"Okay Jordan, it's not that serious," I say out loud to myself. I walk over to the bed and memories that I buried a while ago start to resurface.

Memories from before what happened 14 years ago.

14 years.

I curse myself for allowing them to take over my psyche. I reach the bed and slowly reach out my hand to grab my phone. I turn it over.

TWO NEW NOTIFICATIONS FROM UNKNOWN sits at the bottom under the other tinder notifications I keep getting. I don't know how I keep getting new matches. Rylie must still be logged on to the account from her computer.

That's not what's important right now though. I need to figure out who this random person is that seems like they urgently need to speak with me.

I unlock my phone and hover my shaky thumb over the messages app. I finally muster up the courage to click on it and as soon as I read the message, I drop my phone so fast like it was a pan I just pulled out the oven with no oven mitt.

Like it burned me.

In a way, it did.

+1 (470) 209-5268

Cory

We need to talk

MALAKAI

Insomnia.

Life's greatest gift.

My insomnia comes and goes when it wants too, and I have no control over it.

It got really bad a month ago when I was stressing out over what to say in the speech dedicated to my mom. That night, I fell asleep for 12 hours.

12.

The best sleep I've had since… Well, ever.

I thought my sleep troubles were over and I would be able to go back to my regular scheduled programming. Not the case at all. Ever since then, my sleep has been so staggered and random, so much so, that at one point I was in class and exhaustion hit me like a freight train.

I felt my body drifting into sleep and I quickly excused myself from class and ended up passing out in the library, which was right down the hall, for 6 hours. Luckily it was open later that night due to a club having an impromptu meeting.

I woke up to one of the club members violently shaking me saying they almost called campus police because they thought I was dead.

Anyway, back to what I was saying.

Insomnia.

Insomnia is a female that I had a fling with once, and now, she won't leave me alone. Insomnia was that annoying little sister that constantly nagged and pulled at your leg until you gave her attention.

I thought I escaped her for at least until next semester, but no. She comes rearing her ugly head back in my direction.

So here I am, wide awake at 3:20 in the morning on a Sunday night, staring up at the tray ceiling in my bedroom. I decided not to stay on campus this year because I just wasn't feeling the residence life there anymore.

Don't get me wrong, they have a bunch of cool activities and game nights and things like that to attend, but it just doesn't feel like home, and I never truly felt like myself.

In my room, surrounded by books and my favorite movies, my passions, this is where I'm able to let all my walls down and truly be myself. Not on the football field where my dad wants me to be. Where he wants me to not waste my talents. He's never actually told me that, but I know that's how he feels.

That's the biggest struggle I'm dealing with at the moment, and it's starting to stress me out because I am a junior now and getting close to the finish line.

I need to make a final decision on what I'm going to do with my life and who I see myself being in the future.

I turn on my side to look at the small books stacked on the shelves of my desk and smile fondly at the memories they pull to the forefront.

Seeing as my mom is an author, books have been a part of my life since I was born. Back when I was young, my mom and dad used to always read me bedtime stories. Once I finished reading all the books on my shelves, my mom would go out to buy me more and we would run through those just as fast.

I was always a creative kid, coming up with different story lines and ideas for books but never once voicing them out loud to anyone because I was scared. I would right down my movie and book ideas then hide them under my bed in a shoebox.

One night, I stopped my mom from going to pull a book off the shelf and asked her If I could make my own story. I told her I needed one I could directly relate too and that I even wanted to illustrate it myself. She seemed extremely happy about this, seeing how she was all about expressing yourself through writing and creating stories not just for her but to help other people as well.

The next day she brought home art supplies with construction paper, markers and the gold pins you use to bind papers together.

She sat down with me and helped me bring my first ever vision to life in the form of a book called *Super Kai and the apple tree,* which was basically a book about me discovering an apple that was lost. It rolled far away from its beloved apple tree, and I had to help him find his way back to his family.

My mom loved it so much, she ended up having it self-published and I was able to have it sold at my elementary book fair, so I guess you could say I'm a published author.

Like mother like son some would say.

Creating gives me this feeling that's indescribable, and it's a love that'll never die.

Then I was introduced to the world of football because my dad watched me toss a ball to the neighbor's dog over the fence one summer and swore, I was a golden child, born to be a quarterback.

He enrolled me into camps and signed me up for the neighborhood league to get my practice up. I've been playing ball ever since then and it has sort of become who I am.

Malakai the football star.

Gone and forgotten was Malakai the author, the creator.

The artist.

My mom would ask me from time to time for my opinion on a new story she's come up with, or if I wanted to cowrite a book with her, but I couldn't create stories and play football at the same time.

Now that I'm a junior, star quarterback of my college football team and a Sports Psychology major, it's too late to backtrack in my life.

This is why it's the biggest struggle I'm dealing with right now, and why my insomnia will not go away and let me be for a minute.

I'm struggling between being completely and whole heartedly me and being the me that people see and make me out to be.

Those two Malakai's are completely different people.

I look out my window and notice the sun is starting to rise. Damn, was I really stuck in my head for that long?

I glance at the clock and see that it reads 7:05 am. Well, looks like another night with no sleep. I'm going on 72 hours of no sleep and know that the next time I crash, I'll be out cold for at least a day.

I slide out of my bed and decide to go for a morning run to try and tire my body out, so it'll fall asleep sooner. It was a Saturday and I had nothing planned but knew either Saiyr or Ant would call me with something they miraculously planned.

Slipping on my black huaraches, I grab my apple watch off its charger and head out the house to the cool breeze of the San Diego morning.

Fall time was my favorite, not only because it had the best weather, but because that meant Halloween was coming up and that was my favorite holiday. Seeing everyone, young and old, dressing up and having some carefree fun collectively with no judgement, made my heart swell a little.

Wow, I sound like such a sap right now.

I start my run down towards the cul-de-sac of my neighborhood then work my way back toward the entrance gates. I wave to Sammy, the security guard on duty at the time as I turn right and go bounding down the street.

After about 40 minutes of running, I decide to stop at Einstein Bros. Bagels to get a breakfast bagel and smoothie.

While sitting inside, waiting for my name to be called to get my bagel, I look around at the artwork displayed on the walls. Einstein was probably my third favorite place in the world because their bagels were so good. My bed being number one, and this small hole in the wall book café near my house was the second.

I continue my tour around the shop with my eyes until they land on a flyer posted up by the exit door.

SAN DIEGO FILM CONTEST 2019: UNLEASH YOUR INNER CREATIVITY.

I walk over to it and take a picture of the poster with my phone, reading over all the rules and details of this competition.

SAN DIEGO FILM CONTEST 2019: UNLEASH YOUR INNER CREATIVITY

Your favorite film competition is back and better than ever! After taking a hiatus to work on making this the best opportunity ever, we're excited to say that the annual film contest is back and nothing like before.

- Weekly bootcamp with check ins and advice from Hollywood producers
- Cash prize increased to $50,000
- An all-expense paid trip to Hollywood to get a VIP tour of Warner Bros. Studio

- A special premier of your movie at a red-carpet event with A-list directors, producers, and actors!

Don't be afraid to let your inner creative monster roam free and go all out for this contest! You don't want to miss it! Sign-Ups start October 5th, 2019, See You Then!

Was this a sign?

I mean obviously it was a physical sign, but I meant more on the spiritual level.

This film competition stopped taking place a few years ago and I was bummed that I'd never get the chance to take part in something that big ever again.

Yes my mom would be able to pull some connections and help me get whatever I needed to make my own project like this, but she doesn't know that this right here, film making, is what I really want to do and where all my passion lies.

My dad especially doesn't know, and I don't know why I'm finding it hard to tell them I don't want to be a football player anymore.

"Malakai?" I hear someone call my name over my shoulder and go to collect my breakfast from her hands. "Thank you," I say to her with a gentle smile and walk out the bagel shop.

Anthony's house was just a block away from here, so I decide to pay him a visit.

He has the longest driveway in the history of driveways, and I chalk it up to the fact that his whole family is active. One time they asked me to go out and grab the mail at their mailbox and I had to use my car to go up and get it. I could've walked but I was feeling lazy that day and not up to walking 15 minutes for some mail.

As I approach the gate, I put in the passcode that lets me right in, without having to call the house phone for access.

That alone should tell you me and Anthony's family are tight knit. Anthony and Saiyr are like brothers to me, but me and Anthony knew each other longer.

I've known him since I was six years old because we were on the same toddler football team and our dads ended up forming a connection instantly which naturally transferred to us.

When I get about 5 feet away from the front door, it opens to reveal a shirtless Anthony with a toothbrush hanging out the side of his mouth and a wide grin on his face.

He has a towel wrapped around his waist indicating that he just got out the shower and started brushing his teeth. "Well look what the cat dragged in," he said but I barely understood it because it sounded like a big gurgling mess due to the toothpaste and saliva in his mouth.

He spits it out into the grass and I inwardly cringe knowing Mrs. Davidson will go ballistic if she sees him violating her yard like this. She's a freak when it comes to her yard and flowers.

"Wassup bro," I say and avoid touching his semi-dripping wet body as I walk through the front door. He closes the front door behind me, and I walk up the stairs to his bedroom.

When we get in there, I go out to sit on his balcony and he goes in the bathroom to finish getting ready for the day.

"I was just about to call you," he calls out from the bathroom.

"Oh yea? that's crazy," I say sarcastically because we both knew he was going to call.

"What brings you by?" he asks a minute later, and his voice grows closer with every word until he was out on the balcony with me. He takes a seat in the chair to the left of mine on the other side of the door, making sure not to block the pathway of the entrance.

"Just wanted to chill," I reply looking out at the view of the many trees and buildings we were facing, and the never-ending sky.

I feel his gaze on me and look to see his eyes squinting trying to figure out what's wrong with me. "What?" I say trying to sound as normal as possible and hide my thoughts from showing in my eyes.

"Talk," he finally says, resting his first two fingers on his right temple as he leans back and gets into 'Big Brother' mode. I roll my eyes and give a slight smile because he doesn't miss a beat, and I find myself letting all of what's swimming around my head to fall out.

Ant was the guy you went to when you needed advice and a smart opinion on something, even if it's not the answer you wanted to hear. Saiyr was the guy you went to when you wanted to laugh the pain away and forget your worries for a little while.

Don't get me wrong, Saiyr did have his moments where he got serious and had some good advice to share, but he wasn't always reliable.

I tell Anthony everything, from not entirely wanting to do football anymore, to the film competition and wanting to enter.

Once I finish talking, he just sits there and looks out towards the view, I'm guessing trying to digest all of what I said.

"I had a feeling you weren't feeling football anymore," he finally says, "the way you were dragging yourself up and down the field these last couple seasons were proof."

I smile, still tense and bracing myself for what he was going to say about the film stuff.

"Are you sure this is what you want to do?" he asks, willing me to look at him in his eyes with his tone so he can gage how serious I am about this. I guess he didn't need my answer because my face told him everything he needed to know.

"I support you."

I shoot a look at him a little shocked, as he leans a little bit more in his chair to get comfortable. "That's it?" I say perplexed, "You don't have anything else to say?"

"Was there something else you wanted me to say?" he quirks up an eyebrow and realize he's playing that game where he wants me to get all my feelings and doubts out there like he was my therapist.

Yes, I told him the surface level of what's going on in my head, but he wanted me to spill everything and I just wasn't ready for that yet.

"No," I say sitting back into my chair.

After a minute of silence, Anthony speaks up and says, "So the 28th huh?" and I nod, not knowing if he'll even notice it or not.

"What are you going to do about practice?"

Shit.

I forgot about that. If I'm going to enter the competition, it's required that I attend the weekly bootcamps in the evenings, and more than likely it's going to happen at the same time as our football practices.

I run my hand up and down my hair letting out an audible breath. "I don't know," I say watching a bird land on the balcony railing, wishing I could trade places with it right now.

"Well, you only have two weeks to decide, seeing as the competition sign-up is Saturday after next," he gives me that tone saying I need to get my shit together fast and I know the decision I'll have to make doesn't just affect me.

It also affects Ant, Sai, and the whole football team because they'll be losing their star quarterback.

Yea, they'll have the second string, but he just transferred in from Auburn and the chemistry isn't all the way there with him yet.

"When are you going to tell you parents?" he asks another question I don't have the answer too.

He can tell by my body language and lets out a silent, "Shit bro," but I can just barely hear it.

"I know I say," and watch the bird fly away. If only I could fly away and escape my life, even just for a little bit.

"They're going to be supportive too, you know that right?" he says pointedly looking at me.

"Yea," I reply, and we just sit in silence for a little.

My phone vibrates in my pocket and I pull it out to see Saiyr trying to facetime me. I answer it and see he's outside in a crowded area, all smiles.

"Aye! Just the man I wanted to see!" he says loud on the other end of the phone.

"You're saying that like I'm the one that called you," I say laughing.

"I felt like you wanted to see my beautiful face," he winks. "Who lied to you?" Anthony yells out from his chair.

"Is that Ant farm I hear? Wow, you're having a party and didn't invite me?" Saiyr places his hand on his chest showing offense and hurt.

"I was in the neighborhood," I say, "where are you?"

"Glad you asked! I was calling to tell you to bring your ass down to this food truck festival I found. I was going to call Ant next but I'm glad I'm killing two birds with one stone." He moves to shuffle around some people and says hi to a few that walk past and greet him.

"Send your location bro," Anthony says, never missing out on the opportunity to eat some good food.

"Alright, it's not far from Ant's place so you can just walk here," Saiyr says sitting down on what I assume is a park bench.

"Yea I don't think so," I say, "I'm planning on putting myself in a food coma and walking would be the last thing I want to do." He puts me on pause and a second later, a message pops up on my phone with the address.

"We're about to head there now," I tell him standing up from my seat and heading back inside Anthony's room.

"Alright, I'll be here," Saiyr says then hangs up.

Ant follows me back into his room and grabs his car keys out of the pocket of his gym bag on the ground. He must've had an early workout this morning.

We head downstairs and enter his 3-car garage where his red Mercedes was parked and pull off into the direction of the food truck festival.

Later on that day, after the effects of the food coma subside, we all decide to go to a bar to play pool and throw some darts around.

I remain undefeated amongst our friend group in pool and add a few more wins under my belt. Saiyr is abnormally good at darts and hits the red dot in the center almost every single time, chalking it up to the fact he's the best human being to ever walk this earth.

Cocky bastard.

Anthony's secret talent was bowling, but we didn't feel like playing that tonight, so he wasn't able to gather a single win.

After the bar, we all went back to my place and went in the basement to binge watch horrible comedy movies and laugh at just how horrible they were.

It was around 1am when I heard the first snore roar through the room and instantly knew it was Saiyr knocked out with his head laying onto the bar and his hand loosely wrapped around a glass of apple juice.

Don't ask why he wanted apple juice or why he insisted on pouring it into a glass and drinking it at the bar like it was hardcore liquor.

Anthony and I both heard the snore at the same time and looked at each other while busting out laughing.

"That's your friend," he says to me and I shake my head.

"You introduced him to me, so really that's *your* friend."

I get up and walk over to Saiyr to shake him and tell him to go lay in the basement's guest room. He stirs out of his sleep like a drunken man who's had far too many to drink and needed to get a taxi so he can get home safely.

"Mmm," he says as I guide him to the guest room then close the door behind him when I see that he belly-flops onto the bed. I walk back over and sit back on the couch where Anthony is scrolling on his phone, probably browsing his social media.

"You still having trouble sleeping?" he asks out of nowhere.

"Is it that obvious?" I say placing my hand on the back of my neck and pulling down.

"Uh yea, you look like shit," he says chuckling at me, "You know it's because you're stressing yourself out right?"

"Are we about to have another therapy session?" I say, not really feeling a lecture from him right now.

"I'm just saying, you're harming yourself and need to take care of it. Not trying to sit by and watch you hurt yourself physically and mentally," he says with concern in his eyes.

"Don't worry, it'll be handled," I say, dead-ing the conversation.

He falls asleep a little while later, and I feel my body starting the stages of crashing, and I welcome the sensation.

"It's about time," I whisper to myself, glad that I'll get to be under the sweet trance of sleep.

The feeling comes even harder and I get myself comfortable on the couch, knowing this is about to be a long sleep like last time, hopefully it feels just as good. My eyelids grow heavier and eventually, I'm unable to even lift them. I feel my body settling and then, my conscious is drifting off, leaving my body still on the couch.

Heat.

Sweet Heat.

Warm like a hug from my mother.

Soft fabric under my feet.

I raise my head from my hands and see that I'm in the same position I was in as the dream I had a while ago.

How am I able to vividly remember it now?

When I woke up last time, my memories were just out of my reach and I couldn't touch them. Couldn't retrieve them, then they disappeared.

I wiggle my toes and notice that this time, I can control my lower limbs from the beginning now. The last time I had this dream, I couldn't move them until that girl came close to me.

That girl.

Who was she? I've never had someone like her in my dreams before. Usually when I dream of someone of the opposite sex and it's just use two, they're there to pleasure me sexually and have me waking up with a wet spot in my bed. I don't have those dreams often though, they're rare.

Other than those, my dreams are like everyone else's with wild stories and crazy looking creatures. But the girl that was in my dream the last time wasn't like the rest.

For starters, she was breathtaking. Unlike any other girl I've seen, even outside of my dreams. She was about 5'6 with beautiful hazel brown eyes and green specks splashed in there. Her natural hair was like a ginger coppery red with curls touching just barely missing the top of her shoulder. I'm sure if she straightened it or something I it would be touching her boobs.

Speaking of which, her boobs were a nice size, I'm assuming a B cup judging from the boobs I've handled in the past, and she had a nice perky butt that fit her nicely shaped frame.

She had a button nose with a bridge that didn't protrude outwards and light freckles that peppered around her eyes. When she concentrated, she bit her lip and inner cheek displaying that she had only one dimple in her right cheek.

She seemed around my age, maybe a tad bit younger, but I could tell she had a little feisty attitude about her. She seemed like a strong person. Then it dawns on me that she was just a figment of my dream and my brain was just showing me what my dream girl was like.

Since this is my dream, maybe I can dream her up again and summon her. She was one of the smartest dream girls I've ever seen so maybe we could just have a conversation and she could keep me company while I was in this weird dream world.

A bright light flashes in my peripheral vision, and I look to see where it was coming from.

From the light, I could see a figure walking out, and as their body was fully freed from the giant light orb, the light began to fade and die off.

Blinking, surprised, I noticed that it was the dream girl that I was just fantasizing about. I can't believe I managed to manifest her.

I've never had the same girl in a dream more than once before in my life, so seeing her stand before me now is a miracle.

I look at her face and notice that she looks…what? sad? How is she sad? My dream girls never really had emotions before and did everything I told them.

She looked around before locking eyes with me, and I could tell she wanted to roll hers but seemed too exhausted to do so.

"Hey," I say, shyly and curse myself for sounding afraid to talk to a girl. She doesn't say anything and just walks past the bench I'm sitting.

"Where are you going?" I ask and she keeps walking. I don't know where she thinks she's going because there's nothing but cloud and sky for at least 100 miles.

Why wasn't she talking? Did I mess up her voice box when reimagining her? No, I couldn't have because now that I'm in this dream world I can remember just exactly how her voice sounded.

She had a telephone sex voice with a tiny rasp that made the mass below my belly button jump.

Involuntarily of course.

Or maybe I reimagined her without ears?

"There's nothing out there you know?" I call out to her again, willing her to listen and she stops walking.

Thank you, finally.

"Why are you here?" she turns around slowly, asking me with almost a venomous tone.

"Um," I start to say, confused at the question. "I need to be alone, so leave," she says, and it looks like she's trying to get me to disappear with her mind.

"And what makes you think you can control what happens here?" I say, kind of amused.

"What? just cause you're a 'big strong man' you think you have a say in what I do?"

What? What is she talking about? And how is she trying to kick me out of my own dream.

"Listen sweetheart, I don't know what type of hurt got created and placed into that pretty little head of yours, but I'm guessing I was put here to make it all go away." I stand up and now it's starting to dawn on me that maybe my brain is giving

me a challenge this time around and until I can conquer this girl, she'll keep popping up in my dreams.

A smile forms on my lips. A look of horror flashes on her face. "Don't you dare call me sweetheart and don't even think about coming near me," she shakes her head, "I just need to get myself to wake up from this horrible dream."

That statement stops me in my tracks. Wake up? Dream? Huh?

"What are you —"

She walks towards me then sits on the bench I just stood up from. She places her hands on her temple chanting "wake up wake up wake up" repeatedly and I'm utterly confused right now.

"How are you going to wake up from my dream?" I ask her and she just continues chanting, disregarding me. I crouch down so that I'm able to look at her face.

"Hey," I say softly, reaching out to touch her and then think better of it.

Clearly, I need to take a different approach. "What's wrong?" I ask her and she stops chanting but her eyes are still wide. Was she scared of me? that's a new one.

How am I supposed to handle this? The panic eventually leaves her face and she lifts her head up to look at the beautiful orange and purple swirled sky. I stand then sit next to her, careful not to touch and follow her gaze to the unique never-ending sunset.

We sit there for what feels like hours, not talking, just taking in the view. "When I was younger," she starts to say and her confession shocks me out of the serenity of the moment. "Someone that I gave my heart too, decided to take that heart and leave it beaten and dead in the street."

Silence.

"It took me a while to find where they left it and nurse it back to health, but it'll never be the same. I will never be the same. Now that person is trying to contact me again and it's causing all the hurt and trauma to come back full force, leaving me unwilling to breathe."

I look at her and see that her eyes are squeezed shut like she's trying not to let the emotion seep out of them. Suddenly she lets out a wobbly laugh.

"I don't know why I'm telling you this," she wipes the lone tear that falls from her eye, "Probably because you aren't real."

"I'm as real as they come," I try to joke but it sounds more like a plea. A plea for what, I'm not sure. "Maybe they came back to apologize," I suggest, trying to give her something so she doesn't feel like she wasted her time confiding in me.

"Then why did they wait so long? Why now?"

"Maybe they were scared to face you," I shrug, and she turns to look at me like I slapped her.

"Scared? They could've just talked to me and we would've gotten through it together, but it's too late now. For apologies and whatever else they expect they'll get from me."

There's a rumble in the distance.

No, not yet.

She stands up and wipes both eyes, making sure they're free of any moisture and vulnerability she just let loose. "Thank you for listening," she says to me. "For some reason, this dream world feels like an escape and gives me a chance to catch my breath."

An even louder rumble sounds and the color of the sky begins to change to that dark grey and blue hue. I now know that that rumbling sound indicates the end of my time in my dreams. I wonder if it's because I'm waking up or if it's for another reason.

A cracking sound fills the air and I whip my head around to see that the cloud flooring is starting to drop.

Not again.

Can't I wake up by gliding up to the sky or something?

"Back to reality," the girl mumbles next to me, and before I know it, I'm slipping through the ground and falling into the darkness.

JORDAN

Just like the Joker said, my life isn't a tragedy, it's a fucking comedy.

Or at least that's what I read he said.

I don't even curse like that, but I feel like this situation calls for all the curse words in the book.

It's October 1st now, so it's been one month since Cory started contacting me. Every day he would send messages begging to talk to me and I would immediately delete them every time. Whatever he has to say doesn't matter, because if it was that important, why wait so long?

14 years.

You can't just brush 14 years off like it means nothing. You can't just come back into my life like your leaving meant nothing. Not just to me but everyone else that loved you. I shake my head violently trying to shake off the thoughts that refused to leave me ever since I found out who it was. I skipped my classes this past week and missed the first meetings to the clubs I signed up for online before the messages started.

I'm pretty sure my professors already labeled me as a slacker, and I might get kicked out of the clubs for being a no show. Despite knowing all of this, I just can't bring myself to leave my room.

Rylie stayed with me the first couple of days, but I had to force her to go to her classes because I couldn't have her starting the year off bad like me.

Camille came over on the days she didn't have to work her double shift, which was only about two of them, but I was still grateful for her doing that for me, nonetheless.

Now it's Tuesday and here I am missing yet another class, and on top of that, I'm all alone in the apartment, so the silence causes my thoughts to thump louder in my head. My phone vibrates and I already know who it is before I look.

Maybe: Cory

Please

It always only says one word, but that one word keeps piercing my heart over and over again because that was the one word I spoke to him silently in my head the day after left.

I begged and pleaded just like he was doing now, for him to find it in his heart to come back to us so we can be a complete family again.

But he didn't want us.

Didn't even care. Funny how the roles are reversed.

Just then my phone rings with a facetime call and I see that it's Benny. I haven't told my parents yet and Rylie says she won't tell them either, so every time they call me, I have to fake like I'm happy and everything is okay.

Lying to them and putting on a façade to the people I love most is another hurt entirely, but it's way better than talking about *him*.

I answer the phone and immediately see my baby brother on the other side. Well, not all of him, he just has the top of his head in the camera so I can only see his forehead and his curly dark brown hair.

"Jo-Jor!" he exclaims, and I can't help but smile at him. Leave it to my baby brother to be the one thing that can put a genuine smile on my face when I'm in the middle of so much turmoil.

"Hey Buu! Whatcha doin'?" I ask him in a playful way. He must of stole Ben's phone again, which is something he usually does when he wants to call me. Ever since they taught him that he can access me virtually anywhere with the device in his hand, he's been doing it every time he got the chance.

"Miss you!" he says, then he looks off in the distance and I'm assuming he's just gotten caught red handed.

He starts to run, and I hear Benny in the background saying, "Get back here you little monster!"

I laugh so hard that my stomach starts to hurt. After about 30 seconds of Ben acting like he can't catch up to Jamie, he finally gets him and recollects his phone.

"Hey Benny," I say through giggles.

"Hey Jor, do you want a kid? Because you can have mine," he says smiling down at my brother, "About to make me tear my spleen or whatever organ I was just using."

The love he has in his eyes for my brother makes me happy and sad at the same time. "Nah, I have a feeling you need him more than you think you do," I say as another text message pops up on my phone.

Maybe: Cory

Please

"You don't have class today?" he asks me and the lie slips so smoothly off my tongue, I'm disgusted with myself.

"No, my professor cancelled it. Something about the flu I think, I can't remember."

I rush to get off the phone because I feel my emotions starting to clog and tighten my throat. "I have to go though, want to take this opportunity to study and get ahead in my other classes."

Lie.

Why can't the lies just stop?

"Of course, Jordy, we'll get out of your hair," and just as I'm about to hang up he stops me by saying, "Hey, we're proud of you kiddo."

I just nod in acknowledgment and stare at the phone as it hangs up. "Proud of you Kiddo" echoes in my mind and I hop out the bed and run to the bathroom to release the vomit that's suddenly threatened to escape my mouth.

A couple hours later, during the break Rylie has for the day, she comes to look for me and finds me still in the bathroom.

My stomach was completely empty, and my body still wanted to vomit, but there was nothing else to let go of.

Physically anyway.

"Aw Jordan," she says as she drops her bag and comes rushing to my side. She pulls me into her, and I just let everything out. All the hurt, confusion, anger and abandonment I feel.

I don't usually cry because I've developed a tough exterior over the years and rarely do I ever cry in front of anyone, so I know Rylie's a little lost and uncomfortable right now.

After what feels like forever, Rylie says, "The fact you can still look this gorgeous despite all of this," she shakes her head smiling, "I envy you."

I sit up and wipe my running nose. "Sorry for being such a mess," I say, feeling a little ashamed.

"Jordan don't ever apologize for how you feel. Those are your emotions," she grabs my chin so I can turn to look at her in her face, "And that bastard did some fucked up shit, excuse my French." I nod so she can know that I heard what she was saying and digesting it.

"Whatever you decide to do with him, I'm behind you wholeheartedly. Even if you say you want him back in your life, I will be apprehensive, but I trust you." I smile knowing that I have someone as amazing as Rylie to call a friend.

"No matter what you say, I'm staying here with you for the rest of the day," Rylie says guiding me out the bathroom towards my room, while clasping our hands together, "Now, what liquor do you want? I'll get Camille to stop and pick some up before she comes."

Seeing as Rylie and I are still 20, I don't turn 21 until January 12 and Rylie doesn't until March, we don't drink too often, only when the situation calls for it.

Last time we had wine because Camille was feeling stressed, this time I guess Rylie expected we needed the hard stuff. It's not every day you're hit with what I was hit with, so I'm not opposed to getting blackout drunk tonight.

"Are you trying to go toe to toe with Jim or Jack? Or maybe you're feeling confident and think you can handle both?" She asks as she prompts me to sit on my bed.

"I'll take both," I say, voice still wobbly from the tears a second ago. She pulls her phone out to text Camille I'm guessing, then puts it back in her pocket.

"Okay, the first step to feeling better, is looking better," she gives me a once over, "and sweetie, as beautiful as you are, we need to get you out of these week-old clothes. Strip."

She tosses me a towel from my dresser drawer and goes back out the room. I hear the shower water start and do as I was told before she gets back.

Wrapping myself up in the towel, I hear her go into her room, then head back to mine. When she enters the doorway, she has a speaker in one hand, while her soothing lavender soap sits in the other.

"Come on," she says, and I follow her back into the bathroom. She sets up the speaker and puts the soap on the edge of the tub.

"I dropped some lavender oil in there so it will be mixed in with the steam. Now have fun, take as long as you need. Once you're done, I'll wash your hair then order us some Chinese when Camille gets here. Happy showering!" With that, she closes the bathroom door behind her and leaves me too it.

Did I ever mention I was going to marry her? Because I am.

After my shower, I throw on some black leggings with a plain black oversized t-shirt. The shower I took felt amazing and it feels even better being in some clean clothes.

I walk out to the living area and see that Rylie has the kitchen sink set up like a salon with all her hair products sprawled on each side of the sink. She washes my hair and the massage she gives my scalp feels so good, I feel like I'm in heaven. She puts my hair into some jumbo two strand twists all over, then ties a scarf around it so it'll stay safe throughout the night.

Once Camille gets here, Rylie orders the Chinese and Cam unpacks the grocery bag of stuff she brought for the occasion.

Tubs of cookies and cream ice cream, my favorite, sit next to Kit Kats and Sour gummy worms, which were also my favorites. She then had bottles of

Jim Bean and Honey Jack Daniels in a paper bag from the liquor store.

We ate till our bellies were full and drank until we couldn't form complete sentences. I tried walking to the kitchen to get some water but ended up stumbling into everything. We laugh and laugh and watch my favorite movie, The Wood, and I can't help but feel like the luckiest girl in the world to have people who care about and love me.

I didn't look at my phone once and realize I hadn't felt it vibrate in a while. I instinctively feel around for it and Rylie notices.

"If you're lookin' for your phone," she slurs, "I turned it off while you were showering." She giggles and I giggle back.

"Why didn't I think of that," I say smiling.

"Probably because you didn't want too," Cam says to me, not really thinking and I just stare at her. I didn't want too? Is she implying that I wanted him to text me?

Her eyes widen at the realization of what she just said then quickly added, "I didn't mean like that, I meant maybe you didn't want to turn it off because you didn't want to miss phone calls from Ben or your mom."

"Oh yea, probably," I reply, but I start to feel myself getting back into the mood I was in and it feels even worse since I'm drunk.

"I think I'm going to call it a day," I tell them and try to stand up to walk to my room, but my legs are shaking.

"We didn't even open the ice cream yet!" Rylie says and grabs my arm and pulls me back to sit on the couch.

"Come on Jor," she places her hands in front of her and locks her fingers in a begging motion.

I roll my eyes, "Fine, I'll stay up just a little longer."

JORDAN

14 YEARS AGO

"Okay sweet pea, which color?"

My mommy and I are out shopping for my big girl birthday party. I'm turning six which is a huge deal because I'm halfway to being a preteen. My mom says I'm growing too fast, but I wish I would grow a teeny bit faster.

"Pink Mommy, of course!" I can't believe she doesn't remember my favorite of favoritist colors.

I scrunch my nose at her, and she makes that silly face where she sticks her tongue out the side of her mouth and shuts on of her eyes.

"Ew!" I say because it's kinda creepy. She pokes my cheek and laughs that laugh that always shows off her pretty teeth.

"Don't you think we have enough pink?"

I widen my eyes and gasp in horror, "You can never have enough pink mommy, don't you know?" She laughs again and grabs the pretty pink table sheet thingy from the top shelf and hands it to me. I toss it in the basket I'm holding and follow her around the store.

"Is Daddy gonna be home?" I ask mommy as she hands the store lady our groceries so we can buy them.

She puts them on this magical moving table and the store lady shoots them with her laser beam then puts them in a bag. I wonder if the lady can move things with her mind or shoot the lasers out of her hands.

"He's supposed to be, we'll call him when we get in the car."

I can't wait to get back in the car, I left my Bratz doll in there because I wanted to hold the basket. We also have these cool TVs attached to the back of our car seats and I have my favorite movie Lilo & Stitch playing on them. My Daddy bought it for me for Christmas.

Once we get everything in the car, I hop in my car seat and brush my doll, Sasha's, hair while I wait for my mommy to start my movie. "Ready to call Daddy?"

Oh yea, gots to call Daddy first.

"Yea!" I love talking to my daddy, he's so funny. He works a lot so mommy and me eat dinner alone sometimes, but when he gets home early and surprises me, I gets so happy.

She passes me the phone and I put it to my ear, listening to it ring. It rings a few times and I wonder if he's off saving people at his job like a superhero. My daddy was strong, and all my teachers ask me about him, especially Mrs. Green.

"He didn't answer mommy," I say and hand her back the phone.

"He's probably busy, we'll try again later on his lunch break, okay?"

I nod my head and make Sasha look like she's flying by floating her by the window. My birthday party is tomorrow, and all my friends were coming. Rylie was my best friend of all, and we always hung out. I can't wait to show her all the decorations we got.

We pull into the driveway and I unbuckle myself then wait for my mommy to open my door because I can't open it myself.

Once she does, I grab Sasha and run to the trunk to help take out the stuff we bought from the store.

"You think you're strong enough to carry these?" my mommy asks me, placing both hands on her hips.

"I have super strength mommy, look!"

I grab the biggest thing I see and hold it up, showing off my strength. "Yea you are my little hulk. Go take those paper towels in the kitchen." I don't know why she was laughing, carrying big things was hard work, but someone's gots to do it.

I run in the house through the open garage door and set the big thing down. I look over by the couch and see that we still have our Christmas tree up for Santa to visit me on my birthday.

Christmas was a couple weeks ago but mommy said Santa told her he'd stick around for me. I was his special girl. Just like I was daddy's special girl, so I was double special.

"Where'd my little superhero go?" Mommy comes in the house with bags and I forgot I had to help her.

"Coming!" I run past her and back out to the car.

"You got all the bags mommy," I cross my arms and pout at not finding anything I could help with.

She walks back out to the car, "Yes, but I need your help closing the trunk, I'm too weak."

She shows her arm and how her muscles aren't as big as my Hulk muscles. "Okay mommy, you called the right superhero."

I push my short sleeves of my shirt up and she lifts me high so I'm flying up and I pull the huge trunk door down. "Good work team!" She says and gives me a high-five after setting me down. "Now let's go inside and set up for tomorrow morning."

After putting the tablecloth and the decorations and balloons up, I see that the sun is going down in the sky.

"Mommy why isn't daddy here yet?" I pull my stool up to look out the window in the front.

"I don't know baby, let's try calling him again."

She pulls my hand and we go sit on the couch in front of our TV in the living room. She calls him on her phone, but doesn't give it to me, instead she keeps it by her ear.

"I want to talk to daddy," I pout again like earlier.

"Hold on Jordan." Mommy doesn't sound like her usual self. She must be sad. I need daddy here to make her feel better again. She pulls the phone away from her ear and looks off into space.

"Mommy?"

She doesn't say anything for a second, then turns to me with a weird smile.

"I think it's time for bed sweet pea," she stands from the couch and reaches for my hand.

No. It's too early and I still haven't given Sasha her bath. I hadn't even had my bath yet. And it was my birthday tomorrow. My big girl birthday.

"But Mommy."

"Don't talk back Jordan. Let's go."

I get up from the couch but don't take her hand. I'm mad at her. I'm also mad at daddy because he would've let me stay up and would've played dollies with me.

We walk into my room and she pulls my covers back on my bed. "Don't I need my bath mommy?"

She stops fluffing my pillow and looks at me with the same weird smile. And her eyes are sorta shiny. "You don't have to worry about that tonight, I'll give you a free pass," she reaches out for me to stand in front of her.

"Yaaay!" I run over to her and hug her. "Can we read a book?"

"I'm a little tired tonight sweetie, but I promise tomorrow I'll read you all the books your little heart desires," she pats my bed, "Come on, climb in." I get into my princess barbie bed and she pulls the covers over me. I feel all snuggled and warm.

"You tucked in tight?" she pokes my nose.

"The tightest!" I say. She laughs at me and I'm glad her real smile is back. Then it goes away.

"Goodnight my little superhero."

"Goodnight mommy, I love you," her eyes are extra shiny now. "I love you too baby." She walks over and turns my light off, then comes back and turns my night light on.

Can't forget the night light, even though sometimes I wish the monsters will come play with me. They can't be that bad, plus everybody needs a friend. I doze off then wake up remembering Sasha isn't in bed next to me. I jump out of bed and run and grab her from the couch and run back before my mommy hears.

I doze off and try to remember if I'm forgetting anyone else and then hope I dream about living in a big castle, I love castles....

Something causes me to wake up out of my dream of baby bears and rainbows. The baby bears were all different colors with symbols on their chests. Kind of like care bears but different.

I open my eyes a little and see someone standing above me.

Daddy? I blink a little. It is daddy. "Daddy?"

"Shh, don't wake your mommy," he puts his finger over his mouth. I rub my eye to take away some of the fuzziness covering my eyes. "Where you been? We were looking for you?"

"Yea sorry about that, I was working late." He wasn't wearing his work clothes. He was also holding something in his hand. It looked like a box. I love boxes.

"What's that?" I point at the box and smile.

"Oh this? It's your birthday present," he puts it down on my table by the bed, "don't open it until tomorrow evening okay?" He had on the same weird smile mommy had.

"Can I open it now? Just a peak?" I do my pouting thing that usually gives me what I want from daddy. He smiles and brushes my cheek with his fingers. I squirm because it tickles, and he smiles his huge wide happy smiles. Then he looks sad.

"No, you have to wait princess, okay?" I nod but I'm kind of sad. I want to see my present. I hope it's a puppy, but not an old puppy like Rylie's. I want a baby puppy that's only mine.

"Go back to sleep okay? It's late," he tucks me back in and kisses my forehead.

"Will you make me pink waffles for my birthday? Oh! and a pink cake!?" He giggles but his eyes grow shiny like mommy's.

Why is everyone getting shiny eyes? Maybe it's a disease. I hope I don't catch it. He kisses my forehead again but keeps his lips there for a long time. Then he hugs me hard.

"Daddy! you're squeezing me!" I laugh and he lets go. I feel my cheek wet and see his face is wet.

"Sorry," he laughs but doesn't seem happy.

"So, waffles? in the morning?" He just smiles and stands up from my bed. I feel sleepy again and happy that daddy is home and remember mommy needs him.

"Go check on mommy, I think she's sad," he just stares on me and then turns around. He starts to leave, and I forgot to tell him the most important thing ever.

"Wait daddy! Goodnight, I love you." He stops walking and his shoulders look like they're shaking. Maybe he's laughing.

"Goodnight," he says, but whispers it, "I love you always."

"Oh, and daddy? Please don't leave, we need you tomorrow to set up." He walks out and I fall back asleep.

"It's my birthday!" I jump out of bed and run to mommy and daddy's room. The door is closed, so I knock on the door.

"Mommy, daddy, its January 12th! My birthday! I'm a big girl!" No one opens the door. They must be under a sleepy spell. "I'm 6 today!" I knock again. I hear a noise on the other side of the door.

"Mommy? Daddy?"

Just then, the doorbell rings and I run to see who it is. I use my stool to look out the window and see my bestest friend ever. I unlock the door and hold it wide open. "Rylie!" I jump up and down because I haven't seen my best friend since two days ago.

"Jordan!" Rylie puts down the bag in her hand and gives me a hug.

"Happy Birthday sweet girl," Rylie's mom, my aunt Stacy, said while giving me another hug.

They walk in my house and Rylie hands me the bag she's holding, "Here's a present, but don't open yet."

Why can't I open any of my gifts?

My Aunt Stacy walks towards mommy and daddy's room, "I'm going to talk to your mom real quick okay? You girls go play." I shrug and go show Rylie my decorations.

Mommy eventually comes out her room and gives me a big hug and a kiss. Daddy isn't with her though, but I know he'll come later. The rest of my friends from school and the neighborhood show up and I eventually blow out my candles.

They kept lighting themselves back up though, so I got upset a little. I opened my presents and danced and played. Moms weird smile came back and won't go away. Daddy still isn't home and he missed most of my big girl birthday.

Once everyone leaves, I put all my new toys and Sasha's new doll house in my room. Mom comes in my room after I finish putting my new doll house in my room. She looks sad and her eyes are shiny again.

"Why are your eyes so shiny mommy?" She sits on my bed and pats the spot next to her, I run over to her and jump on my bed on my belly. "Did you see that mommy? I was basically flying!" I laugh and look at her, but she isn't laughing.

She isn't even smiling.

"What's wrong?" I turn and sit on my butt so I can get a better look at her face. "Is it because daddy had to work late again? It's okay, I'm a little mad at him but only one of us should be mad. He probably didn't mean it."

She shakes her head and smiles a little. "How did I get so lucky with you?" She clears her throat and straightens her back and looks at the ceiling. I cock my head to the side at the silly question, "God put me here, remember?" She laughs and I smile because I made her happy again.

"That's true." She looks back at me and doesn't say anything for a while. "Your Daddy isn't coming back."

Huh? What was she talking about? I just saw daddy last night. Was he going on a top-secret spy mission? Did he get eaten by a bear? I hope not, I love bears.

"What do you mean mommy?" She lets out a long breath like she was a dragon breathing fire.

"I mean...he decided that he doesn't want to live with us anymore."

"Is it because I was mad at him today? It's okay, you can tell him I'm not mad anymore, he can come back." I shake her arm a little and she turns away to look out my window.

"It's not because of you sweet pea, it has nothing to do with anything you did. You're perfect and your daddy knows it," she wipes her eye because they started leaking, "He just thinks we'll be happier if he wasn't here anymore."

"But I was happy with him here too," I feel my lip tremble a little and get sad inside. I want my daddy.

"I know you were, but sometimes, God has other plans for people, and I guess he assigned your daddy a new plan."

I don't like it.

"Can we tell him to bring daddy back?" I need my daddy.

"No baby, we can't question God's plans." She gives me a hard-tight hug, kind of like the one my daddy gave me last night. "But you know what?"

She says as she pulls away from me. "Me and you are going to be just fine without him, you know why?" My eyes are leaking now because I really want my daddy and I can't make them stop. "Why?" I sniff.

"Because I love you and our love can help us conquer anything we want." She's smiling a real smile now, but it doesn't make me feel happy.

"Will daddy ever come back?"

"I don't know sweet pea."

She doesn't know? But she always has the answers.

I wish I could ask my daddy.

She hugs me again, "I love you my darling girl."

"I love you too mommy."

Weightless.

Conscious.

Alive.

As the bright light fades, I look around to see I'm once again, back in the cloud world of my dreams. I walk a little with no set destination, just taking in the serenity of it all, and the beautiful view of this never-ending sunset.

As I'm walking, I notice a familiar object in the distance with an even familiar figure sitting on it.

"You can't be serious," I say under my breath.

I walk up to him and he lifts his head from his hands once I get near. Why was his head always in his hands?

"You again?" He had the verve to say to me in my own dream.

"I should be saying that to you," I retort back, crossing my arms. He scoots over on the bench, gesturing for me to sit down next to him.

I take the seat, but it's not because he told me too, and sit on the very edge so I still had my own breathing room.

"This is a little weird," he says looking off in the distance.

"You told me to sit here," I say back, knowing what he meant but finding it odd that he found it weird.

Maybe my subconscious slipped into his Dream brain. "No, I mean the fact that we keep meeting each other like this," he waves his hands around in the air to emphasize where we are.

I look out into the same direction as him and don't say anything.

"Last time we were together you said something that caught my attention," he starts off saying.

"I did a lot of things in the last dream I'm not proud of," I say, remembering how I let my emotions get the better of me in my own dream.

"You said that it was just a dream or something, and you tried to wake yourself up," he says completely bypassing what I just said. I nod my head not following what he's saying.

"What did you mean?" I turn my head to look at him and he's already looking at me. How long has he been looking?

"I meant that I'm actually dreaming right now and none of this is real," I do the same hand gesture he did a minute ago. He has a weird confused expression on his face and I'm trying to figure out why.

"What?" I ask, feeling oddly weird now. He doesn't say anything, just places his hand to his chin, scratching at his lowcut beard. He really was gorgeous and looked like he should be a sculpture in a museum somewhere.

"What?" I say again, impatient this time.

"It's just," he trails off, still in deep thought, "I'm dreaming too." His words shock me and cause me to whip my head back in his direction. I almost caught whiplash.

"What do you mean you're dreaming too?"

"I mean exactly what I said. I went to sleep last night, thankfully, and woke up, or rather, arrived here."

I sit there unable to move, and extremely confused. "So, what are saying?" I ask once I'm able to speak again.

"I'm saying that obviously this isn't just a regular dream. Somehow, our dreams were connected for some unearthly reason." He turns his body so that he's comfortably looking at me now. He waits for my response and I fail to form any words.

What he's saying can't be possible right? We leave in the real world, not some fantasy. I shake my head refusing to consider what he's saying.

"Okay then since you're having trouble, what's your name?" He asks me.

"Jordan," I say, "Jordan Jameson." My voice is a little shaky when I first speak but then my confidence seeps back into my tone once I repeat my name.

"Nice to meet you Jordan, I'm Malakai Woods," he extends his hand out and I just look at it then up at him. He pulls his hand back awkwardly, "Okay then."

"Sorry, I just don't really know you like that," I say trying not to sound rude. "It's all good," he says with a smile, "why don't we just get to know each other then?"

I turn my body toward him and sling my right leg over the bench, so now I'm straddling it like I'm riding a horse. "Okay Jordan Jameson, how old are you?" He says with a joking tone.

"I'm 20 years old, turning 21 in a couple of months."

"When's your birthday?" He asks.

"Uh uh, it's my turn to ask the questions", I say as I wag my finger out towards him. This game of 20 questions could be fun. I love interviewing people.

"How old are you Mr. Woods?" I ask in my best interview voice.

"I am 20 turning 21 in a few months," he mocks me, "now when is your birthday?"

"January 12, what about you?" I quirk an eyebrow. "April 14," he says with a smile.

"So, we're the same age?" I ask.

"Are you wasting your question on that?" He asks amused.

"No, and it's not even my turn."

"Okay then, are you in college?"

"Yep," is all I say.

"Are you not going to tell me where?"

"You didn't ask that," I say smiling. "So, you're a smart Alec, noted."

He taps his temple and laughs. "Are you in college?" I ask, ready for him to give me the same one-word answer. He surprises me when he says his reply.

"Yep, a junior at San Diego State University. Currently an exercise science major but that's soon to change." His admission causes me to give mine.

"I'm a junior at Clark Atlanta University, currently a business major just because I needed a major." He looks at me cocking his head, I expect him to ask about what I just said, but he goes a different route.

"Do you have any siblings?"

I smile as I think about Jamie and his bubble personality, "Yes, just one. His name is Jamie and he's two years old."

"He must be amazing judging by the way you get when you talk about him." I nod and ask the same question back to him.

"No," he replies, "I'm an only child but I didn't grow up alone. My best friends are basically my brothers without the blood. It would be nice to have a little brother or sister of my own though." He sits as he contemplates asking his next question I'm guessing. I hope it's not if I have any hot friends.

"Why were you sad the last time we were here?"

She seems unprepared for my question and shifts to where she isn't looking at me. She puts her leg back over the bench, so now both legs are on the same side and looks out across the soft cloudy horizon.

Even when she's uncomfortable she's still gorgeous. Now that I know she's an actual living human, I'm even more intrigued by her. Want to know if her skin is as soft as it looks. How good it'll feel to have her body pressed against mine in a non-creep kind of way.

I like cuddling and I'm not afraid to admit to that. I knew asking this question could go one or two ways. She could either shut me out completely and go back to her cold clipped ways, hiding the glimpse of goofiness I was able to witness. Or she could realize I'm not a bad person out to get her and open up to me a little.

She looks like she's about to talk and tense my body in anticipation for what's about to come out of her gorgeous lips.

"When I was 5, the night before my 6th birthday, my birth father walked out of my life." I don't say anything, willing her to go on with my gaze on her profile. She continues to relay the memory of her 6th birthday and how her father never showed up.

"Did you ever open the present he left?" I ask her once she's done with her story. "No, I threw it deep in my closet and haven't thought about it since." She gives a sad chuckle. "Honestly, I haven't really thought about him until recently." She plays with the bracelet she's wearing.

"I'm sorry that happened to you," I say trying to comfort her.

"It's okay," she says, "wow it actually feels good to talk about this out loud." She gives a small smile, probably towards herself because she still doesn't look at me.

"I love my friends and everything, but our spa drinking nights only help me so much." I make a mental note to ask her about said spa nights if I ever get the chance to talk to her again after today.

Or tonight.

Or whatever time it is.

"Why haven't you talked to them?" I ask, genuinely curious about this girl and her life.

"I didn't want to burden them with these heavy emotions I'm feeling. That's also why I haven't told my parents that...." she trails off, wondering if she's saying too much.

"What?" I ask. She looks at me, trying to decide if she should say anymore. I give a reassuring smile, or at least what I feel is a reassuring smile and urge her to continue. Thankfully she does.

"My father, Cory, started messaging me a couple of weeks ago asking to speak with me." I try to suppress the shock that flickers on my face.

"What'd you tell him?" I ask. She shakes her head, "I haven't replied. I just keep deleting them. I still haven't told my parents that he's reached out." She finally looks at me, "I don't know how it would make them feel." "What are they like?"

She then goes on to explain how understanding and calm her mom is, how corny and funny her stepdad Ben is, and how giggly and smart her brother is.

I see the love in her eyes and feel it radiate off her in waves of beautiful heat. They're so lucky to have each other. "From the sound of it, I'm sure they won't be upset with you if you decide to respond to him."

She shrugs her shoulders. "I don't know."

"I think, if anything, you should talk to your mom. You said you haven't talked about or asked about your dad since that day, right?" I feel like I had a eureka moment just then, "Maybe she can put into perspective how exactly she felt and what happened that night before. I'm a firm believer in closure, because you can't fully open new doors if the old ones aren't under lock and key."

She looks as though she's contemplating what I'm saying. "Enough about me," she says shaking off the thoughts swirling in her head. "Tell me about you. Why are you changing your major?"

For some reason, my anxiety and stress doesn't come to me as I explain to her my current situation and how it's been a struggle for me to grab a hold of my destiny.

"If I'm going to talk to my mom, I think you should talk to yours too. Even if you aren't ready to talk to your Dad, *at least talk to your mom." She shifts so she's back turning her body to me. "Also, I think it's so cool that she's the author of one of my favorite books 'Once in a Pink Moon'."*

"Yea, that's one of my favorites too," I say proudly.

"So next time I see you, you're going to have already talked to your mom?" She asks quirking an eyebrow, looking a lot like Anthony in that instant.

If we were in an alternate universe and she was my friend in San Diego, I could see the two of them together.

Almost.

A little.

I could also see her with me but that's wishful thinking. No girl wants a dude who doesn't have his shit all the way figured out.

"Only if you're going to talk to yours also. I don't want to be the only one having fun out here," I shoot her one of those smiles that usually has girls dropping their mouths to the floor. She, of course, isn't fazed at all. We hear a rumble in the distance.

"I'm starting to think that's our cue to go," I say like it wasn't obvious. We sit there together as we watch the earthquake open a ripple in the ground. That ripple then turns to a hole the size of a pond. That pond then expands until it swallows both Jordan and I into its dark mouth.

MALAKAI

The drive to my mom's house is the longest drive I've ever taken in my life. Even that one time the guys and I decided to road trip to New Mexico didn't take this long.

I've been so stressed out these past couple months that I've barely had time to relax. Stress tends to take over everything you know and do if you let it. Right now, not only was I dealing with a shitload of stress, but I also had a good amount of anxiety mixed in with it due to what I was about to do.

I was about to tell my mom the decision I made for my life. I don't know what happened to me, but I woke up suddenly with some newfound courage this morning.

A sense of determination if you will, that caused me to hop out of bed and decide it was time I confided in my mom, telling her what was going on in my head.

My final decision came to me during practice a couple days ago while I was going through a few drills with my team. I had the football up in the air, ready to throw it down to the wide receiver, when suddenly, I just put my arm back down.

Coach was screaming at me from the sidelines and my teammates were looking at me like I grew three heads. Something in me just told me to stop and I let the football drop out of my hand.

I walked off the field toward the coaches. Anthony and Saiyr ran up to my left and right side.

"You okay bro?" Anthony asked looking concerned.

"You need us to take you anywhere?" Saiyr asked, sounding the most serious I heard him sound in a while.

"Yea I'm okay," I said as I walked then thought about how I actually felt, "Actually I'm more than okay," I said smiling. Saiyr looked confused as hell but Anthony just nodded in understanding.

"What the hell do you think you're doing Woods? Get your ass back on that field," coach said as I approached him.

"No can-do coach, I quit." Saiyr whipped his head around and looked back and forth between me and Anthony. I looked at him with the biggest smile on my face, "I'll explain later bro," and patted his shoulder.

I started speed walking then broke into an all sprint because I wasn't getting to my car fast enough.

When I got to my car, I opened the door then looked back at the crowd of football players that gathered around coach. I noticed Anthony trying to calm down a screaming and irate, balding old white man and laughed as I climbed into the car.

I never felt so alive.

I wish I could go back to that feeling. Now as I pull into the driveway of my parents' house, I try to suppress the urge to vomit.

"Calm down Malakai," I breathe to myself, "you're working yourself up for nothing."

But was it really for nothing? My life was about to completely change and if I didn't have full support from my parental unit, I don't know what I'd do. I'd probably go crawling back to the coach saying it was just a fluke and I wasn't feeling like myself. On my hands and knees, trying to get him to take me back.

I shake my head at the crazy scenarios I think up in my head and turn the key in my car so it can shut off the ignition. I sit in the car a few minutes more.

Okay, maybe a half an hour more.

My mom isn't expecting me today, so she doesn't know I'm out here. She could easily look at the cameras, but I know she's working right now, trying to create her next best seller.

I open my car door and step my foot out, "you can do this," I say, talking to myself again. I fully get out and walk around the car, up to the front door and silently curse before I knock on the door. I pace back and forth, laughing at myself for thinking she's going to hear that knock all the way from her office. I pace a little more, then I hurry up and jab the doorbell before I can run back to my car and drive away.

A couple of minutes later, my mom opens the door wearing her square reading glasses which sit on the lower part of her nose bridge and her eyes peeking over the top of them.

She had on her silk Versace robe and underneath, she was wearing one of my school's spirit t-shirts with her black Nike sweatpants and slip on house shoes from Target. Humble yet still showing she has some type of 0s in her bank account.

"Malakai?" she takes the hand she was holding to her chest and places it on my cheek. She then pulls me into a hug while she says, "What are you doing home?" She gives me a kiss on both cheeks, European style and walks back into the house, assuming I'd follow.

As I close the door behind me, my stress and anxiety levels shoot through the roof.

"Was your practice cancelled today?" She asks as she rounds the corner, headed back towards her office.

"No, I just wasn't feeling well," I say, which is not entirely a lie, my stomach is battling a war with my intestines right now.

She walks into her office and sits back down in front of her iMac, and I take a seat in one of the chairs across from her desk. I sling my right leg over the right arm of the chair and slouch down, getting comfortable.

"How's the book coming along?" I ask her, trying to figure out how I'm going to get the words I need to say out of my mouth.

"It's going great, you know the first 20,000 for me are always the easiest," she looks up from her computer screen and winks at me, "It's the middle part of the story that gets me." I nod and take in the beautiful scenery of her office.

When you first walk into the office that's separated from the rest of the house by dark brown rustic barn doors, the first thing you notice are the floor to ceiling windows covering all the right wall. There's a huge area rug with a black and white kind of tie-dye design to it, covering almost all the dark hardwood flooring.

There were two bookcases on the wall straight across from the door covered in all my mom's favorite books as well as all the books she's published over the years, even unreleased ones. In the middle of the two bookcases on the wall, was a big canvas painting of an old 1937 Underwood typewriter.

Her desk was not in the middle of the room, but more towards the wall with the bookshelves and paintings. She had a nice dark brown desk with shelving on both sides and a black leather chair she used as her desk chair.

Across from the desk were two accent chairs, both black leather with dark wood trimming and accents. The chandelier overhead looks like a spiderweb of lights and the ceiling was all black, giving the room that dark shadow feel. If you didn't know my mom, you would guess this was my dad's office because of all the masculine feeling features.

The only sound in the room is the sound of the water running on her tabletop fountain, her nature sounds playing very low on her computer and the typing on her keyboard where she brings the stories in her head to life.

After a minute of us sitting there in silence, me screaming at myself in my head to stop being a pussy and just come out and say what's on my mind, my mom stops typing and looks up at me.

"What's eating you?" She asks, cocking her head to the side. She squints her eyes as if willing my inner thoughts to seep out through my pores and take the shape of a person.

I look at her and give a shy boyish smile and place my hand to the back of my neck, pulling down on it. I breath out and straighten up in the chair. "What do you mean?"

Stupid question.

I don't even know why I fixed my mouth to ask that question like she wasn't my mom.

"Well, you've been acting weird for the past couple of weeks and dragging your feet around like someone's killed your dog," she says as a matter-of-factly. I let out a nervous laugh and stand up because I need to do something besides just sitting there.

I pace back and forth in front of the floor to ceiling windows that give us a perfect view of our Alice in Wonderland garden out back.

"You can talk to me Mal Mal," she says in her loving mother voice.

Mal Mal.

I haven't heard that nickname since I was about 10 years old and told her I was grown now so she could just call me Malakai. I wish I had that 10-year-old courage with me right now.

Just say it Malakai before you go crazy and they put you in an insane asylum. Look at me talking to myself in third person. I stop pacing and keep my body turned towards the windows overlooking the garden as I release the weight I've been holding in since I decided I wasn't happy.

"I quit the football team," I blurt out. I hear her audibly gasp and before I give her the chance to say anything, I keep going, trying to get it all out before I get scared again.

"Yes, I know I went to that school on a football scholarship and yes, I know that I'm choosing the worst possible time to quit, but I just wasn't happy anymore. I don't want to be a football player and I figured I should quit now before it's really too late and I'm a senior about to get drafted to the NFL."

I take a deep breath, preparing myself for what I'm about to see before I turn around and face her. When I look at her, I'm punched in the face by the shock that I feel. I expected to see disappointment, anger, sadness, irritation, anything but the huge smile that she's sporting. She almost looks as if she's proud of me and that she's been waiting on me to do this for a long time.

How could she have seen this or expected me to do this? Or maybe my mind is playing tricks on me and displaying what I hoped I would see on her face. I blink a few times, trying to see if her smile was just a façade but low and behold, it's still plastered on her beautifully created face.

"What?" I say confused. She looks down and shakes her head, letting out a soft chuckle before she looks back up at me.

"You know how long I've been waiting for you to say that?"

What? What is she talking about?

"What do you mean?" I say, still shocked she's not angry at me. "I could tell from the beginning that you didn't really care all that much for football," she starts saying and leans back in her chair, "I only saw you truly happy when you were telling all of your crazy stories and creating scripts and skits for you and your friends to perform."

When I was younger and we had family dinners with Anthony's family, eventually Saiyr's too, we would put on miniature plays that were written by me.

I would put the costumes together, set up the stage in our huge living room, and direct everyone and give them "acting lessons". Doing all those things was me exercising my true passion in the world and I didn't even realize it at that young age.

Thinking back on it now, I know I'm making the best decision I could ever make for my life. This causes some of the stress and anxiety I feel to fall away.

"Why didn't you ever say anything?" I ask her, smiling a long with her because her smile is contagious, and I'm no longer worried about what she'll say.

"I was waiting for you to fully realize it yourself and then come to me a step closer to who you're truly meant to be." Wow my mom was amazing.

"So, you're not disappointed in me for ruining my future?" I walk to my chair and sit back down as I brace myself for her answer.

"Of course not. Yes, it won't be easy changing majors from what you're doing now, but as long as you're happy I'm overjoyed." She stands up and rounds her desk, then sits on it so she's directly in front of me and looks into my eyes.

"I'm so proud of you Malakai for taking a step out of your comfort zone and grabbing a hold of your future," she brushes her fingers on my cheek, "And I'm so proud of the man you're growing to become."

She pulls her hand from my face and grabs both of my hands and holds them in hers, about to drive her final thoughts home.

"I believe in you and know that you'll excel at anything you set your mind too, whether it's being the biggest film writer in Hollywood history or creating a new society on Jupiter." She tightens her grip on my hands to emphasize her final point.

"Because of this, I'm not worried at all about where you'll end up because I know wherever that is, you'll be happy with your life."

Starting to feel my emotions clogging my throat I pull her into me for a hug. "I love you mom. Thank you."

"No, thank *you*. Thank you for coming into my life and being the best kid, a mom could ask for. I love you more." She pulls back then kisses my left temple. "I know you haven't spoken to your father yet so don't worry, I won't tell. I'll let you do it."

I nod at her, "Thanks Mom."

I stand up from my seat and she lets go of my hands, pulling me into another hug. "Just know, despite what you might think, your father will support you all the same, just like me."

I don't say anything in response, just walk back over to the window, looking up at the sky and how dense the clouds look. She goes back to sitting behind her desk, but she doesn't continue her typing just yet.

"Did you tell Anthony how you felt?" I look back at her, wondering why she's asking me this.

"Yes, I told him a couple weeks ago, why do you ask?"

"I figured you did because I saw him at the grocery store the other day and he looked like he was hiding something and was giving me short clipped answers," she laughs and I laugh too, picturing Anthony trying to play it cool while harvesting a huge secret like this.

"Poor Ant, I'll call him and say he's in the clear when I go upstairs."

"I'm glad you have friends as good as those two crazy boys," she says shaking her head, then goes back to working on her book.

"Alright, I'll be upstairs. Call me if you need me." I walk out the office and before I close the door behind me, I look at her typing and smile at her. She feels me looking and gives me a smile in return then goes back to looking at her screen.

I close the door and thank God for me being so lucky to have a mom as amazing as her.

As I step out the shower, towel drying my hair, I check my phone and decide to see what the football team group chat was talking about.

I put the group chat on do not disturb because I knew they'd blow me up asking why I left and blah blah. I open the thread with 40 new messages and immediately regret it.

Most of them are angry texts saying I ruined their chance of winning the championship and that leaving in the beginning of the season was a bitch move.

Others said I was a fake and then I see messages with Anthony and Saiyr defending me and I'm grateful for my friends for having my back through whatever.

After that, there are messages from the other players saying they'll miss me and tell the second-string quarterback that he has some big shoes to fill. I was also the captain of the football team, but I know that title will automatically go to Anthony seeing as he was the assistant captain.

Me, Anthony and Saiyr were the faces of the football team, and even though losing me will place a huge dent in the program, they'll survive without me.

After laughing at a few text messages and memes that are sent by Saiyr clowning different members of the team, I close out of that group text and open the one with just Saiyr, Anthony and me.

I send them a request for a group facetime call and prop my phone up on the counter as I start my night routine. Saiyr is the first to join the call.

"Are you going to tell me what the hell is going on now?" he immediately says, and he sounds like a concerned father. I laugh at his serious face, but he doesn't even smile a little bit. I put toothpaste on my toothbrush and start telling him what I told Anthony a couple of weeks ago.

In the middle of me telling my story, Anthony joins the group call then I tell them both what happened when I told my mom.

"Damn," Saiyr says once I finish telling my story, "So when are you telling Mr. C?" I shrug and spit the mouthwash I was gargling out into the sink.

"You know sign-ups for the competition start tomorrow?" Anthony chimes in, chewing on a double double burger he just got from In-N-Out.

It was already October 4th, meaning I had to either tell my Dad tonight, or tomorrow morning before the sign-ups are opened online.

I wet my face towel and wash my face while talking. "I might just go up to his office in the morning since he has to work the first half of the day for the new deal he just landed."

My dad owned his own marketing company titled CWM, Christian Woods Marketing, and it was one of the top marketing firms in the country.

"You just want to go to his office and do it because you know he'll be busy and won't have time to think about what you said," Saiyr says with a knowing smile. I hate that my friends knew me so well.

"Nah," I jokingly lie, "I just don't feel like doing it again tonight. I already went through that talk once."

"Yeah whatever you say," he replies laughing. "Ant if you don't stop inhaling that food and savor every godly bit," he talks towards a loudly chewing Anthony.

"Shut up," Ant says with a full mouth. We eventually hang up after talking for a while longer and they tell me how chaotic practice was today. They say coach blew a few blood vessels in his eyes and had to go to the hospital.

Saiyr hangs up because he was going to a house party tonight and Anthony says he was going to meet him there after he went home to change. I tell them I'll pass because I needed to rest, but I don't think sleep will come easily to me tonight.

I go and lay down in my bed, shutting my eyes trying to will myself to sleep. Insomnia is the most annoying thing on the planet.

After about an hour of doing this, I decide to go give the Zzzquil I had in my medicine cabinet a try, so I can fall into a sleep coma. It was now 12 am and I was wide awake with no hope for a good night's sleep. I go grab the Zzzquil and read the recommended dosage on the back. I add a tad bit more than they say, just a tiny bit for extra power, then go back and lay down.

After about 30 minutes, I start to feel that familiar slip of my conscience into the dark abyss of sleep.

JORDAN

Today is the day. Today is the day I get the answers I was never looking for.

Today is the day that I get the answers I never wanted.

I never wanted to think about him again, but once again, he took away my ability to choose. Cory was a door I didn't mind abandoning, but something told me that closing doors was important if you wanted to grow as a person.

I can't remember who said that though. As I take out the last bantu knot, I put in my hair last night, I smile at the milestone I was making. Today I was going to finally ask my mom about my birth father.

Today I was finally going to hear her side about the incident that took place 14 years ago. That incident that always leaves a subtle sting in my gut when my birthday rolls around.

It was a Friday and I was trying to finally leave the dorm and breathe fresh air. I was going to spend the weekend at my parents' house, and I told them I'll watch Jamie for them so they can get a much-needed date night, as well as a break.

I pick out my hair to give my bantu knot out some volume and go put on my electric blue Old Skool Vans. I was wearing a thin cropped hoodie with some low waisted ripped light wash jeans.

Rylie was in her morning Friday class, thankfully, I didn't have a class on Friday, but at this moment I kind of wish I did. I could of went to at least one of my classes this week, seeing as I suddenly have a definite pep in my step.

I text Rylie telling her I'm heading out and grab my car keys. Benny dropped them off along with my Black 2008 Nissan Altima about a week after I moved in, but I had yet to drive my car. I didn't have anywhere I needed to go, and if I did, it was within walking distance of the campus.

The joys of living in the heart of the city.

Once I get to my Nissan, I get in and feel on my steering wheel. "I missed you," I say to my car and start the ignition.

As I'm driving, I get a call from Cam and answer it right away. "Hey Cam," I say as I pull to a stop at a red light.

"Hey J," She says as I hear her shuffle with the phone, "Hold on, I'm putting my earphones in."

More shuffling.

"Okay, I'm good now. How ya feeling today?" The light turns green and I ease my way down the road.

"I actually feel pretty good today, I'm headed to my parents' house for the weekend."

"Are they cooking?" I laugh at her immediate question.

"No, I'm actually going there to finally ask my mom about…." I trail off and can feel the nod she gives on the other side of the phone.

After a beat she says, "Are you ready for this?" I give myself some time to think, even though the answer was clear as day to me when I woke up this morning.

"Yes, it's time. I'm almost 21 and I want to finally have all the answers to my life."

"I'm glad you're finally there Jor. You know Rylie and I are rooting for you one trillion percent." I hear someone call for Cam in the background. "I gotta go, my 15-minute break is over, surprisingly."

I roll my eyes. I'm pretty sure it's against the law to only have a 15-minute break if you're working a 10-hour shift. "I can't wait til' you quit that job," I say.

"You and me both my little Jor. You. And. Me. Both."

When I pull up to my house and park at the curb a little behind the mailbox, I push the garage door opener, and notice that both cars are gone. I'm not surprised seeing as it's only 1:15pm.

Jamie was at his daycare and my mom was going to pick him up after she gets off work at 3:00pm. Benny doesn't get home until around 6:00pm, so I'm not expecting him until right after dinner is ready.

I get out and go into the house through the garage door. I let down the automatic door and unlock the actual door connected to the house with my key. The garage door leads you right to the side hallway next to the kitchen, so when I walk, that's the first room I head towards.

I open the fridge to examine the contents and pull together a nice fruit salad with coconut water on the side for my brunch. I grab the fruit bowl and head to the living room and turn on Black Mirror on the big 65" Smart TV.

After two episodes of Season 5, I hear the garage door going up. I look in my fruit bowl and make sure I didn't eat it all without realizing. I always purposely left the best pieces of watermelon for Jamie because I knew he loved them. The fact that I even saved him these pieces is a perfect representation of how much I love him.

A few moments later, I hear the garage door open and hear his little feet pounding on the hardwood floor, bounding straight for me. "Jo-Jo!" He says as he runs into the legs I had propped up on the square white coffee table.

"Hey Buu!" I say as I pull him up into my lap, "How was daycare?"

"Fun!" His enthusiasm always gives me extra energy. It also quickly drains said energy within a few minutes. I hand him the bowl of fruit and he inhales the few pieces of watermelon. "Hey Mom," I say over my shoulder as she turns the oven on to 450.

"I could've preheated that for you," I say, and put a squirming Jamie on the ground. He runs into his play area in the left-hand corner of the living space.

"Hey Jo, that's okay. I still have to prepare everything before it goes in." I stand up from where I'm sitting and think now is a better time than any to bring up the burning questions scorching my tongue.

"Mom, can I ask you something?" I say as I take a seat at the island. She's rummaging through the fridge and cabinets getting all the ingredients ready to start preparing dinner. Turning to me quickly, she opens up the package of meat, "Of course. Hit me." I play around with the lint on my jeans before my next sentence rolls out.

"It's about," I look up at and breathe in the courage I need to finish my sentence, "It's about Cory." She immediately stills, and I'm surprised she doesn't drop everything all together. She gently puts down the chicken she was seasoning and turns to face me. The expression in her face shows a tiny hint of sadness.

I hope this conversation doesn't make me cry.

She leans against the counter and rests her hands on both sides of her on the counter. "I know we haven't talked about him since.... *that* day, but I think I'm finally ready to ask the questions I've been wondering about." I play with more lint as I try to gauge her reaction.

"Where did this come from all of a sudden?" She says looking bewildered.

I tell her about how Cory started texting me that day we were on the phone and how he hasn't failed to text me at least twice a day asking to speak with me. She listens to my story intently and doesn't say a word. Once I'm done, she just sits there staring at me, then she smiles.

"You know I've been waiting for this day for 14 years?" She turns the oven off then circles around the island and takes a seat next to me. "You have?"

"Yes, darling girl. I knew eventually you would want to know more about that day and why he left."

"What if I never asked about him?" I say scrunching my eyebrows together. "Then the full story would just die with me," she says smiling and we both give a soft laugh. The light heartedness of the conversation makes it easier to ask my questions.

"So, what happened that day? Why did he leave us?" *Leave me.* She straightens up in her seat as she begins to recall everything that led up the events of that day.

"Let me start from the beginning. Cory and I were high school sweethearts. He was the captain of the football team; I was the captain of the track team. I despised cheerleading, but everyone wanted me to be the captain of that too." She shook her head and gave a small smile as she takes a trip down memory lane.

"We went to prom together and won prom king and queen. We were the face of true love for our high school. For a while, that love knew no bounds. We were whole heartedly head over heels for each other and would never do anything to hurt one another. We got married right after high school."

She shifts in her seat and I knew that the next part of the story wouldn't be a happy one.

"One day, I got home early from work and find some high heels at the front door. They weren't mine as you could imagine, so I walked to our bedroom and low and behold," she says looking like she didn't want to remember this part, "He was there, in my bed, with another woman. There was the love of my life, showing me just how deep in the clouds I was thinking that nothing could ever rupture what we had.”

A lone tear slides down her cheek and I wipe it with my thumb, forcing my anger to stay at bay.

“After that, I kicked him out, changed the locks, all that good stuff. About a week later, I felt sicker than my normal heartbreak sickness. I was throwing up a whole lot and I looked so pale that I could’ve passed for a ghost. I ended up going to the doctor because I didn’t want to end up literally dying over a broken heart. That was when I found out I was pregnant with you.” She recalls, sniffing and wiping her tears.

“I contemplated whether I should tell your father or not, but I knew, without the shadow of a doubt, I was keeping you.

I didn’t have a plan, was fresh out of college barely making ends meet. Couldn’t land a job, but I knew somehow someway, we were going to be okay.”

“I ended up calling him and telling him I was pregnant, and he begged and pleaded claiming his cheating was a fluke. I took him back, not because I believed him, but because I wanted you to grow up with a complete family. I should’ve known you can’t glue the pieces back together with Elmer’s glue, hoping it’ll stick.”

She lets out a sigh. “Anyway, I let him back in our lives and he actually seemed like he changed his ways. He went to every doctor’s appointment and was present through the whole journey.”

"Over the years, I had my moments where I suspected he was still stepping out on me, but I never actually had the hardcore evidence to prove my suspicions. One day, I decided to follow him when he left for work. Mind you, I was 37 weeks pregnant, and I followed him all the way to his boss's house. I know what you're thinking, maybe they just had a meeting set up at the house, no big deal."

She shrugs her shoulders. "I thought that up until his boss's wife answered the door in a see-through red lace garter set and nothing else."

I audibly gas and she just nodded her head in an 'I know right' fashion. I hear a loud bang and look over to where Jamie is playing with his toy train set. "Not too rough baby," my mom calls out to him before she continues back to her story.

"So, the amount of stress from that situation sent me into an early labor, but luckily I was already full term with you. My water broke right outside of the house and I had to zoom to the hospital before I called and told him that it broke. When he arrived, he reeked of Chanel no. 5 and had a faint lipstick smear on his neck. If I hadn't known where he was, I would've thought he just had a tiny scratch on his neck."

I try to picture what I would do in a situation like that and accidentally let "Shit" slip from my mouth. I immediately apologize.

"It's okay, I already know," she chuckles.

I'm glad she's able to laugh about this situation now because I know dealing with all of that while you're pregnant is probably one of the worst things ever.

"His affair with his boss's wife went on for the next few years, all the way up until the day before your birthday." I look at her shocked, with the widest of eyes.

"I didn't confront him about it for so long because any emotion I was feeling, I knew would rub off on you, and I wanted you nothing but happy. As long as he was being a good father to you, I was willing to put up with a little heartbreak to see you happy until I gathered everything I needed to get a divorce."

I quirk an eyebrow at her questionably. "Since I was the one who handled the money, I paid our bills and also put some money away to the side for us when it was time to take that leap. That day before your birthday was the last straw. He had never missed a birthday before then and would even help in preparing the decorations for the party." She shakes her head, anger flashing across her features before she continues.

"That year I guess he had enough of that perfect dad act. That day we went to the grocery store to pick up the last decorations, I knew he was at *her* house. I thought calling him would remind him that he had a daughter who was turning the big zero six, but he didn't even bother to pick up. I knew he knew the phone call was about you.

When we got back to the house and I tried calling him again to no avail, I realized that that was it. You can hurt me, but you will never *ever* screw over my baby." She looked me dead in the eyes when she said the last sentence, the intensity of her gaze causing me to squirm in my chair.

"I had to put you to bed early to get everything I needed together without your curious eyes wondering. After I put you to bed and went back in my room, he had the nerve to say he was 'working late'," she put the last two words in air quotes. That again reminded me of Benny.

"I called him immediately after that text and of course, it went to voicemail. I went off on him in the voicemail telling him I knew what was going on and I will not let him sit here and fuck over the best thing that's ever happened to us. I ended the call by telling him we were getting a divorce. He literally sat there and spent the whole day with her knowing that he had his 5-year-old princess waiting in her castle. I threw all of his shit kindly in a garbage bag and set it outside on the front lawn."

"He came home that night begging the same way he did all those years ago, but this time it was different. This time I had someone else I was living for. I had you. And I had money to sustain us, as well as an interview for a job I applied to a couple weeks before. Once he realized I was for real, I guess he felt the best course of action was to completely remove himself from our lives. I couldn't believe he could leave something as perfect as you, but then I thought about it. He was in our lives, but he wasn't actively present, so he didn't fully know how great he had it."

"Telling you he left was the hardest thing I've ever had to do, and I was so afraid on how you'd take it. But my little girl was way stronger than I could've imagined." She wipes a tear I didn't realize was running down my face.

"After that day, you acted like he didn't exist. You never even mentioned him again. Yes, you were hurt and heartbroken, but you did your best trying to keep going with your life." We were both crying now, and an oblivious Jamie was now coloring in one of his coloring books on the floor.

"There were times when I would hear you crying at night and times when I would see you looking a bit distant, but most of all, I saw you trying to not let your demons win."

"But in a way they did win Mom," I say wiping my cheeks. "I was never able to let myself love a boy or even fully like a boy because I felt like they were going to leave me. I still can't even bring myself to call Ben dad because I feel like he'll eventually leave too once he realizes he's had enough of me."

My mom shakes her head violently at that. "Ben loves you like you were his own. You are just as much of a daughter too him as Jamie is a son. He's nothing like Cory."

I put my head down and she places her finger under my chin, urging it back up so that I'm looking her in her eyes. "Your father leaving was not in any way your fault. It had nothing to do with you or me, but everything to do with him and whatever demons he was battling within."

She cups my cheek and uses her thumb to brush a falling tear. "And you want to know the most important thing?"

She gives me a warm genuine smile as she gives her next revelation, "I forgave him. And it's okay for you to do the same. Don't let a grudge bury you into the ground and take away your ability to see light. If you decide to forgive him and want to form some type of relationship, that's okay, you aren't betraying me. If you decide to never want anything to do with him, that's okay too. Whatever you do, just make sure you end that chapter of your life so you can start a whole new book. One where you actually live with no worries or regrets."

I let out a long slow breath as my biggest worry leaves my chest. Deep down, I felt like the little part of me that's curious to know what it's like to have my real father in the picture, was betraying the love and obstacles my mom went through to help me live a better life in spite of the harm he's caused our family.

She told me it wasn't betrayal wanting to let Cory back in, and that was something I didn't know I needed to hear until now.

Did that mean I did want a relationship?

We sit there crying a little more until a hungry Jamie comes waddling over asking for his gummy snacks.

We laugh and pull ourselves together. My mom goes back to preparing dinner and I round the island to give her a hug from behind. "Thank you, mom," I say, "For everything."

Still.

Quiet.

Peaceful.

Lifting my head up from my hands, I turn my head to the figure walking up to me and smile.

'Well look who it is,'' I say scooting over to give her room to sit on the bench. She smiles and it practically undoes me. A genuine smile that gives a hint that the talk with her mother probably went just as good as mine.

"So, did you do your homework?" I ask, wanting to nudge her shoulder but unsure how she would take it.

'I always do my homework.'' She gives me the 'was that even a serious question' look.

I put my hands up in defense. "Well excuse me," I laugh, "how did it go though?"

She chews on her lower lip as she contemplates how to say her next words. "Honestly, I wish I had that talk with her earlier. Hearing her say the words that she did really changed my perspective on the whole situation."

I felt her newfound happiness radiating off her and couldn't stop the wide grin from spreading across my face. She told me a summary of the story of her parents and what led to the tragic events of that one January day.

"That's one hell of a story," I say still trying to reel back in my shock, "Sounds like something you'd see on a movie."

"Yea, a Lifetime movie maybe." We both laugh then she turns to me, getting comfortable. "How about you? What'd your mom say?"

My smile stays on my face as I tell her the stress I went through that whole day and how I almost shit my pants driving there. She laughs and shows happiness in her eyes when I tell her about my mom's never-ending support and how I'm excited to start this new journey in my life. Jordan didn't know it yet, but she was someone I would consider a friend now.

Being able to talk to her so openly and candidly is what caused me to cling to her so fast. Yes, at first, we didn't know what the hell we were experiencing, but now that we know that it's more than just a dream, we're able to treat one another like real human beings.

I finish my story and I stand up from the bench. I wanted to take a little walk with her down the never-ending stretch of clouds and sky, so I was hoping she'd follow me with no complaints.

As I walk a little way away from the bench, she gets up and matches her strides with mine beside me. "So, have you decided what you wanted to do about your dad?"

I turn my head to her as I ask the question, hands in the front pocket of my joggers. She shakes her head.

"No, not yet. Apart of me wants to just block the number and be done with him, but deep down inside, I can't shake that feeling of 'what if' ya know?" I nod my head in understanding.

"I think you should open the present he left you that night," I shrug and continue, "and use whatever is in there to fuel your final decision." She looks at me like she's considering what I'm saying. "Plus, I'm just really curious to see what's in there."

I laugh and she tries to scowl at me but fails and laughs too. "I don't know, I might."

We walk further and I turn around to see the bench starting to fade into the distance.

"When are you talking to your dad?" she asks me. I put my hand on the back of my neck and pull down. "I have no choice but to do it tomorrow, since that's when sign ups start."

"You can't sign up any other day?" Her curiosity is cute. "Technically yes, but this competition is on the first come first serve basis and there's only 30 spots. Did I mention it was the biggest film competition of its time?"

"You did, multiple times," she says sighing while smiling. I smile with her and something small flickers in my chest. I ignore it.

"I'm just really worried my dad will be highly pissed at me and say I failed him as a son," I shake my head at the fact I'm even thinking like this about my Dad but I think about all possible scenarios in every situation.

"Do you honestly think he'll say all of that?" She stops walking which causes me to stop too.

"Yes." I shake my head after thinking. "No, but it's still something I'm mentally preparing myself for."

"Maybe after you tell your dad, your insomnia will chill out a little bit." I forgot I told her about my insomnia. I hope she's right. "Hopefully. We'll see though."

I continue our walk and she's right alongside me. "When you wake up, do you remember me?" My question comes out of nowhere but I'm glad I asked it. She thinks hard.

"Now that I think about it, no I don't." I try to not let the little pang I feel in my chest show. "But the advice you give and the sense of courage you leave me with still lingers in my mind. It's like a distant memory of someone I once knew. Or like a quote I remember reading in a book once."

That provides me a little comfort. "Same with me, I don't remember you, but I remember the feeling you give me." She shoots her eyes to me, "not like that, I barely know you. But I do consider you my friend a little now." I smile at her and she gives a shy one back. Was she blushing? Maybe I'm just seeing things.

"Maybe if we try to will ourselves to remember, a sliver of it will stay with us when we wake up?"

"Why do you want to remember me Jordan Jameson?" I quirk and eyebrow at her and give a smile.

"I just want to better understand what it is that we are in. Like what we can and can't do or why we were placed here," she was blushing, "that's all."

"Uh huh," I say and as I look off in the distance, I see that we were coming up on yet another bench.

Or was it the same bench? Weird.

That gentle rumble in the distance makes its way to our eardrums. "Already?" I say under my breath. I feel like I just got here, and I wanted to talk to her more.

Wanted to pick her brain. Figure out all her favorite foods. What made her tick. What made her happy. If she snorted or cried when she laughed hard. Or both.

What the hell is wrong with me? Why do I want to know this about a random girl? Get a grip on yourself Woods.

"Well, I guess that's it for us tonight," she says beside me. We get up to the bench and sit down. The rumbling gets closer and closer.

"Same time tomorrow?" I ask her.

"Sure, why not?" She says and actually winks at me. I would've thought my heart fell for her then if it wasn't for me literally falling into the now familiar black abyss.

Malakai

I woke up smiling and determined.

I don't know what's been going on with me lately, but this newfound motivation is welcome to stay forever.

I look over at the clock to see that it's 9:30am, so my dad should be in his office. Signups start at 3:00pm today, so I need to hurry up and get a move on.

I get up and shower, then throw on some black and white plaid slacks with a cream-colored cashmere sweater and my black Roberto Cavalli suede loafers. I figured since I was seeing him at his office for an important "meeting", I might as well dress up a little.

I grab my phone and call his work number to make sure he's in his office. "Hello Mr. Woods office, how may I help you?"

"Hey Jenny, it's Malakai, is my dad free?" Her tone goes from clipped professional to warm and loving.

"Hey Mal, he's about to go in for a meeting, but he should be out around 12. Did you need me to give him a message?"

"Yea, tell him I'm bringing lunch today."

I can hear her smile through her words, "Aw that's so sweet! Okay, will do. See you at 12!"

Jenny has been my dad's personal assistant for about 4 years now. She's in her early 30s, and I look at her like a big sister. She's one of the nicest, caring people I know and she's well on her way to a much-needed promotion. I'm grateful to her for making my dad's work life so much smoother so he's not working late nights every day.

I check my Apple Watch and see that it's 10:45, so I have about 10 minutes before I need to head out. His office was in downtown San Marcos, which was about 40 minutes away from where we lived in La Jolla. I figured I'd stop and get us some brunch from my favorite brunch spot, Brockton Villa.

I call ahead and order our food so that when I get there, I can just pick it up and go straight to the office.

When I get to Brockton, a lot of the people there know me as the star quarterback from my college, and a lot of the others know me as the guy who always orders the Chilaquiles.

After talking to a few people I know from around the neighborhood, I start making my way to my dad's office. The ride there is one million times better than the ride I took to go talk to my mom. This is probably because I've already told one of my parents my life plans, and she was already behind me 100 percent.

I know my dad will probably be the same way, but I'm just worried he won't fully understand. I'm worried he'll always have that thought of "why did he ruin his life like this" or something. I shake off the thought as I zoom down the highway toward San Marcos.

"Hey Mal!" Jenny jumps up from her desk and gives me a big hug.

"Hey Jen," I say smiling back, "you look good. Who's the lucky man?" She swats at my chest, blushing. "Shut up," she rounds her desk and sits back down.

I place the food bags in my hand on the ground next to me as I talk to her. "What? I'm just saying you don't do the whole make up thing unless there's someone you're seeing." I give a knowing smile.

"His name is Chase, and it's still new so that's all the information you're going to get," she shakes her head smiling.

"Chase," I play with the name on my tongue, "I like him already. As long as he keeps you happy."

I pick up the food bags. "He does," she smiles and looks as though she's thinking about him. I look at my watch and read 12:15. "Is he out of the meeting yet?"

"Yep, just got out 10 minutes ago."

I point a finger at her with the food bag still in my hand, "Alright. Be good out here, don't do anything I wouldn't do." She laughs and I wink at her then head down to my dad's office.

He had floor to ceiling glass windows all around his office; even the wall and door facing toward the cubicles scattered around were all glass. He had the ability to frost them over whenever he was having an important phone call or private meeting, but when they weren't frosted, anyone was free to come in.

He wasn't a mean boss, but he wasn't a push over either. Everyone in this office respected and loved him and I'm proud to call him my dad.

As I walk up to his office, I say hi to a few of his employees, then push open the door to his office.

"Malakai!" He says standing up and rounding his desk. He pulls me into a firm hug and rubs my back while he does. We pull away from each other and he grabs one of the food bags I'm carrying.

"Hey Dad, I figured I'd bring you lunch since I wasn't really busy."

"Judging from where the food came from and the smell, I already know you're about to put me into a food coma." He laughs, "Thank you so much son."

I shrug like it's no big deal and my anxiety starts to build inside of me. He frosts the windows of his office so we could have some private father son time.

His desk was all black and sitting in front of a gorgeous view of San Marcos. In the far-right corner of the office, he had a mini bar where he would mix drinks for some of his faithful clients or even new clients if they were feeling comfortable enough. To your immediate left, when you walk in, he has a black leather couch against the wall with a dark brown coffee table in front of it. Frida Kahlo's "Still Life Parrot" painting is hung on the same wall the couch sits against.

I sit down on the couch and pull the contents from the bag I had, splaying them out across the coffee table. He pulls his out and does the same onto his desk.

We start eating and he tells me about the meeting he just had with a potential new business partner. My dad participated in a lot of business to business marketing, but just recently ventured in the business to consumer marketing realm. He was one of the biggest marketing firms, and he wanted to provide some sort of classes or training to teach people more about the importance of marketing and what it all entails.

I tell him about school and how I'm glad I'm not on campus anymore this year. "How does the team look this season? Do they seem championship ready?"

I knew he would ask me about football seeing as it's basically the biggest thing I'm doing in my life right now. I swallow hard on my food and gulp down some of the bottled water I got from his bar before I reply to him. I look over at him, and he's just chewing away at his food, waiting for my response.

"About that," I rub the back of my neck, "I ..." damn why was this so hard, "I quit the team."

He choked on the water he started drinking and I wince. "What?" Is all he manages to say as he wipes the water off his suit jacket.

"I quit the football team."

"When? Why? Is this a joke? Are you pranking me?" He looks around for some hidden cameras and I breathe out the breath I didn't realize I was holding.

"I wish I was," I say then immediately change it, "actually no I don't." I pull down on my neck. "I quit the team a few days ago."

"Why? What's going on?" He has genuine concern in his eyes, and he gets up from his desk to come sit next to me on the couch.

"You know I've been playing football for basically my whole life." He nods and waits for me to continue. "Yes, I like playing it and I like the hustle and bustle of it all, but," I look down at my food suddenly losing my appetite, "but my heart isn't in it. I'm not fully happy."

He leans back in his seat and lets what I said sink in. "I thought you loved football. You would always beg me to take you to camp and sign you up for little leagues."

He wasn't lying, I did do all these things but not because I loved the sport. "I did it because I loved seeing the look on your face when you watched me on the field."

My dad was a football player growing up but had a serious knee injury that cost him his senior year in high school and his spot on the college team. He's fully recovered now but it took years of physical therapy.

"I felt like it was selfish of me to be so good at football and not want to play, knowing you loved the sport so much and it was ripped out from underneath you."

I don't look at his face, but I feel the violent shake of his head. "I loved the proud look on your face whenever I made a good pass, won a game, or even lost a game. You were just proud to see your son following in your footsteps."

I use the fork in my hand to play with my food. "I was thinking about telling you I didn't want to play football after high school, but when I got the scholarship and the spot as the star quarterback as a freshman, I couldn't just decline that opportunity. I knew it would crush you."

He places his hand on my knee, and squeezes. "Look at me," he says in a serious almost stern voice. I do as I'm told and finally see the many emotions that are swimming in his eyes.

It's hard to grasp all of them, but the few that I can pull out are sadness, anger, and disappointment. I knew he would be disappointed in me but seeing it on his face hurts a whole lot more.

"I don't even know where to start," he says shaking his head.

After a beat he says, "Well first, thank you for telling me all of this. I can see that this conversation was well overdue and for that I'm sorry."

He's sorry? Shouldn't I be the one apologizing to him?

"I'm sorry that you felt you couldn't come talk to me about this earlier. I'm sorry for pushing my dreams onto you at such a young age." He blows out a long breath. "Ultimately, I'm sorry for having my head so far up my ass that I didn't see that my own son was suffering." He lets out a disbelieving scoff and I place my hand on his arm.

"You didn't force your dreams on me dad, it was more so just me wanting to honor the legacy you left behind, even though it wasn't what I really wanted to do."

"What is it that you really want to do?" He looked like a little boy the way his curiosity flashed on his face.

"I'm glad that you asked," I give a timid smile as I think about the things I have planned for my future.

"I want to get into film making and film production." I immediately follow it with, "I know it doesn't make the best money starting out, but I believe in myself and know that I'll be successful."

He gives a half smile, "I should've known you loved doing that since you always put on shows as a kid." He laughs at the memory, "It was so cute watching you boss Anthony and Saiyr around in those costumes you put together." I smile at the memory too.

"So, what's the next step?" He asks me.

"Well, first, I'm going to talk to my advisor and see about switching my major. Then I'm going to ask what's going to happen to my scholarship now that I'm off the team."

He nods, "Seeing as you're already a Junior, you know you'll probably be in school a year or so longer?" I nod knowingly.

"As long as I'm pursuing my true passion, I don't mind weathering the storm a little longer."

He looks at me with a gleam in his eye that causes me to break eye contact because I feel too exposed. "I'm so proud of you son, and I wish I was half as smart and courageous as you at your age."

"Aw dad stop," I say feeling my face grow hot. "I'm serious son, I look up to you," he chuckles. "Also, I don't know why you felt the need to tell me it'll make money. I'm not in the least bit concerned about your future. Both your mom and I know that you're destined for greatness."

"I'm still mad I didn't notice this sooner; I will never forgive myself." Dad says as he walks me outside to my car. We talked more about my future and I told him about the competition. He seemed genuinely excited for me, which caused my excitement for the competition to spark back up again.

"It's okay dad, you know now," I place my hand on his shoulder when we get to my car that's parked on the outside curb.

"It's not okay, that just means I don't know my son as well as I thought I did." He opens my door for me. "You know what? This calls for a father son bonding retreat somewhere deep in the woods, secluded from the rest of the world."

"Dad, we're black. We don't do that."

We both laugh, and I close my car door while simultaneously putting my driver side window down. I glance at the clock in my car when I start it and see that it's 2:10pm. I had time to get home and sit on my computer as I watched the clock tick by.

"Alright son, are you going to be home tonight?"

"I'm not sure, you know Anthony and Saiyr, always popping up or making plans at the very last minute." I put the car in drive.

"I'll see you later then, be safe, I love you," he taps the top of my hood and steps back onto the curb.

"Always, I love you too," and with that I speed off down the road towards my house.

When I get there, my mom isn't home. She said she was visiting her little sister, my Aunt Gi-Gi, and to call her after I talked to my dad. I would make that call once I finished signing up for this competition.

I get to my room and run straight to my iMac. I go onto the San Diego Film Contest website and still had 2 minutes before 3:00pm hit. The traffic on the website was high and I was nervous that I wouldn't be able to sign-up because the site would crash.

I twirled in my chair and think on the conversation I had with my dad. I really had the best parents that a kid could even ask for. My phone timer went off that I set a couple weeks back after finding out about the competition. I immediately refresh my browser and thankfully, the site doesn't crash. I hurriedly enter my information in the specified fields and hit submit.

CONGRATULATIONS! YOU'RE IN!

You are now one of the 30 lucky participants in the 2019 revamp of the San Diego Film Contest. I guess the early bird does get the worm ;)! We will send a formal application form to the email you provided on the previous screen. This is just so we know a little bit more about you and what you plan on doing for this competition. It'll also show us if you're a good fit for the competition, or if we should give your spot to someone who's more fit for the position. Good luck to you and this new exciting journey you're about to embark on!

Best of luck,

The San Diego Film Contest Team

"YES!" I scream out into the air and jump up from my seat, knocking my desk chair back. All the stress, anxiety, and insomnia I dealt with up until this point was more than worth it. Seeing that congratulatory message felt so much better than my college acceptance letter.

I'm already picking up my phone. I don't even know what number I'm dialing because I'm too excited and just letting my fingers do all the work.

"Hey bro," I hear Anthony's voice on the other end. I hear a little girls voice in the background asking him if he wanted pink or purple nails. We switch over to Facetime.

I immediately knew he was at Saiyr's house and Saiyr's little 4-year-old sister, McKenna, was giving him one of her infamous makeovers.

"Pink please," he says and looks off camera to watch her put the paint on his nails. "I got in," I say barely containing my excitement, "I'm in bro."

He shoots his gaze back to the camera and shoots his eyebrows up. "Really!?" he puts his fist on his mouth to cover the "O" that formed there.

"Hey! You messed it up!" McKenna whines in the background.

"Sorry, Ken Ken, hold on." He gets up and walks through the house.

"Wow, Congrats Kai! That's huge. I'm guessing the convo with your pops went well?" He opens a door and I hear a shower going in the background. He walked in the bathroom to where I assumed Saiyr was taking a shower.

"Aye Sai, Mal got into the competition," he says to him through the shower curtain. I hear the curtain slide a little and Anthony immediately covers his eyes. "Come on bro," he says and Saiyr grabs the phone from him a second later.

"If you didn't want to see, you shouldn't have barged in Ant." He turns his attention to me. "Is this true Woods? This better not be a joke."

"It's true," I say smiling hard.

"WOOHOO!" He screams on his end of the phone and his mom yells at him to keep it down from another room. "SORRY!" He yells again, "I'm proud of you bro, I knew you could do it."

"Can I have my phone back now," I hear Anthony say in the background and laugh. Saiyr gives him back the phone and I hear the shower curtain slide again. Anthony turns from the shower then uncovers his eyes. He leaves the bathroom and goes back to where McKenna was waiting for him.

"Pull up to Saiyr's house bro, I'll tell his mom to make her spaghetti. We're going to celebrate tonight too."

Saiyr's mom made the best spaghetti in the world. "Alright, I'll come over there right after I call my mom."

"Bet," he says and then we end the call.

Seeing their reaction to the news reinstated that I was making the right decision and my family knew just how important this was for me. I call my mom and then my dad, both of whom were very excited for me and not surprised.

They told me they wanted to celebrate with me tonight, but I told them I was going over Saiyr's house. My dad said they would come to Saiyr's house later tonight as well, making it a big family affair.

I loved how close everyone was and having my family all come together to celebrate me taking the first step towards my dreams is surreal.

I grab my car keys and head back out the door, the happiest I've been in a while.

JORDAN

Saturday morning, I woke up with a decision. I was going to tell Cory that I didn't want a relationship with him. I went all these years without him and now that I finally have a choice on whether he will be in my life, I don't really need him.

After all, I had my mom, Jamie, and of course Benny, who's been more of a dad than Cory will ever be. I still can't bring myself to call Benny Dad, though, but I'm sure once I close this door for good, that time will soon come.

I don't know what it is though. I know I told my mom I felt like Ben would leave, but that wasn't the only reason why I couldn't call him dad. It's like all these years, I felt like I was betraying my birth father by calling Ben dad, even though he betrayed me to the worst possible degree. I held onto a tiny bit of hope that he would come back into my life, and now that he finally made his appearance, I wanted to tell him to go fuck himself.

I was done being a victim to his selfishness. I was done letting him define my life when he clearly didn't give a shit about it. I was done with the whole idea of him. I know that making this decision would cause other people to have "what-if" scenarios for the rest of their life, but I already played those what-if scenarios over and over in my head for the past 14 years.

What would a little more do?

I still haven't told Ben about my dad contacting me, and I don't think I ever will. Not because it's none of his business, but because I don't want him to feel like I considered giving his spot as my dad back to its original owner.

Me being able to make my own decision now gives me a strong sense of empowerment. Not to mention, I woke up feeling at peace with this decision and knowing what it meant for my life. I also woke up with curiosity nagging at the back of my mind, wondering about the gift that's been sitting in my closet for the last 14 years. I haven't thought about that gift since the night he left me, so why was I suddenly thinking about it now. I almost completely forgot about it.

I roll out of my bed at my mom's house and walk sluggishly over to the closet. I'm a little nervous to see what's in the box and laugh at myself, because it's probably another doll like the Sasha one I carried around with me as a kid.

I open the door and look at some of the big winter coats I left here hanging up, and a few shoe boxes sitting on the top shelf above them. I moved some of the shoe boxes around and pull out the small box with red wrapping and a gold bow in the center. It looked like a Christmas present, but he probably pulled it together last minute. I walk back out of the closet and close the door behind me.

I place the present on my desk and just sit down and stare at it for a few minutes.

"Should I open you or throw you away?" I say to the box. The fact that I'm sitting here talking to a box tells me I've reached a new level of crazy. I stand up, grab the box then go set it down on my bed. I stare down at it a little more, and then hear my stomach growling.

"Alright, eat first, everything else later." I nod in agreement with myself, then walk out of my room to get some breakfast.

About four hours later, I'm back in my room again. I didn't mean to be gone this long, I honestly wanted to tackle this task today and be done with it. However, when I got downstairs, my Mom had asked if I wanted to run to the store with her really quick. I had to go because she wanted me too, and I figured she probably missed making grocery store runs with me.

Then when we got back, Rylie called me asking how to clip her own ends because she didn't feel like going to the hair salon. Then I figured we should catch up with Camille and ended up talking to them majority of the time.

While on the phone with them, Jamie made a mess, spilling his bowl of oatmeal all over the floor and himself, so I had to clean that up while mom cleaned him up.

Now I'm here, ready and willing to tackle this thing. Sure, some of my courage wavered a little bit, and some anxiety creeped into my blood stream a little bit, but I'm just as empowered as I was this morning. Or so I tried to convince myself.

I sit down next to the present on my bed and just stare at it. "You can do this Jordan," I say to myself under a hushed breath. After a beat, I just grab the present and start ripping the wrapping off it. Once all the wrapping was off, I turned the box around because of course he wrapped it upside down.

It was a jewelry box from Pandora. On top was a little folded up piece of paper that was taped right over the Pandora symbol.

Before looking at the paper, I unlocked the box and inside was a heart key necklace. There was a bigger heart in silver that served as the top of the key, and a smaller heart that was supposed to go in a locket and open it, laced with diamonds. It was beautiful.

I close the box, then take off the note from the top. You can tell the note is years old, because it now has a yellow colored tint to it and the material feels a little dated.

I unfold it and see that it's a letter from Cory. I sit back against the headboard of my bed so that I'm propped up and comfortable while I read this.

DEAR MY ANGEL JORDAN,

I CAN'T EVEN BEGIN TO DESCRIBE THE PAIN I'M FEELING FOR WHAT I'M ABOUT TO DO. I KNOW YOU PROBABLY WON'T UNDERSTAND OR BELIEVE ME, BUT I LOVE YOU WITH EVERY PARTICLE OF MY BEING. I LOVE YOU SO MUCH, THAT I HAVE TO PUT MY PRIDE AND SELFISHNESS ASIDE, FOR YOU TO LIVE A HAPPY AND FULFILLED LIFE. I'M SO SORRY FOR ANY GRIEF OR HURT I CAUSED YOU. I'M SO SORRY THAT I COULDN'T BE THE FATHER THAT YOU NEEDED ME TO BE. I'M SORRY I COULDN'T CHANGE. HOPEFULLY THIS TIME AWAY WILL TEACH ME HOW TO BE A BETTER MAN. I'M SORRY I LET YOU AND YOUR MOM DOWN. I KNOW WHAT I DID AND WHAT I'M ABOUT TO DO IS INEXSCUSABLE. PLEASE FIND IT IN YOUR HEART TO KNOW THAT I NEVER

MEANT TO HURT YOU GUYS. YOU WERE THE BEST THINGS TO EVER HAPPEN TO ME. I AM LEAVING YOU NOW TO WORK ON MYSELF AND TO TACKLE MY INNER DEMONS. ONCE I MANAGE TO DO THAT, I WILL COME BACK TO YOU GUYS A NEW, BETTER MAN. ONE YOU COULD PROUDLY CALL DAD. PLEASE WAIT FOR ME MY DARLING ANGEL. PLEASE GIVE ME TIME TO GROW. I KNOW THIS IS A LOT TO ASK OF YOU, AND I'M SORRY. BUT I DON'T WANT TO LOSE YOU FOREVER. PLEASE.

WITH ALL OF MY LOVE,

DAD.

I don't even feel the tears that are falling down my face, until I see them staining the letter I'm holding in my hands.

How dare he? How dare he say because he loves me, he had to leave. I'm so infuriated with him, that my head starts to hurt. If you loved me, you would've stayed, and we could've all worked on it together as a family.

He put my mom and I through hell because he was still *growing*? This is why I made the decision I made, because actions speak louder than words. That man doesn't care about me, no matter what he says or how many times he says it.

I'm so mad, that I'm itching to give him a piece of my mind. I grab my phone off the charger on my desk, and quickly scroll to our text thread.

Endless messages of him begging please met with no reply, only fuels my anger more. I was about to show him what him being gone for 14 years did to me. Let him hear the venom and hurt in my words as I gave him a piece of my mind.

I press on his phone number and put the phone up to my ear. It's only 3:00pm, on a Saturday so wherever he is in the country, I know he's awake.

It rings one time before he answers the phone. It's like he was sitting around waiting for this call or something. I hear breathing on the other end and just sit there. No one says anything for about 10 seconds, we just listen to the other person breathing.

I have no doubt I sound like a mad man who just ran 30 miles with all the hard breathing I'm doing, but I don't care, I'm pissed off and rightfully so.

Growing impatient, I finally say "Hello?" and hear an audible gasp on the other end of the phone.

"Jordan?" I hear a man say in a gruff voice. He sounded like he'd been crying, and it catches me all the way off guard. I don't say anything, and he keeps going, "Is that you?"

He sounded like he was smiling on the other end of the phone, all happy to finally hear from me. I roll my eyes and open my mouth to release the fury of words I had jumbled up in my head, ready to be thrown at him.

What comes out of my mouth surprises not only me, but the man on the other end of the phone.

"I'll tell you where and when."

"So, you'll meet with me?" he says choking on a sob. I grip the phone tighter not wanting to hear this stranger of a man break down. It was uncomfortable to say the least.

"Oh thank you, thank you so mu-"

Click.

I end the call in the middle of his sentence because I couldn't take it anymore. What did I just do? I was supposed to tell the man who betrayed me to fuck off and forget I even existed, but I ended up betraying myself. Most of all, I didn't even know where this man was located.

Did he stay in Atlanta all these years? Or did he move across the country and start a whole new life? Was he successful? Was he single?

I shake these sudden thoughts out of my head. "Just when I thought I had everything figured out," I say to myself.

After being stuck in my head for the next two hours, I got exhausted thinking about this situation. I was finally ready for it to be done with and for me to close the can of worms, but I ended up tripping on it and spilling all its contents on the floor. Now I'm left to clean it up. I needed a momentary distraction and knew just who to turn to for a few minutes of bliss.

My idea of bliss was clearly not the same idea Jamie had. I took him to the park in the neighborhood so I could get out and get some much-needed fresh air, and so he could have fun and exhaust his energy.

There were some kids on the playground already who were three times Jamie's age. That didn't stop him from taking the role as the "King of the Playground" claiming the other kids to be his "royal servants".

He made them "fetch" his sand bucket from the sandbox and give him their toys so they could play in peace with no interruptions. He also made them push him on the swing and bow down to him as he stood at the top of the slide overlooking the rest of the playground.

At that point, I had to intervene and tell him it wasn't okay to make anyone his servant. He threw a little tantrum and I ended up taking him back to the house. I knew letting him sneak and watch a little bit of Game of Thrones that one night a while ago was a bad idea.

I figured since that episode didn't have sex in it, he'd be fine watching a snippet. Man was I wrong. So utterly wrong.

Since Jamie wasn't giving me the peace I needed at the moment, I opted to call Rylie since she would never let me down. I called her on facetime and she immediately declined it.

Okay, maybe that was an accident?

I try calling her again, but on a regular phone call this time and got the same result. A few seconds later, my phone buzzed. I looked down at the notification that popped up on the top of my screen.

Rylie:

Hey Jor, you okay? I'm out with a friend right now. Call you as soon as I'm home! x

A friend? She met someone? And didn't tell me? Yea, I'll have some words for her later. I tell her I'm okay and send the emoji with the raised eyebrow. I'll try calling Cam. Hopefully she isn't working right now. She declines my calls as well. My phone buzzes again.

Cam:

Sorry babe, I'm working a double right now :(. Everything okay?

Me:

Yea, just bored. Call me as soon as you can.

I wanted to tell them about Cory, but I didn't want them going all crazy and in protective mode. I just wanted a chill conversation.

I look at the time and it's only 6:00pm. My mom and Benny went out on a date about an hour ago, so it was just me and Jamie in the house. He was playing with his toys in the living room and I was sitting on the couch, just flipping through channels.

"You want to watch a movie Buu?" I ask him, already knowing his answer.

"TROLLS! TROLLS!" he says as he runs over to me and jumps so he's sitting on the cushion next to me. I go onto the Hulu app on the TV and play the Trolls movie.

After watching Poppy and Branch save their family and friends for the second time on repeat, I glance over at a sprawled-out Jamie knocked out sleep. It was almost 10:00pm at night and I'm surprised he didn't fall asleep sooner.

After we watched the movie the first time, he was yelling "AGAIN AGAIN!" until I had it playing once more. He fell asleep about halfway through the second cycle, but I didn't turn it off.

I loved this movie too.

I pick up a sleeping Jamie, and go put him in his room upstairs, which is directly across the hall from mine.

After I tuck him in, I go downstairs to shut the TV off. Just as I'm doing that, I hear the garage door opening and go to open the door to greet Mom and Benny.

"Finally, the kids are back," I say placing my hands on my hips.

"Yea, I brought her back before curfew. That should earn me a gold star," Ben says as he opens my mom's door and lets her out.

"Me allowing you to take my Mom out *was* your gold star." We all laugh, and they tell me about the movie they went to go see, Joker. It came out yesterday, and I couldn't wait to go see it myself. I already knew a few quotes from it that I could relate too.

I eventually make my way upstairs and feel myself starting to get sleepy. Cory flashes in my mind, and I remember the contents of his letter.

I sit on my bed and look at the box that holds the necklace inside of it. So many emotions were going through my mind and I wish I could just sort them all out and throw them away one by one.

I lay my head back and throw my arm over my eyes. Rylie and Cam still didn't call me back and I really wish they would right now. I needed to talk to someone, and at this point, I didn't care how they'd react. I just wanted to get my thoughts together and figure out where to go from here.

I feel my sleep starting to pull me under, and let go of my thoughts enough, to allow it to take me. My body grows heavy and my mind grows lighter.

Tomorrow I'll figure it all out.

Tomorrow.

Hovering.

Gliding.

Bright.

So Bright.

As I open my eyes, I see I'm standing a few feet away from Malakai. The fact that I know who he is now blows my mind.

He's not just the Adonis of my dreams anymore. He's an actual real person. I still can't wrap my brain around that simple fact. I walk towards him and he lifts his head up, giving a broad smile.

"Long time no see," he says as he scoots over when I approach. I take the seat next to him and can't help the smile

that spreads across my face. This man was beautiful on the outside, and as I got to know him more, I was starting to see he's beautiful on the inside too.

"You seem happy," I say to him as I take in his beautiful smile and the dimples he's putting on display. I still sort of wished I had two dimples instead of the one in my left cheek, but I also like it because it makes me different.

"I am, extremely happy," he says looking down at his hands, still smiling.

"I take it the talk with your dad went well?" I ask, already knowing the answer.

"It went just as good as I could've imagined, if not better." He turns his body to me so that he's facing me. "I also signed up for the competition and got in!"

"Wow! I'm so proud of you Malakai!" I almost hug him but think better of it. We're friends now, but I still don't know his boundaries or anything. Plus, I'm not trying to complicate our friendship.

He goes on to tell me the events of the day he told his dad he didn't want to be a football player anymore. I think it's interesting how one's life can turn out completely different if they just expressed their feelings a lot sooner and trusted that it'll turn out okay.

It's never too late to change your life or to take control of it.

He finishes his story and then I shake my head smiling. "I'm so happy for you, really, that's amazing Malakai." He nods and then smiles at me. "What?" I ask, his smiling too contagious.

"It was thanks to you that I even had the courage to do what I did. Thank you," I shake my hands in front of me protesting what he just said. "No way, that was all you, all I did was provide a tiny push."

"Exactly, and because of that push, I am now the happiest man alive, so thank you. Seriously."

We look at each other with an intensity, and something in my chest flutters. He then clears his throat and I look away, hiding the blush that creeped up in my face. The hell did that come from?

"So um," he rubs his hands on his legs, "Did you make a decision on what you were going to do with Cory?" I let out a long breath.

"I thought I did," I stand up and walk two steps away from the bench, kicking the cloud ground, watching fragments of it drift away like a cloud of smoke. "What do you mean?" he says from the bench.

"Well, just like you, I woke up with the sense of determination and knowing exactly what I was going to do. I was going to tell Cory to stay out of my life for good, and then..." I drift off.

"And then what?" He asks me, standing up and walking towards me. He was so close that I could feel the warmth radiating off him and smell the Listerine that was on his breath. How the hell was that possible?

Also, I'm glad he has good hygiene. I wonder what else about him was good. I shake off the thoughts my mind was drifting too. What the hell Jordan, focus. He quirks an eyebrow *waiting for me to continue. Why did he have to look so good when he did that?*

"And then I guess you asking about the gift last time stuck in mind somehow, and I went and opened it."

"Wait, you remembered me asking about the gift?" I look up at the surprise on his face and quickly shut down what he's thinking.

"Not necessarily, I was just curious about the gift in the closet all of a sudden, and now I figure it's because you were asking about it."

"So, what was in it?" He sounded impatient and I think it's funny how bad he wants to know what was inside.

I go back to the bench and sit down, and he sits next to me. Closer than usual but I try not to pay too much attention to that. I tell him about the necklace, and recite the letter word for word, surprising myself that I had remembered all of what it said. When I'm done, he sits there taking it all in, rubbing his chin. "Shit," Is all he manages to say. "Yeah I know," I say playing with my hands.

"I'm guessing that had you second guessing your decision," He says next to me.

"It had me more than second guessing. Next thing I knew, I was calling him telling him that I'm going to pick the time and the place of our meeting," I say turning to him. His eyes grow wide and rubs the back of his neck.

"Damn Jordan, is that what you really want?" I let out a long breath. "I don't even know anymore. I just want this to be over. I want to go back to living my life with no bullshit."

"Were you really living with no bullshit though?"
His question hits me as if someone had just punched me in the face. I sit and think about his question. Maybe he was right, maybe my life was always fucked up and the "no bullshit" part was just a façade.

I hated Cory.

Hate him.

Hated.

I don't even know anymore. I'm so conflicted. "What should I do?" my voice sounds small. Unlike me. Malakai shrugs next to me.

"I think you should do whatever your heart tells you to do. Ignore that voice in your head for once and just go on gut instincts." He taps his right temple with his forefinger. "That voice in your head will have you going crazy for no reason at all. Trust me, I know," he lets out a chuckle and that causes me to smile.

Silence that voice in my head. I could do that couldn't I? Stop overthinking everything and just go with the flow? My whole life, I've always been a planner, never really did anything spontaneous if I didn't have all details laid out in front of me. But then again, that life I was living wasn't real was it?

It was time to rewrite my story. Change the narrative. Sprinkle in a few plot twists. I was going to come out a new and improved Jordan after I handled this situation.

"You know, we give good advice," I say to Malakai as a matter of factly. "Yea, we just don't take it," he says laughing and I laugh too.

We sit in silence and stare at the orange and purple sky we've come to know quite well. I look at the cloudy ground and decide to do something a little different. I stand up from the bench and then walk a little way away before laying down on the ground.

Wow this felt amazing. Why hadn't we thought of this sooner? This could heal all the back problems I have in this life and the next.

Malakai laughs from the bench, "What? was my bench too uncomfortable for you?"

"Yea, you're laughing now," I yell over to him, "But wait until you feel this." I turn my head and give him a sly smile. I got him curious. "How does it feel?" he says starting to stand up.

"Like a Tempur-Pedic on steroids. The best thing ever created. Like heaven," I say in a sing song tone. He lays down next to me, so close, that our elbows almost touch. My hands are interlocked on my chest and my legs are laying out in front of me. He mimics my position.

"Wow, you weren't lying Jameson. This is heaven."

"Have I ever steered you wrong Woods?" I say laughing. "No actually, no you haven't," he laughs back. We lay there for what feels like forever. The longest we've ever stayed in this world together.

"Can I ask you something?" he says breaking the silence. "Of course," I say, curious as to what his question would be.

"Do you think we would be friends out in the real world?"

I don't expect this question, so it takes me a second to answer.

"Yea, why not?"

He sits up from where he was laying and looks at me. I turn my head and look over at him. "I'm just asking because you're probably the coolest girl my age that I've ever met, and I wish we could be friends in real life too."

"Aw, like wise. I don't really have guy friends. Or even talk to guys at all but talking to you is refreshing. Maybe one day we could meet. Like in the movies. A chance encounter type of thing."

He scoffs, "Yea right. When would you ever come to San Diego?" he asks, doing the eyebrow quirk thing again.

"I don't know, maybe one day I'll want to go there for vacation. Or maybe you'd want to come to Atlanta. Everyone wants to come to Atlanta."

He mulls this over in his mind. "I have thought about going up there a few times."

"See, Exactly."

"So, if you saw me in real life, you would be my friend?" He asks in a serious tone.

"What's up with all the questions?" I say, propping myself up so that my hands are supporting me from behind.

"I was just wondering." He turns his head back towards the sky and I stare at his profile. Before I ask the question that is on my mind, I hear the rumbling in the distance. "Well, my taxi is almost here," I say to him, not wanting to let go of this peace just yet.

"Let me walk you the front then," he says in a joking tone.

"How kind of you sire," I say standing up. He stands up and bows moving his arm out in a half circle motion. "After you ma lady."

I curtsy to him, then head towards the bench. He walks beside me, and the rumbling just gets louder and louder.

"You ever wonder what the hell that rumbling even is?" he asks me when we approach the bench. I sit down and realize I never actually thought about it, just accepted it.

I shake my head, "Not until now." I think it over a little bit. "Maybe it indicates one of us waking up. Or maybe it's an alarm clock," I suggest.

He shakes his head, "I took out the batteries from my alarm clock because it got annoying."

"That's the whole point," I say laughing. He sits down next to me as the rumbling draws closer. "I'll catch you later Jordan Jameson. Remember, you got this okay?" I nod my head smiling, "Same to you Malakai Woods. Break a leg in this competition."

"Actually, that's a theater referen-"

And before I could hear the last of his sentence, I was falling.

And falling.

And falling,

Until I crashed.

MALAKAI

It's been a couple months since sign ups, and I've been impatiently waiting for the email to tell me where the first bootcamp class will be.

After I got in as one of the 30 participants, they had to go through this whole process of ruling out people who don't fit the criteria or changed their mind about joining the competition.

Once they had the final 30, we had to take drug tests and they had to do criminal background checks on every single one of us. Now that the whole entry process is over and done with, I keep checking my email every 30 minutes for one from the film contest team.

I haven't been getting a good night's sleep because I've been too busy coming up with ideas for the movie that I'm going to make for the competition.

From what I've heard, they email you a secret email telling you the theme of the contest this year, and your movie must focus around that theme. Just for good measure, I've been trying to come up with different ideas for a lot of different movie themes so that when I get the email, I can already have an idea lined up.

Thinking about this has taken up so much of my time and energy, that I've started to fall a little behind on studying for my finals.

Now it's the night before my final for my Ethics in Sports and Exercise class, and I haven't looked at any of the notes I've been writing in class before this moment.

I've been so wrapped up in my new life, I forgot I still need to do good in these classes I'm already in this semester before I can start my new Media Studies major classes.

"Can we take a break?" Saiyr whines while he spins in circles in my desk chair.

"We literally didn't even start yet," Anthony says from my accent chair in the corner, "At least look at your notes for 10 minutes before you start complaining."

"I honestly might be up all-night studying for this class, you guys don't have to stay that whole time." I say, biting on the back of the pen in my hand.

"Nah, we're staying here until you know about 90% of those notes like the back of your hand." Anthony says, showing me the back of his hand.

"But we will take much needed snack breaks in between," Saiyr pointed out.

We study for hours, they quiz me, I quiz them. We take breaks to eat and give our eyes and brains a break from all the information we're trying to cram into them.

At around 4:00 am, of course they're both knocked out. Anthony fell asleep in the chair, which also reclines. Saiyr is laid out on the floor with the pillows and blankets he took from the guest room down the hall.

Of course, I'm wide awake. I stopped studying for my final a couple of hours ago and decided to start storyboarding for the movie ideas I came up with so far.

Once 7:00 am hit, I wake up Saiyr and Anthony and we all start to get ready. They take turns showering in the guest bathroom, and I shower in my bathroom. Since they both basically live here, and we're liable for falling asleep at the other person's house with no prior notice, we all leave some clothing in each other's guest room.

Once we were all dressed, I drove us down to the school since our finals were at the same time. I walk into the class, say hello to a few of my associates, and start on my final.

"I feel like this was my best semester yet," Saiyr says as he dips a fry into his ranch. He pulls the fry up in the air and feeds it to himself like it were a woman feeding him grapes in a jacuzzi. The ranch drips onto the side of his mouth and I shake my head.

When we finished our first round of finals, Saiyr said he was hungry (no surprise there), so we stopped at Duke's, this Hawaiian restaurant around the corner from my house. We had a table outside and were looking out at a beautiful view of the ocean.

"My advisor says that since I'm just now starting my major classes, I will only be in school an extra semester." I say taking a bite into my Poke Taco after I speak.

"That's good, I was worried you'd be one of those super seniors who stay in college for like 10 years." Saiyr says trying to lick the ranch off the side of his mouth with his tongue.

"Nothing wrong with that," Anthony says sipping his drink, "Some people just have no idea what they want to do for the rest of their lives, which is understandable."

"I didn't say there was anything wrong with it, I just would hate to see Kai go through all of that stress. Lord knows he doesn't need anymore." They both laugh and I just keep eating my tacos.

I check my email on my phone because I realized I haven't checked it since I've gotten out of my last final of the day.

ALRIGHT FILMERS TIME TO KICK IT INTO HIGH GEAR!!

The competition is officially starting! Below are the directions and information to when and where the first class will be located! Remember these classes are mandatory so be there or else you're kicked from the contest! The class tonight is going to tell you what this year's theme is! See you there!

The San Diego Film Contest Team

I nearly choke on my Taco because this email was sent when we were leaving the school.

"I know those tacos got a little kick to them, but they aren't that spicy," Saiyr says raising an eyebrow at me. I grab my wallet and throw a 20 on the table.

"I gotta go," I say walking fast towards the doors leading back inside the restaurant.

"Call us when it's over!" Anthony yelled after me already knowing where I'm going. I don't respond.

It was 6:30pm and the first class of the contest started at 7:00pm but they asked us to arrive at least 10 minutes early. It was also in La Mesa which was about 25 minutes away without traffic.

I slide into the driver's seat of my car and put the address from the email into my Apple Maps. It says that it'll take me about 35 minutes to get there. "Shit," I say already changing the gear in my car so I can zoom down the road.

"This would happen to me."

Glancing at the time in my car for the thousandth time, it was now 6:50 pm and I was in traffic. I was only 10 minutes away from the building I needed to be at, if only everybody and their mom wasn't on the highway right now.

I look in the rearview mirror and see the piled-up traffic behind me. I figure if I take a few backroads, I'll only be a couple minutes late.

After maneuvering my way off the highway, I take the backroads the rest of the way and make it at exactly 7:01pm. I get out of the car and run towards the propped open door that a person wearing a badge was about to close.

"Wait!" I say as I get up to where he was about to kick the door prop from under one of the doors.

"Well well well, you made it just in time!" The guy says too me giving me a broad smile.

I glance at the badge on his neck that tells me he's a part of the film contest team and that his name is Eddie.

"Come on in," he beckons to me with his left hand and as I step through the door, he places that hand in between my shoulder blades as if to glide me in.

He closes the doors behind me, and I let out an audible breath. "Follow me over to this table and we'll get you signed in, sound good?" he asks me. I just nod my head trying to get my thoughts back together and take in the fact that I almost lost this opportunity before I could even put the tip of my toe into the water.

The class lasts for only two hours and was just an introductory session explaining all the rules of the competition. Someone ended up walking out because they couldn't dedicate all their time to this project and participate in the weekly check-in sessions that would be held.

These sessions are there to ensure that each participant is where they need to be as far as preparations for their movies go. They also explained to us that surprise popular A-list Hollywood producers will attend a session at random giving out advice and secret tricks to the trade to all willing participants.

Lucky for me, Winter break is starting next week so I can focus all my time to this film contest for the next four weeks. No football practices or extra event games to get in my way, I can solely focus on what I love to do.

"How was it?" My mom asks as I close the front door to the house behind me. I walk over to where she's standing at the corner of the hall that leads to her office. I give her a peck on the cheek, and she rubs mine simultaneously.

"Honestly, it was great. I'm excited to start prepping and storyboarding." I jerk my head toward the kitchen, quietly telling her "lets walk and talk because I'm starving".

"What's the theme this year? Tell *me*." She sounded like a little kid begging their parents to tell them what was in their Christmas present box. We walk past the hall that lead to her office, down the middle of the two-sided staircase, and went into the open spaced living room area with the open concept kitchen to the left.

"I'll tell you once Dad gets home," I say shaking my head at the woman who's supposed to be my mom but sounding more like a little sister at the moment. We get to the kitchen and I look in the fridge for some left-over chicken and rice. She stands to my left, leaning her hip onto the marble waterfall countertop on our island. She sticks her bottom lip out and crosses her arms in a pout.

"He won't be here for another 30 minuteees," she whines, dragging out the word minutes like she was 5 years old.

"Mom, that didn't work when I tried that on you as a kid, so it's definitely is not going to work on me."

I scoop out some rice from the pot and put it on a plate.

"Fine, I won't tell you my news either then," she turns her head up and huffs out a breath, turning her body away from me.

I shrug, "That's fine with me," I laugh, and she lets a smile break out across her face. She looks back at me, "You're just like your Dad."

"Yea but I get my good looks from you," I say winking at her.

"Way to hit a man where it hurts," I hear a voice say from behind me and whip my head around. I put my hands up in defense as I see my dad grabbing his chest like he was just stabbed there.

"I'm just being honest," I say laughing.

He walks past me and gathers my mom into his arms. He kisses her like he was deployed away for some years and was finally coming back home. I can only hope one day that I find a love that's half as good as theirs.

"Alright alright," I say as I lightly punch my dad in the arm. "You guys can do all of that in the bedroom far away from mine later tonight. And I mean much later, like after I fall asleep later."

My dad belts out a hearty laugh then nuzzles my mom's neck one last time before letting go of her and patting me on the back a little too hard. "Cock block," he whispers in my ear and I snort at his unexpected dig.

"Tell me about the session," he says as he takes the wooden spoon out of my hand and scoops out more rice onto my plate, then taking it for himself and adding some pieces of chicken on to it.

I stare at him heating up my plate in the microwave and he just whistles while watching the plate twirl around through the peeking window. He takes it out the microwave and grabs a spoon, scooping up some rice and stuffing it into his mouth.

"What?" he says once he realizes I didn't say a word and was just staring at him.

"I'm officially divorcing you as my dad," I say to him but grab another plate from the cabinet.

"But the session was cool. They told me what to expect and told us the theme of the competition this year."

My mom does an impatient dance where she stands, and I chuckle at the immature parents that I've been blessed with. I wouldn't trade them for the world though.

"What is it?" he says but his words are distorted because of the food he had in his mouth. I tap my chin and scratch my head like I'm trying to remember what they told me.

"Just say it already! I'm getting grays over here," my mom says.

"Okay okay," I say, "the theme this year is ..." I drag it out a little longer just to piss them off and it works.

"Deliverance," I finally say, and my mom makes an O with her mouth.

"Oooo, that sounds fun to play with. Do you have any ideas yet?" she asks me. I can already see her coming up with a new book to write like she isn't currently writing one already.

That's my mom, her creativity is always flowing. That's where I get mine from. "It's funny because I've come up with multiple ideas for other themes but not that one."

"Maybe you can flip one of the ones you already thought of to make it fit the actual theme," my dad says shrugging, thinking it was the simplest answer. "I could do that, but I don't know. I'm going to think on it more tonight."

"When's your next session?" he asks me as he takes a bite of his chicken. "I'm not sure, they said the session will be at random for us and we won't know about them until the day of."

"They're going all out this year I see," my mom says as she walks over and takes one of my dad's chicken breasts.

"Hey!" he protests as she takes a huge bite off of it and smiles shyly like she didn't do anything wrong. I talk to them for a long time after this and then my phone buzzes in my pocket. I glance at my apple watch to see what the notification was, hoping it wasn't an email surprising us with a midnight session the same day as the intro session.

I wouldn't put it past them.

Anthony:

?????

Saiyr:

Saiyr liked "?????"

It was a message from Ant in our "Brother Bears" group chat. Saiyr named it that years ago and we never changed it. I call them on group facetime and relay the same thing to them that I told my parents.

"Any fine ass girls in the competition?" Saiyr asked.

"Really?" Anthony said sounding exasperated, "Do you ever think about anything besides girls bro?"

Saiyr looks as though he's really contemplating this. I see the moment he has a eureka moment and comes up with something that he thinks about.

"Sex," he says smiling and I bust out laughing.

Anthony puts his hand on his forehead but he's smiling too, trying to hold in his laugh.

"There was a cute girl sitting next to me, but I didn't ask her name. I was too focused on what I was going to do for the competition."

I prop my phone up on the lamp that's placed on my desk. Sitting in the chair, I lean back, bouncing back and forth.

"As far as actors are concerned, you know we're down. I've been practicing my Oscar speech," Saiyr says as he pretends to tighten an imaginary tie on his neck.

"Once I figure out the story, you will be the first actors I have in mind," I say to them.

"If there's any kissing scenes, I want them all," Saiyr adds in, "Don't be afraid to get as explicit as possible. I look good nude."

"You must really want me kicked out of this competition?" He laughs and all 3 of us continue to talk about the contest, our futures, and of course, girls. I don't get any sleep that night due to me trying to figure out the perfect story that'll depict deliverance in the most unique way.

JORDAN

"So, is it serious?" Cam asks Rylie as me, her and Rylie walk to the escalator that will take us up to the main part of Atlantic Station.

We were coming to watch Joker finally before it left the movie theater. We also wanted to look around and shop for Christmas presents for our family (and secretly each other).

"I think so," she replies once we get on the escalator, "We still haven't had that talk yet."

"What? the marriage talk?" Cam says scoffing. "No," Rylie swats her arm lightly, "The 'what are we' talk, we're just going with the flow."

Remember that time when Rylie didn't answer my phone call because she was hanging with a friend?

And never called me back? Yeah, turns out she was "hanging out" with Zavier. One of the boys that helped us move into the apartment during move in day.

The same Zavier that hit me up on Tinder asking me why I was on a dating app. He ended up becoming a cool acquaintance I would wave and say hi to from time to time when I would see him at school.

Once I asked Rylie why the hell she never called me back the day after she dodged me, she told me she went out with Zavier but just as friends.

Apparently, one day when she was waiting in the courtyard for me while I was in class, he approached her saying "Hey, you're the other girl I helped move in a couple of months ago?"

She was apprehensive and gave him dry answers, but he ended up sitting across from her anyway. He left before I got there but she said ever since then, she would suddenly see him everywhere.

Sometimes he would be with a group of guys and run up to her, leaving them behind, just to walk her to wherever she needed to go. She eventually stopped being dry to him because he was cute, funny, and a "chivalrous gentleman".

Then she agreed to hang out with him, which was the night I was watching Jamie and opened the present my Houdini father left me before he did his infamous disappearing act. They went out for ice cream and walked around Piedmont park like a romantic couple in the movies.

They've been seeing each other since then, but they weren't official yet seeing, as he didn't officially ask her, and she seemed scared to ask. She probably thought she would make him panic and think that she'd want to get married and start a family the next day.

I was happy for her because she's been so happy since she's given him the time of day and chance to get to know her, but I'm still mad that she didn't tell me about it right when it happened.

"I didn't think it was important to tell yet, I was going to tell you about him once we hung out the first time," she had said when she called me back the next day after their first hang-out-date-but-its-not-really-a-date date.

"I think you should ask him; it's been two months. What do you think J?" Cam says turning to me as we walk off the elevator towards the Regal movie theater.

"I think since Ry is the one in the relationship, she knows more about it than us," I shrug one shoulder, "But If there is a little voice at the back of her head screaming trying to figure out if Zavier feels the same as her, then she should ask." I cock an eyebrow at her giving her a look that I know for a fact that she has that voice. I knew my best friend all too well.

She plays with a stray hair she left out the back of her ninja bun. I liked that we all were naturals and we all had different length hair. Mine touched just above my nipples, Rylie's was at her shoulders, and Cam had hers styled into a short cut that was too short to grip for braids but long enough to see her little curls popping. Cam and I were the only ones with our hair dyed.

Me with my Orange coppery colored hair, SZA and Rihanna inspired, and Cam had hers like a pastel pink cotton candy which went perfectly with her caramel colored skin.

"I don't know," she chews on her bottom lip, "I might ask him next time we hang out."

"It would be nice to know ASAP, before you buy him a Christmas present and he looks lost like 'Oh we were getting gifts?'" Cam tries to sound like a guy while mocking what she thinks Zavier will say. Rylie and I laugh at her horrible attempt and she scrunches her nose at us.

We order a big bucket of popcorn and 3 bags of sour gummy worms before we went to take our seats. I sat in the middle holding the bucket, Rylie and Cam picking out of the bucket throughout the movie. Once it was over, I dump the empty bucket and suck out the last of the slushy Cam bought when she went to use the bathroom in the middle of the movie.

"That movie was way better than I was expecting," Ry says as we walk back out to the setting sun.

I look off to my right where I had a perfect view of the beautifully colored orange and purple sky. Like a never-ending painting that brings serenity to my soul. It also brought a faint familiar feeling and a flicker of forgotten memories that don't make it passed the wall they're locked behind.

"It was so good, I low key want to watch it again," Cam says off to my right. A shoulder bumps into mine lightly and I'm pulled out of my trance to look at a concerned Rylie.

"You okay?" She asks me with her eyes. I nod and look to where Cam is popping a sour gummy worm into her mouth. The warm feeling that was starting to fill into me while staring up at the sky, fades just as fast as it came.

"That's probably my favorite movie of the year," I say giving my opinion, "Beautifully written and even more beautifully executed. The acting, the feelings it left me with," We walk towards the stores across the street from the movies.

"Made you want to go start a riot wearing a clown mask," Cam finished my statement, smiling.

"Exactly," I reply with a wide mischievous grin like the Cheshire Cat.

We go window shopping all over the outdoor mall strip, and I find a few things I wanted to get Jamie and my parents. We pass by a Pandora Jewelry store and it reminds me of the heart key necklace that Cory bought me from there.

I still haven't called him to tell him the time and place to meet. He's calmed down on texting me and started texting me once every other week saying, "You still there?" or "Did you change your mind?"

It annoyed me that he kept texting me because it reminded me that I still haven't closed that door and that I'm stalling, but I'm just not mentally ready to see him. Now that I have a choice, I'm not going to force myself into something I'm not ready for like he did to me. I also didn't tell my friends that I called him or even opened the present he got me. I just told them that he cut down on texting me whenever they would ask about the situation which wasn't all that often.

It's not that I don't want to talk to or confide in my friends, because I do want too *so* bad. I just don't feel like thinking or giving that situation the time of day again just yet.

After our window shopping, we all go back to Rylie's silver 2018 Volkswagen Jetta. It was Saturday and we were all staying at Rylie's house that night.

Next week I had my last couple of finals to take before I had a whole month to myself for winter break. Maybe that's when I'll set up the meeting with Cory because I need my head to be completely focused on my classes right now.

I haven't missed a class since that week I was down bad from Cory's forced reentrance into my life. Back when I slipped into a depressing state and didn't do anything school related. I've been ahead of my homework once I got my usually over productive self-back.

I'll be damned if he messes up finals for me too.

We pulled into her driveway that led to a huge 8-bedroom, 9-bathroom, light-bricked three-story house. Her parents stayed in Buckhead which was where the more well-off residents of Atlanta stayed. To say that her family was well-off would be an understatement.

Her Dad created this unique software that gave Microsoft and Bill Gates a run for his money, quickly becoming his top competitor. He went from being a small start-up businessman that worked out of a studio apartment, to this multi-millionaire with a beautiful family.

Rylie was their only child and she was also a daddy's girl. She wasn't a spoiled entitled brat, nor did she ever flaunt the fact that her parents had money. She was just a normal girl like anyone else, which is why she insisted on staying on campus and going to college on academic scholarship.

She also wanted to leave the nest to get away from her helicopter mom. Her mom worked with her dad and was his publicist. They met in high school just like my mom and birth dad.

They all went to the same high school too, so they know everything about my parents and my Lifetime inspired life.

We pulled up to the side of the house where there were 6 garage doors, three on either side of the driveway, separated by an open columned hallway up ahead. She pulls into one of the three on the right side and puts the car in park.

We usually hang out at Rylie's house more than mine because she had so many things we could do in her house. There was a gym, bowling alley, theater, game room, spa, pool, bar, and so many more things.

Her movie theater was able to get new releases even though they were still at the theater because her Dad had connections, but we still preferred to go out to traditional theaters. We didn't want to turn into hermits that never left the comforts of a home.

I basically lived in this house before we went off to college and before my mom was pregnant with Jamie. Now I like to spend my time at my parents' house so I can hang out with my brother and help them out whenever they need it. I'll bring Jamie here once he gets a little older.

We walk in through the gym entrance, and I feel down at my stomach area to remind me just how long it's been since I've exercised. I used to be able to run 10 miles no sweat, but now? I couldn't even run to the mailbox at the front of Rylie's big ass lawn without collapsing on the ground heaving for breaths.

It takes us 10 minutes to get to the kitchen where we see Rylie's mom, Aunt Stacy, cooking what looks to be chicken alfredo from where I'm standing.

She's blasting Luther Vandross and Cheryl Lynn's "If this world were mine" on the kitchen's Bluetooth speakers.

She sways her hips to the music while dashing some seasoning into the big pot, simultaneously twirling her wooden spoon. She looked like Ursula when she was concocting that potion to steal Ariel's voice in the Little Mermaid.

"Mom," Rylie says sounding embarrassed at the show her mom was giving us. Cam giggles next to me as Rylie's mom almost drops the seasoning in her hand into the pot. She whips around, surprise etched on her face and her hand thrown to her chest.

"Jesus Rylie, you scared me. When'd you get home?" she says breathing hard. She always was overly dramatic. I shake my head and chuckle. She turns the music down so that its now softly playing in the background.

"We just got here," Rylie walks towards her mom and peers into the pot she was stirring. "I was coming to see if we had any food or if I should order pizza."

"Oh don't worry about that," Aunt Stacy says as she gets her bearings back, "I decided to cook a meal for you girls. It's been years since I've done that."

Cam and I go to hug Aunt Stacy one by one in greeting. "That's really thoughtful of you," Cam says as she pulls back from her hug.

"Thank you so much," I add, "We really appreciate that." Aunt Stacy gives us a warm smile.

"You girls were always so respectful. How'd I get so lucky to have all three of you in my life."

"Mooom," Rylie drags out, "Are you having mood swings? Is your cycle on?" She makes a show of acting like she's checking her mom's temperature. Aunt Stacy swats Rylie's hand away from her forehead laughing lightly.

"I can't just be appreciative?" She turns back to continue mixing the pasta. Rylie turns too us in a "do you see what I'm seeing" look and I just shrug. Rylie's mom doesn't usually cook because, let's just say, she doesn't have the "knack" for it.

Rylie's dad, Uncle Rick, usually does all of the cooking when he got off work, if not him, then it would be Ry. Rylie's mom hadn't cooked for us in like 6 years.

"We're going to my room now, call me when the food's done," Rylie says as she leads us to the spiral stairs to the right of the kitchen. Luther Vandross's voice fading more and more as we ascend the stairs.

"I don't know what's gotten into my mom lately, she's been so…" Rylie waves her hands in the air searching for a word, "perky."

I close the door to Rylie's room since I'm the last one to walk in. "Maybe she's going through the big '*M*'" Cam offers, emphasizing M.

The M meaning Menopause for those who are lost.

"Maybe that's it," Rylie taps her chin with her finger, "That would explain the weird moods and mood swings.

We change into pajamas that we found from Rylie's walk-in closet that came with its own island and runway shoe closet. We eat the pasta her mom made and laugh reminiscing on old times.

We choose to watch our sappy romance movies in Rylie's room instead of the theater room because we didn't feel like making that walk across the house. It was too huge for all that. After the last movie goes off, it's about 1:30am and I'm surprised both Rylie and Cam are still up.

We finish laughing at a story Rylie was telling us about Zavier trying to tie a cherry stem in his mouth but ended up choking, and she had to perform the Heimlich. The laughter dies down and we just lay in silence, in a three-way cuddle-spoon situation on Rylie's California king bed.

"Jordan?" Rylie asks, breaking the silence. Her tone sends worry down my spine and I can already the direction this conversation is about to go.

"Yeah?" I reply, trying to sound clueless.

"How's the situation with your dad?" She turns around to where she's lying on her stomach and can look me in my eyes.

I turn to my side and rest my head in my hand, propped up on my arm. I sit and think on whether I had the energy to talk about this now. I consider the fact that I kept this from both of them these past couple months and decide to stop prolonging the inevitable.

"I called him," I say simply.

"What!?" Cam says shooting up from where she's laying so she can look at me over Rylie. Rylie doesn't give off a reaction.

I nod, acting as if it wasn't a big deal even though I was still screaming at myself on the inside for wanting to see him.

"A couple of months ago," I say and see the flicker of hurt swimming in Rylie's pupils for my not telling her. "I didn't want to freak you guys out about it," I say laying back down on my back so I could avoid the hurt in both of their eyes.

"I didn't tell anyone yet, I wanted to understand how I felt about it first. I just needed to deal with it on my own."

There's a long silence before Rylie finally says something.

"What did you say to him?" I relay the events of the day that led to the phone call, even the part where I tried to call them.

"Wow," Camille says as she lays on her back, digesting what I said.

"I'm proud of you," Rylie says smiling at me, "I'm hurt you didn't tell me earlier, but I understand your reasons. You needed time to think for yourself without outside opinions affecting your judgement."

This is why I loved this girl. She was so understanding and got everything about me. I pull her into a hug and Cam joins in, squishing Rylie in the middle. We break apart after a long minute.

"So, when are you going to call him back?" Rylie asks.

"I was thinking about doing it right after my last final exam on Thursday." I say playing with the lint on the pink pajama pants I was wearing. "I was going to say we should meet up somewhere kind of private but also public enough for him not to kidnap me or something," I joke but also half serious. The world is getting crazy and this could very well be an imposter.

"Do you need us to go in undercover?" Cam says sounding excited. "I've always wanted to be an actress. Me and Ry could act like a couple or something sitting at a booth behind yours."

I consider this idea. It would be more comforting knowing my friends are close by. I also know that I need to do this alone. Well, almost.

"Maybe you guys could wait in the car while I'm talking to him or something? Just in case?"

"Of course!" Rylie says throwing her hands in the air theatrically. "We need to make sure our girl is safe."

We go back to cuddling on the bed and I feel myself starting to drift off. My body grows heavy and I feel my eyelids start to flutter, entering REM. My conscious feels like it floats out of my body as I completely succumb to the feeling.

Heavy.

Dark.

Anticipating.

I raise my head up from the position I'm more than familiar with by now. I look to my left already knowing what I'll find there. She walks towards me as radiant as the sun, looking like an angel as she always does.

"Nice pajamas," I say to her smirking. They were pink with chocolate cupcakes and white frosting all over them.

"Ha Ha, very funny," she says in a mocking tone as she walks closer towards me. I stand up and resist the urge to pull her into a hug. I feel like I haven't seen her in forever, and if I were to remember her outside of my dreams, I would've been worried I'd never see her again.

I don't know what it is, but I've grown a liking to this girl. She stops in front of me, our toes almost touching. "Where've you been?" I ask her, cocking my head to the side. I give her a once over and she blushes.

"Where's your shirt?" She asks me, trying to keep her eyes up at my face. I laugh at how cute she looks when she's trying to hide her attraction to me. I look down and realize she is indeed right; I am without shirt. I suddenly remember why.

"I was running on the treadmill at my best friend Ant's gym, trying to get inspiration for my movie, and I guess I ended up crashing as soon as I got off." She seems to relax a little bit.

"Oh, I thought you were probably shagging your girlfriend or something," she says looking away from my face.

"Shagging?" I say laughing in disbelief that she just said that too me. She walks away, I'm guessing to hide her embarrassment, and lays down on the cloud ground. I follow suit, lying next to her, making sure to be close, but not close enough to touch.

"If that's your way of asking if I'm single," I say after a few minutes, "Then yes. Yes I am." She starts to protest that that's what she wanted to know but I cut her off, "I haven't had a girlfriend in a couple of years."

Silence.

More Silence.

Maybe she didn't hear me.

"Did you love her?" She finally asks, but I almost don't hear her because she said it so quietly. I think about this question.

"At the time I guess I thought I did," I turn my head to look at her, "but ultimately, no. I was just very much in like."

"Why did you think you did?" she asks with her head turned to the sky. I sit up and prop my arms behind me.

"Because I would do anything for her. I always wanted to see her happy. She made me happy. I was attracted to her. There just wasn't that spark," I glance back at her, "The spark that causes you to do stupid things and move mountains to ensure that it never dies. The spark that has the ability to break through the darkness inside and radiate within you even in the afterlife."

She intakes a sharp breath. "Geez," she says. I shrug up one shoulder, "Yea. She just never had me wanting to be stupid. It was too picture perfect if you will." She finally looks at me and I give her a smile. She returns it.

"How about you Jameson?" I say, inwardly hoping her answer is similar. She looks disgusted by the fact that I even asked her that question.

"Nope, never want to be."

I look at her confused. "Really? Why?"

She looks back at the sky. "I just don't believe in it."

"So, your past boyfriends didn't give you hope?" I say, trying to figure out why she would say such a thing about such *an important emotion. "Never had one." Why does she sound so nonchalant about this?*

"Ever?" I say in disbelief.

"Nope."

"Ever been on a date?"

"Nope."

I shake my head in disbelief. "Can I ask why?" She plays with the lint on her pajama pants, biting her lower lip. "People claim they're in love, but in the end, they just leave."

"That's not true," I say in protest.

"Just look at the divorce rate," she says putting her arms out in front of her like she's presenting an imaginary chart, "They're the highest they've ever been."

"That doesn't mea-"

"So, people claim they love you 'til death do us part, but don't hesitate to leave at the first sign of trouble." I start to realize why she believes all of this. "Jordan," I start to say.

"I don't need your pity," she spits out and stands up, walking back towards the bench. I stand up following behind her.

"I'm not pitying you," I say to the back of her head, "I'm just trying to understand you more."

"For what?" She spits back. Her sudden change in mood has me faltering a bit. She was the one who brought this up.

"Well for one, you're my friend and we talk to each other. Help each other in ways we didn't think possible." I step closer. "I'm just trying to help you sort out your thoughts, that's all." She drops her head down and I use this as an opportunity to circle around her so that we are facing each other.

Somewhat anyway, since I'm just looking at the top of her head.

"I just don't want to fall in love okay?" She finally looks up, pain swimming in her light brown pupils. "I don't want to be hurt and go through the same thing my mom went through. I've lived through it once; I refuse to live through it again."

I want to hug her. Pull her to me and bury my nose into her curls. I want to comfort her more than I'd ever wanted to comfort Lisa, my first "love". I ball my fists at my side to keep from touching her and settle for providing the comfort through my voice.

"It's okay to be afraid," I tuck my hands in my pockets to prevent from brushing my fingers across her cheek, "but you can't let that fear keep you from living. To live is to be alive. And even though you'd look beautiful either way, I'm sure everyone would prefer you alive." I smile at the chuckle that escapes her mouth.

"There's the smile that I know and lo-...like."

I need to be careful not to throw that love word around. She nods her head and I take that as a sign that she doesn't want to talk about this anymore. She turns back to go lay on the clouded ground and I sit across from her, crisscross applesauce style.

"So, tell me about the competition, how's it going?"

"We had our first two sessions, and there's only two more before they give us the equipment and we have a week to record and submit our movie."

Her eyes grow wide, "Wow, that's not really a lot of time is it?"

I shake my head, thinking about how that's not even half of my problem. "And on top of that, I'm still trying to come up with a unique way to show deliverance in a short film while also leaving the watcher wanting more and moved with so many emotions."

She nods slowly, trying to understand where I'm coming from. "And if you don't figure it out?" I shrug trying to show I don't care as much when really, it's been causing me headaches ever since I found out the theme,

"Then I guess I'll try again next year." She gives a lopsided smile, showing off her one dimple.

"Even though we haven't known each other all that long, I can see straight through you Malakai Woods." She points a finger at me and squeezes one of her eyes closed as If she's about to shoot a sniper at someone a few yards away.

"What do you mean?" I say, silently hoping she can actually see straight through me. I want to be able to be completely naked in front of her. Figuratively of course.

"I can tell you want this more than anything in the world and losing will cause you to be really devastated." I nod letting her words roll around in my brain.

"You're not wrong," I say.

"I also know that you will come up with the best idea and everything will turn out fine. In fact, I'll even help you right now." I shoot my eyes to hers, shocked.

"You will? Do you know anything about film making?" I say it not in a condescending way, but a genuinely curious way.

She shakes her head, "Not really, but I have watched tons of movies in my day from many different genres. I know what makes a movie good or not. I like to call myself somewhat of a film critic."

I could kiss her right now.

Out of happiness of course.

And on her cheek. Definitely her cheek. The one on her face.

"I also kind of want to try something," she adds. She moves to where she is now resting on her knees.

"Something like what?"

"Well you know how you have the ability to control your dreams? And are able to manifest any creature, person or object?" I start to see where she's going with this.

"You want to see if we can do that here?" She shrugs one of her shoulders, "why not?"

Why didn't I ever think of this? I'm always trying to control my dreams, well before these started happening anyway. And before I met her.

"The only thing I found that I couldn't change in my dreams was the location and scenery."

"*Aw man, there goes that trip to the Eiffel Tower I was planning,*" *I say jokingly.*

"*Shut up,*" *she says, and she closes her eyes in concentration. She looks like Bonnie from the Vampire Diaries when she was trapped in that dimension with Damon, trying to use a spell to set them free.*

Something sparkles in front of us, first it looked like a little shiny firefly covered in glitter, then it materialized into a sheet of paper. My eyes grow as big as the sun.

"*What the hell?*" *I barely speak out. Jordan opens her eyes and they then mimic mine.* "*It worked! It actually worked!*" *She jumps up from where she was sitting and does a little victory dance.*

"*You try!*" *She points at me after her dance. I sit in the same position she did. I close my eyes and focus on the object I want to create. I feel a warmth start to grow and sizzle inside of me and I try to mix my object with that warmth. I feel sparks like electricity flow through me and I can hear Jordan's sharp intake of breath.*

Once the warmth fades away, I open one eye and peek at what I created. "*You did it!*" *She says holding up the ballpoint Bic pin I manifested, to go along with the paper she made.*

"*Does that make me somewhat of a warlock now?*" *I ask, quirking up an eyebrow.* "*Sure, only if I'm your queen-witch master,*" *she winks.*

I wink back, "*more like my personal tinker bell.*"

She laughs and my heart laughs back.

Whoa.

Calm down Mal's heart.

"Alright, let's get planning."

She picks up the paper and writes **MALAKAI'S FILM OUTLINE.**

How'd she know my name was spelled like that. Malakai is usually spelled with a y like "Malachy".

"How'd you know my name was spelled like that?" I say amused.

"Just guessed. Call it a friend's intuition."

With her help, we come up with three amazing ideas and all I need to do is pick one.

"That was easier than I made it out to be," I say, elated that I'm back in the game as far as where I need to be in the competitions stage. "Yea, you had help from the best person alive." She says confidently. I liked when she had her confidence on the forefront.

"Eh, second best. If that." I keep my gaze on the paper, admiring her beautiful penmanship.

"Whatever." She laughs as she stretches her legs.

It feels like we've been here for hours. I wonder what time it is in the real world. I also can't help but feel like our time is coming to an end. Not just in this dream, but in this freak dream REM world all together. She was getting close to that closure she needed in her life, and I was already taking control of mine.

I helped her though her obstacle and she helped me to learn how to live for me. I don't want this to end. I don't want to forget she existed because she's a key role in my life right now.

"Thank you," I say as I try to keep the emotion I'm feeling, out of my voice. "It's no problem, I only helped with little details." She looks over the paper.

"No, seriously, thank you. For everything. For being you."

She slides her eyes up to meet mine and we just stare at each other for a long time. I feel myself starting to lean into her face, which is so close to mine that I could feel her breath on my lips. Before it's even remotely clear on what I want to do, the familiar rumble starts in the background.

No no no. Not yet.

I need more time. Here. With her.

I need to tell her I wish I could be there with her, holding her hand as she talked to Cory. I need to tell her I want her with me in San Diego, when I premiere my movie during the contest.

I wanted her to be a friend to the real me.

A friend. Yes, that's what I wanted.

The rumble grows louder, and I fold the paper and tuck it into my back pocket. I grab the pen without fully thinking and write my name on her bicep. I don't touch her though, I only let the tip of the pen graze her soft looking skin.

She looks down at what I wrote and up at me confused. I shrug.

"I'm testing my own theory."

I wanted to see if my name would stay there after she woke up. Wanted to see if she'd be able to remember me. Remember this world. She took the pen and wrote her name on my chest. She also was careful not to touch me. She wrote it on the left side, Over my heart. More than likely it wasn't intentional, nor did she think about the placement. It was probably just the most open thing she could see.

"Call me when you wake," I say with hope in my tone.

"Hmm, I don't know. Sleeping with you might not be that memorable." She says smiling.

I laugh. I didn't realize that the rumbling had been growing louder and reached us because I was too focused on how close she was too touching me.

Before I knew it, I was falling, but it also felt like I was floating at the same time.

I was happy.

Smiling.

Even though I was being swallowed by the dark.

Malakai

"Welcome to the third class filmers! We are so close to the end; can you taste it?"

A bubbly blonde headed girl who looks like she's in her late 20s, speaks at the front of the class. Next to her, three other members of the film contest team stand there, smiling, their employee badges dangling from their neck.

"This class is dedicated to storyboarding and drawing out your idea. Miranda will come around and pass out the story board template we prepared for you guys," she stretches out her arm towards the cute, short, middle eastern looking girl wearing a black hijab.

Miranda raises and waves her hand to show us that she is, in fact, THE Miranda the bubbly blonde just mentioned.

"We also have a surprise guest coming tonight, so be on the lookout for a familiar face because we won't even tell you when he pops in."

I wonder who it is. I bet it's one of this hot shot Hollywood producers who only care about making money and looking good for the cameras. Those types of people don't care at all about the beauty of film making and leaving your watchers with something memorable.

When bubbly blonde's speech is done, I start to think on the idea that came to me when I woke up a couple days ago. It was perfect for what I wanted to convey and aligned with the theme of the contest.

I don't know how I didn't think of it sooner.

I rub at my left peck muscle, remembering the rash I woke up with that same morning. It didn't itch or anything, but it was warm to the touch like it was irritated. I draw out the storyboard and go to start working on the script.

"Why this scene before this one?" I hear a voice say from behind me. I turn to look at the scene the man is pointing too.

"It makes the most sense. Having the protagonist face his demons and then reach his goals." I say it like it's obvious, and I assume it's one of the other participants thinking they know everything.

"Don't you think it would be interesting to make the protagonist think he beat his demons by reaching his goals, but come to find out they were just hiding behind a bush?"

I stop writing the script I was drafting and turn to face this person who has *so* much to say about my writing. My jaw goes slack and I'm paralyzed with shock.

"Ma…" I say but my mouth doesn't finish the sentence. I've never been awestruck before. I don't like it. I look stupid.

I pick my jaw up off the floor and scramble to collect my balls as they rolled away.

"Matthew Weiss," the man before me says, extending a handout to me as he flashes his megawatt smile, "But you can call me Matt."

I shoot my hand out to shake his. "Malakai Woods."

I give him a firm shake as my confidence slowly creeps back. Matthew Weiss was probably the biggest actor of my generation. He starred in hundreds of movies, playing multiple different roles.

He has about 20 Oscars sitting in his huge mansion too match. He was also my favorite actor of all time, and a man I looked up too (after my father of course). Not only was he the most talented well-rounded actor who gave Denzel Washington a run for his money (sorry Denzel), but he was also a philanthropist, an activist, and an all-around positive person. If perfect existed and was a full, blood pumping, breathing human, it would be Matt Weiss.

"You're Sydney's son," he says too me with recognition in his eyes.

"You know my mom?" I say sounding like a five-year-old who's just met Santa.

"Of course, we have a few mutual friends. She also is the author of some of my favorite books," he taps his chin in thought, "She's always talking about you too."

My eyes shine with adoration for my mom and the fact she was talking to Matthew Weiss about me.

"Loved the speech you did for her too, I watched it on YouTube the other day. Your mom told me you were in this competition when I bumped into her in passing last week."

I can't believe my favorite actor knows who I am. I also can't believe my mom kept the fact that she knew MATTHEW WEISS and never told me.

"Decided to search you up to see if you had any work and saw the speech. Beautiful words."

Matthew Weiss looked *me* up?

The Matthew Weiss.

I clear my throat trying to hide the meltdown I'm having in my head right now.

"Thank you so much, I was really struggling with what to say." Why would I say that? Now I don't seem reliable.

"That's how I am when it comes to my speeches. I just hand it over to fate and let it control what I say," he wiggles his fingers out like he's controlling a puppet, "you could call me Pinocchio."

"So, you never tell a lie?" I feel myself asking without thinking. He laughs.

"I used to lie a lot, but as I got older, I asked myself. What's the point? I'm really prolonging the truth coming out and when it does come, it'll be 20 times worse than what it could've been. So now I just tell it like it is and say whatever comes to my mind. Meticulously of course."

He winks and my adoration for him grows more. "So, let's talk film, shall we?"

I shake out of my starstruck-ness and listen to the advice he gives me about my story board.

"If you apply the changes we went over, or if you decide to say screw me and you know what's best for your movie, I'll still watch either way. I have a feeling I'm going to see a lot more of you in the future."

Matt (yes, I call him Matt now) pats his hand on my shoulder. "Now let me go help these other young and struggling directors."

I laugh and he flashes me another smile before he walks off.

"What?" My mom says quirking one eyebrow up at me as she looks up from her computer.

My dad places the book he was reading in the chair across from her desk, the same chair I sat in when I told her I quit the team and placed it on the top of his crossed legs. He looks like he's trying to figure out what I'm upset at my mom about.

"Two words," I say holding up two fingers with my palm facing me, leaning on my shoulder in the door frame. I wait a few seconds and she leans back in her chair.

"Am I going to have to guess?" she says amused. I shake my head but still don't say anything. I want to drag out the anticipation. My dad smirks from where he's sitting.

"Matthew. Weiss."

My dad's smirk turns into an all-out grin. He looks at my mom's face and busts out laughing. Her face morphs from concern, to relief, to apologetic, to amused.

"He was the surprise guest huh?" she asks as she crosses her arms. I walk in the office and sit in the chair next to Dad. "Why didn't you tell me? You know he's my favorite!" I throw my arms in the air dramatically.

"There was really nothing to tell," she says, "I only see him in passing, or for like five seconds at social events whenever I'm in Hollywood. I didn't want you to get your hopes up and exaggerate our friendship in your head."

I lean forward and rest my head into my hands. Such a familiar position. A distant memory flickers at the back of my mind.

"So dramatic," my dad chuckles next to me.

The memory is gone.

"Dad, it was Matthew freakin' Weiss," I refrain from using the actual word that I want to use, "If it was Michael Jackson or Prince, you'd feel the same way too." I turn to look at him and I see him nodding in agreement.

"He seemed like he was very interested in the movie I was drafting up," I add.

"Oooo, let me see let me see!" My mom says, sliding her computer monitor out of the way. My dad places the book I now see is *The Kind Worth Killing* by Peter Swanson, on the empty desk space in front of him.

I stand up and walk to the doorway where I left my bookbag. I pull out my planning notebook and walk back, splaying it out on the desk space she provided me.

We talk more about my plans and my mom gives me a few ideas and pointers. My dad does too, but I like my mom's better.

Don't tell him I told you that though.

We order Chinese and eat it in my mom's office, laughing and talking and being all family like.

I think about Lisa and how our relationship was good for what it was. I wonder what she was doing. If she found someone who's willing to be stupid for her. I hope she did because she deserved it.

Why am I even thinking about this? Oh yea, because my mom brought her up asking if I'm dating. Why do moms do that?

Once we finish eating our take-out, my mom goes back to writing her book and my Dad goes back to reading his. They were such a cute couple and perfect for each other. I hope I find somebody I can be completely myself with and isn't afraid to take risks. Someone who meshes with me and fills all the gaps and holes on the inside.

I need to call my friends. I can't be left alone tonight thinking about a love I probably won't have for another ten years.

"If it isn't my favorite guy on the planet. My Mal Mal!" Saiyr says as he picks up the phone. This man is always doing something. He looks like he's in a crowded house party and I can barely hear him over the music. "Ant!" he calls off into the distance ahead of him.

Moments later I see Anthony's side profile in the frame.

"Sai what the hell," he says as he blocks his eye from the bright light of the screen.

"It's Mal Mal," Saiyr says and I can tell by the way he keeps saying my nickname that he's had one too many to drink.

"Oh, wassup bro," Anthony says as he smiles still blocking the light from his eyes. "Where are you guys?" I ask wondering why I wasn't invited.

"Some guys from the team threw an impromptu party after practice and word spread fast, I guess," Ant chuckles on the other end of the phone.

"We were going to invite you, but I knew you had your session today," Saiyr chimes in, "plus I checked your location when we got here, and you were still in La Mesa."

I know it may seem like me and my friends party a lot, but we really don't. We're chill people, sans Saiyr because that man does party a lot.

Ant is the most chill out of all of us but enjoys spending his nights out and about from time to time.

I don't mind the party scene myself, but I won't ditch important work to go grind against a few random girls I don't know. Saiyr on the other hand...

"You can still pull up bro, the party is just getting started," Sai yells out and people chant and whoop as he says this.

"Nah, just pull up when you're done, I'll be up." I say laughing at my friend.

Anthony flashes a look of concern, "Your insomnia still bothering you? You need to go to a doctor or something. They'll be able to help."

I shake my head.

"They're just going to shove pills in my hand and send me on my way. No thank you." He doesn't say anything because he knows I'm probably right. The music grows louder as he walks to wherever the speakers are.

"I'll be there once I leave here which will probably be soon," he says as he sits down on a couch.

I think it's Rummel's couch, one of the offensive linemen.

"Okay, just call when you're outside. Make sure Saiyr doesn't do anything stupid," Ant nods and ends the call.

I log into my Instagram after God knows how long, and check what I missed. I go to my notifications and stare at the top one, smiling.

THEMATTHEWWEISS STARTED FOLLOWING YOU.

I look at the second notification and see that he commented a fire emoji under a picture of me celebrating a win with my football team last year.

I wonder if he's saying the picture itself is fire, the fact that the team won, or the fact that I gave up a life that I knew and stepped out on a whim to chase my dreams.

I shake my head. I doubt he thought all of that by looking at a simple picture. I'm thinking too much into one emoji.

I scroll through my page and see that it needs some serious renovating to better represent the new Mal.

I go and archive my old photos and once I land on the ones of me and Lisa, I find myself drifting back to the thoughts that were in my mind earlier. About how I'll find the love of my life in ten years. Something tells me it'll be a lot sooner than that. Another something tells me I've already met my soulmate; I just didn't know it yet. Or maybe I did…

Anthony came to my house alone because Saiyr ended up going back to Britney, the cheerleading captain's, dorm room for the night.

I don't have to spell out what for. They've been "intimate" for a while now, ever since my mom's release party.

I wouldn't say they're in a relationship, more so like fuck buddies. Anthony was a single pringle like me, so we both bask in our loneliness for the rest of the night. I bring up girls he's dated in the past and he did the same for me.

We work out why it didn't work out in the past for us, and what we hope for in a future relationship.

I show him my storyboard and the start of the script for my movie and he chooses which character he feels like he'd play the best. I tell him that's too bad because he's going to have to audition, and I'll put him with whatever character *I* feel is best.

We play the new Modern Warfare game on my PS4 until he's passed out on the floor.

I go back to working on my script, silently willing sleep to creep up on me so I could get a good night's sleep like Anthony. And like Saiyr because I know he's sleeping good right about now.

I think about the last time I had sex and inwardly shiver. It's been a long minute. Somehow, entertaining the idea of finding a girl around here to talk to doesn't seem so appealing.

I write until I see a peek of the sun out my window, trying to play peek-a-boo with me by hiding behind the clouds.

The view engulfs me, and I go out on my balcony to watch the sun rise the rest of the way, never falling victim to a sleep induced coma.

I'm ready for this competition to be over so I can finally have my sleep back.

Jordan

"How were your finals?" Ben asked as I opened the passenger door to his red Audi coupe.

Since this was my last week at CAU before winter break, I left my car at home this past weekend and Ben dropped me off at school. I just finished taking my last final of the semester and felt like I could breathe again.

Only I couldn't because I still had a nagging situation I had to deal with.

I slide into the cream-colored passenger seat and buckle my seat belt. I place my bookbag on the floorboard in front of me and plop my head back on the leather headrest.

"That bad huh?" he says as he drives off into the busy Atlanta traffic. I turn my head slightly toward him so I could give him a silent message with my eyes. He chuckles and shakes his head.

"I'm so glad that time is O-V-E-R for me. You're almost done though kiddo." He turns his blinker on to get in the next lane. "I have a surprise for you. To congratulate you for getting through finals."

I perk up in my seat and give a half smile, "What is it?" I ask.

"It talks!" He says trying to look horrified.

"Ha Ha," I slide back to a slouching position, "I'm just exhausted. I've been up since six this morning and have been over working my brain since then."

He smirks at me. "You Gen Z's and your first world problems," he sticks out his bottom lip in a mock pout. I lightly punch his arm and he acts like he's about to veer off the road in traffic.

"BEN!" I shriek and he just gives a big bellied laugh in response.

"Okay Okay," he says, and he turns into a parking lot a couple minutes later.

My eyes grow wide and my mouth instantly salivates. "Surprise!" He says as he hops out the car and rounds the front to open my door.

He brought me to my favorite donut spot ever, Sublime Doughnuts. They had the best Strawberry N' Cream and Honey Glazed Cinnamon Swirl donuts. I lick my lips as I climb out of the car door Ben held open for me.

"Thank you so much!" I say as I hug him tight and hurriedly walk into the front door of the shop.

This location in Southwest Atlanta had a warming vibe to it. It was a small little shop with a leather couch towards the back-window seal tabletop. At the window, there were metal barstools that gave you a view of the parking lot out front. Tiny round wooden tables with old vintage looking chairs that you'd find in your grandma's house with the plastic still wrapped around it, were all over the shop.

The walls were painted like a sky with little clouds around and the ceiling lights also looked like little clouds floating in the sky. Behind the counter you could see freshly cooked donuts set up along the back wall. As we wait in line, I take in the sky mural all over the walls and the cloud like lights, a flicker of a memory trying to break free from its mental prison.

"What can I get for you?" A voice says breaking me out of my thoughts. She looked like she's been trying to ask me this question for a minute.

"Sorry," I say, and I order my favorites. Benny orders a dozen of my favorites for me to take home later. I'm so grateful for him. He then orders another dozen, inside of it would be six Raspberry Filled Hearts with Dark Chocolate (for my mom), three Orange dream stars (for Jamie), and three Caramel Apple Fritters (for himself).

I go grab a seat at one of the empty tables along the left wall as he pays for the order. He saunters over to me and takes the seat across.

"How's work?" I ask when he sits down. He was a pediatrician at Children's Healthcare of Atlanta. He just took on a young boy, Conner, with leukemia and I know with cases like these, they usually hit him hard.

Ben was a very loving person who grew bonds and relationships with his patients, treating them like they were his own kids.

He lets out a deep sigh and scrubs his face a little. He gives me a weak smile and that tells me things aren't going so well. "Conner isn't doing so good right now. His blood cells are changing, and it's caused him to have an infection that's affecting the amount of oxygen reaching his body's tissues."

His weak smile ends up falling, "He's not responding well to the antibiotics, so it's looking like we might have to do a full-on blood transfusion."

"Oh no," I say softly, sad that a young child and his family must go through all of this. Also, sad that Ben, the nicest person on the planet, has to deal with all of this loss around him and be so positive.

Lord knows I would be beyond emotionally drained.

"It's just, he's only six years old. He has so much life to live," he extends his hands out as if showing something off, "He should be out there worrying about which slide he's going to go down first, not which day is his last." The pain swimming in his irises is so evident that it causes me to try and keep my emotions down.

"Sorry to damper the mood," he says with a sad chuckle.

"No, it's okay, really." I reassure him.

The girl behind the counter calls out our order number and Ben goes to pick up the boxes. He opens the shop door with his back and holds it open for me, then runs to open my car door.

He never lets me, or my mom open our own doors. We started toward the house, and I decided to lighten the mood with some music. I hooked my phone to his Carplay and scrolled to my music app.

A few seconds later, J.Cole's album *KOD* plays through the speakers and I turn the volume up. J.Cole was Ben's favorite rapper at the time, so I knew he would appreciate this gesture.

He turned his head to me with a wide grin. "You done messed up now Jor," he says getting excited then starts reciting all the words to the second song on the album.

We both rapped the whole thing on the way home, dancing and having fun, not caring about the drivers in the cars next to us staring at us like we were crazy. The traffic allowed us to get through the whole album with no interruptions.

When we pull into the driveway, I see that my mom's car isn't there. Ben opens my door for me then pulls the donuts from the backseat and takes them into the house. I walk in with him and go set my bookbag in my room. I come back down the stairs.

"Where's mom and Jamie?" I ask him once I get to the bottom.

"She took Jamie with her while she hung out with Stacy for a little while." He plops down on the couch and I plop in the accent chair to the right of it. I lean in and open my box of donuts that sits on the coffee table in front of us.

"So that means you actually have to cook something edible?" I say, cocking up an eyebrow.

He throws a pillow at me and I dodge it. "Hey! I can cook. I was going to order pizza but just for that, I think I'll make the pizza myself."

"Oh no," I whine, then I remember something. "Actually, we don't have the ingredients to do that so jokes on you."

He looks up from his phone that he grabbed a second before I said this.

"Jokes on you actually, I'm ordering them on Instacart," he says as he shows me the phone screen that is indeed, on the Instacart app. I throw the pillow he threw at me moments ago, back at him.

About thirty minutes later, his Instacart order is delivered and we splay out all the groceries across the island. "Want to make this a competition?" I say to him.

"I'm listening," he says intrigued by my question.

"Whoever makes the best tasting pizza wins and doesn't suffer any consequences, while the loser is on dish washing duty for a week. I'll bring mom in on it too, so she'll leave all the dirty dishes in the sink so the loser can clean them."

He ponders what I said, rubbing his chin. "I like the way you think. It's on," he extends his hand out to me and I shake it.

I start to gather my ingredients for my pizza, and he moves his pizza to the countertop behind me, so I won't "steal his ideas". We work in a comfortable silence, but my mind starts to think about Cory and all the events that's happened in the past few months.

I realized I still haven't told my parents that I talked to him, nor did I tell Ben that he even hit me up in the first place. Maybe now is the perfect time to bring that up.

"Ben," I say into the air as I work.

"Mhm?" he responds in concentration.

"Why do you love my mom?"

I hear him stop working and turn towards me. I don't turn towards him though, I just casually spread the alfredo sauce over my premade pizza dough.

"What do you mean why?" he asks confused, "Where is this coming from?" I add a little more alfredo sauce.

"I guess what I mean is.. why'd you decide to take a chance on her?"

On *us. Me.*

He walks around where I'm working, to the other side of the island with the barstools and stops until he's aligned in front of me so he could see my face. I don't look up from where I've been spreading alfredo sauce in the same place for the last few minutes.

I feel him trying to find a reason in his head, or at least that's what I think he's doing anyway.

"Well, I seen your mom bring you into the office a few times when I was just starting my residency a few years back. I always thought she was the most beautiful thing I've ever seen. You guys were never alone though," he doesn't fully say it, but I know what he means.

Cory was like Voldemort in this house, the unspeakable.

"I would just admire her from a distance a few times and the bond between the both of you would always pull at my heart strings a little." He chuckles at the memory and I smile remembering how much fun my mom and I had back then.

"One day I just happened to be jogging in Historic Fourth Ward Park. I didn't usually jog but that day I was feeling spontaneous. I grabbed some running shoes from the back of my closet and went at it the best I could. I wasn't unfit because I went to the gym regularly, I just wasn't a runner." I'm still not looking at him, but I giggle thinking about him running because he still doesn't run to this day.

That had to be a fluke. Or fate.

"Anyway, I was jogging in Historic Fourth Ward Park, and I was coming up on the playground area and noticed your mom sitting on a bench. I haven't seen her for a long while and always wondered what happened. You were on the jungle gym; she was sitting alone, and I was a little winded from jogging for 30 minutes straight."

"I approached her, and she actually recognized me from our few interactions at the hospital. She seemed a little down and I tried to provide comedic relief to see her beautiful smile. Since that day, we would hang out occasionally as friends and she would open up to me a little bit more. And then I met you."

The tone of his voice caused me to look up at his face. Adoration and what felt like love were on display in his dark brown eyes. I want to look away because of the intensity, but for some reason I don't.

"Your mom and I's relationship started to blossom. I fell for her strength, perseverance and undeniable beauty. She was also funny but not as funny as me of course. Once we established we were going to try for more, she allowed me to meet you. You were such a go-getter. A force to be reckoned with. I was so grateful that you allowed me into your life."

I shrugged it off like it was no big deal, trying not to get emotional. I really don't like getting emotional.

"You were nice, and you always brought me candy and ice cream."

He laughs and I give a half smile. "The way to any woman's heart is sweets. Lesson I learned from my youth. But to answer your question, I fell in love with the both of you. It wasn't all that hard to do either."

"Is it hard to stay faithful?" I blurt out. My eyes go wide because my filter decided to be nonexistent at the time.

He looks at me as if I grew two heads. Then I see when realization dawns on him.

"Is this about..." And he doesn't say it, but I know he's asking about Cory. I let out a long sigh.

"He started texting me," I finally tell him. He rounds the island so fast that I can barely see it happening. He grabs my shoulders and whips me around so he can check for any signs of hurt or bruising or whatever protective dads check for.

"Are you okay? Has he hurt you?"

I shake my head. "No, nothing like that. All he did was text me asking me to see him."

He takes a step back and gives a sigh of relief then is immediately back in protective mode. "When did he start?"

"A couple months back. I told mom about it already but..."

"You wanted to know how I felt about it?" He finishes my sentence for me. "You don't know how happy that makes me." I look at him confused.

Why does that make him happy?

He shakes his head. "Something this major has happened in your life. Something that has nothing to do with me, yet, you're worried about how it will make me feel. You're worrying about me when the only thing you should be worried about is you."

I take in his words while he grabs my hand and guides me to sit on the barstools. Now we are in the same position my mom and I were in when I told her about my birth father a few weeks ago.

How ironic.

"How did him contacting you make you feel? Did you respond?"

I told him about the roller coaster of emotions that I've been through the past few months and how I called Cory back and it didn't go as planned.

"You and your mom are the strongest women I know. If meeting him is something you need to move forward with your life, I'm all for it. Just know I'll be there with you the whole way. Whether that's holding your hand or cheering from the sidelines. I'll always be here for you." He pulls me in for a hug and I hug him back, squeezing my eyes shut.

While we're hugging, he says in my ear, "Oh and to answer your question. No, I've never thought about stepping out on your mom. It's not in my DNA to do something like that."

"Thank you for taking a chance on a single mother and her sassy kid."

We both laugh and release each other from the hug. We look at each other in the eyes and so many words are said through our pupils.

Ben claps his hands together. "Alright, let's get back to this competition. I'm going to make my dishes extra dirty just for you."

Gliding.

Soaring.

Falling.

Falling.

As the bright light dims, I move my hand away from my eyes. I smile when I see Malakai sitting there on his stone bench. It looks like he's holding something. I walk over to him and he looks up at me with a smile. His smile is so radiant that it fills me with warmth.

"It's about time you got here, I was starting to think you were going to stand me up." He puts his arm out to hand me something.

My gaze moves from his face to the object in his hand. It was a rose. I smile hard at him.

"I see you're getting use to your newfound powers. This is sweet of you, thank you." I take the rose and put it to my nose. The smell that enters my nostrils is not that of a regular rose. This smell is much more sweet and angelic for lack of a better words.

I close my eyes and let out a slight moan. When I open them again, Malakai is staring at me intently.

"What?" I ask.

"Nothing," he says and scoots over. I take the seat next to him and then I remember the mark we left on each other our last visit to this dream world. "Hey, did my name stay on your chest when you woke up?"

He shook his head, "No, I just woke up with a rash that was hot to the touch. How about you?" I shake my head as well.

"Same for me. What about the paper that we worked on?"

"That actually wasn't even in my pocket. So I'm guessing whatever happens in the dream world..."

"Stays in the dream world," I finish his sentence for him.

"That's disappointing, I wanted to hang out with you. Put you in my movie since you helped me with the idea." He did sound genuinely disappointed. Surprisingly, I was too, just a little bit. I mean we are friends and we have confided in each other, but that's only because this isn't real. Our friendship *wouldn't be what it was if I met him on the street somewhere, before all this dream stuff started. We'd probably be associates but nothing more.*

"Speaking of your movie, how's it going?" I put the rose to my nose again, inhaling its unearthly addicting scent.

"Oh, guess what?" he says excitedly, and I flinch because it catches me off guard. "Matthew Weiss knows who I am." He sounded like a fan girl and it made me laugh. It was cute to see him so giddy from meeting somebody as famous as Matthew.

He told me about everything that transpired when Matthew Weiss looked at the plans for his movie. He also told me he confronted his mom about not telling him that she knows his biggest inspiration. I'm kind of jealous that he got to see the drop dead, better than Trevante Rhodes and Kofi Siriboe, jaw dropper that is Matthew Weiss.

Yes, I have to say his full name when I address him because he's Matthew Weiss. Malakai, however, just calls him Matt. He can do that though now that they're cool with each other.

"I finished writing the script yesterday too," Malakai says, finishing up his eventful story. "Now I just have to get my actors together so we can film it. The last session for the film contest is next week and that's when I'll get all of the equipment from them."

"That sounds really good Malakai, I'm so happy for you."

He nods and grants me access to his perfect set of pearly whites that always has me a little off kilter. "But enough about me, what's been going on with you?"

I like how he doesn't ask about Cory upfront, but more so in a way that he wants to know more than just my father. "Well, I passed all my finals so that's a blessing." I put the rose down in between us and just look down at it. "I also plan on calling Cory within the next few days. I just wanted to enjoy my break for a while before shit hit the fan, ya know?"

He chuckles, "The calm before the storm."

"Exactly," I say chuckling back.

"Any plans for your birthday?" he asks me. I realize that my birthday is approaching fast and I haven't even given it one lick of a thought.

"No, I honestly don't even like to celebrate it. My family just makes ne a cake, I open gifts and that's that."
"Why?" He asks but I know he already knows the answer. I decide to entertain him for a bit, what's the harm?

"It reminds me too much about that day Cory left." I don't know why it's so easy for me to talk to him about this situation. Maybe it's the atmosphere or because it's a dream.

Or him.

I wave off the quick thought that appears in my head before I start to overthink it like I do everything. "Besides, I'm not much of a party person, more of a homebody."

"This is your 21st though right? You should at least have one big blowout to celebrate you being considered an adult in society. Besides, I'm sure once you close that door to the past, *it'll make it so much easier for you to enjoy and celebrate the fact that you're alive still."*

I give him a lopsided grin, "You're always so deep."

"Growing up with a writer as a mom, you really learn how to use your words," he laughs.

"Well, since our dreams seem to be far in between, then we have to celebrate right now, come on." He gets up from the bench and gestures for me to follow him. He walks a ways away to a spot on the cloud ground he deems as good enough. Even though it looks the same all the way around us.

What is he planning?

I see him shutting his eyes in concentration, and energy starts to surge in the air. Before I know it, he's generated a blanket and laid it down on the ground. Next came a basket that looks like one made for a picnic. He makes balloons, champagne glasses, and even a gift. I stare at the decorations he set up before me in awe.

"Wow," is all I manage to say. "I know right," he says rubbing at the back of his neck, "I didn't even think I'd be able to do this. It was just a random idea." He plops down on the blanket and opens the basket. He pulls out a round cake with only my name on the top in icing. He also pulls out some sandwiches and chips.

"Can we eat this?" I ask bewildered.

"Honestly, I'm not even sure. I'll be the test dummy though."

I sit down across from him and he takes a bite from what looks to be a chicken salad sandwich. As he chews, his eyes grow wide in astonishment.

"Oh wow," he repeats after every chew. He finally swallows then looks at me with his mouth open in shock. "You have to try this. Now."

He hands me a sandwich of my own then works on opening his back of nacho Doritos. I take a bite of the sandwich and I swear it tastes like a hug from an angel. It was a taste I've never experienced before. It was different, but also had that classic chicken salad sandwich taste. I let out a moan and he stops trying to open his bag of Doritos and looks at me.

I close my eyes as I indulge in the flavors of this sent from heaven sandwich. If I could, I would only eat this for the rest of my life.

I open my eyes back up and he clears his throat, quickly returning to opening his bag of chips. "What?" I ask, curious to know the reason for his weird reaction.

"What?" he says back in response.

"Why were you staring at me like that?" I ask, quirking up my eyebrow. "I was just trying to see if you were experiencing the same thing I did, that's all." He finally gets his bag open and starts chomping away at the Doritos.

From the look on his face, I could tell that they had the same affect the sandwich had on his taste buds. I pick up one of the champagne glasses and he picks up his in response. He puts his in the air to make a toast.

"To Jordan's 21ˢᵗ birthday extravaganza. May it bring you peace and prosperity. Happy Birthday!" we clink glasses and take a sip.

"Thank you so much for this. You didn't have too," I say when I put my glass down. "But I did," is all he said in response before he went back to eating.

After eating and talking about everything and nothing at the same time, we put all the stuff to the side and laid down on the blanket staring up at the sky.

"You should open your present before it's too late," he says in the air. I forgot all about the little gift bag he imagined up. I sit up and reach to my right to get the gift bag. He sits up too and watches me intently. He looks a little nervous. "I hope you like it."

I go through the tissue paper and see a round sphere at the bottom of the bag. I pull it out and see that it's a snow globe, but not just any snow globe. This snow globe had a cloudy bottom with me standing up pointing at something in the sky and Malakai sitting next to me, looking at whatever it is I'm pointing at. The bench was also in the globe and I was wearing my favorite oversized Michael Jackson t-shirt which made me smile.

"Thank you so much, it's perfect." I shake the globe and notice that instead of snow coming down from the stop, the ground beneath me and Malakai shake, causing everything to swirl around the globe, but as it settles, everything goes right back to where it was like nothing ever happened.

"It's so you never forget about this place and our friendship. Even though you probably won't have it when you wake up."

"I still appreciate it all the same."

"The smile she's giving me right now makes it hard for me to stay still. I want to pull her into an embrace, feel her warmth, and I do just that. Without even thinking, I reach over and pull her into a hug.

At first, she's shocked and hesitant, but then she gives in.

Right when she does that, a powerful heat starts to form between us. I then feel that familiar surge and cackle of energy course through my veins and cause sparks to shoot in my nerves. It feels how I feel when I'm creating something, but ten times more powerful. The heat between intensifies to the point where it starts to burn.

Suddenly, a bright white light forms around us, and it gets too bright.

Too hot.

Too fast.

MALAKAI

I shoot up out of my sleep, confused and disoriented. I'm sweating profusely, causing my shirt to stick to my body. I gasp for air as I take in my surroundings.

I'm in my room. I'm so hot all over that I throw my shirt over my head and run quickly to the bathroom to jump in the cold shower.

I place my hands against the shower wall in front of me and allow the cold water to shoot down my body. I feel instant relief and slow down my breathing. "What the fuck?" I whisper to myself. What the hell happened to me?

Once I'm out the shower and my body temperature was back under control, I walk back over to my bed. My sheets were soaked with sweat and hot to the touch. They feel as though they were just taken out of the dryer.

I gather all my sheets and pillowcases, then walk to the laundry room down the hall and toss them in. I come back to my room and realize that it's still dark outside and wonder exactly what time it is.

I look at the clock on my nightstand and it says 3:30 am. What the hell am I doing up at 3:30 am?

I lay back down and try to go to sleep, but I'm unsuccessful. I decide I might as well do something productive since it's looking like I'll be up for the rest of the night. I go on my phone and look at the ad I put on Backstage in search of some aspiring actors or even experienced actors looking to be a part of my film. It's pro bono work, but I told them they'd have the opportunity to be broadcasted to tons of A-list Hollywood producers and directors.

I've gotten tons of replies since I posted it on their a few days ago, so now I need to set up an audition time so I can see how good they are at acting. I'm putting my all into this short film and need it to come at as close to perfect as possible.

I come up with a plan as to where and when I'm holding the auditions and reply to the inquiries.

Hopefully the casting is a cake walk.

A few days later, I'm standing outside the venue where my mom had her book release ceremony a few months back. Christmas, also known as the deadline to submit your movie, is next week Wednesday, and today was Monday so I needed to find my actors today or else I'm screwed.

This venue was the perfect place to hold my auditions because not only did it have that theater room with a stage and seating, it also was big enough to hold all 150 of the actors that responded to the Backstage ad listing.

After putting up the signs that tell the actors where to go to sign-in and wait for their name to be called, I walk back in to make sure everything was set up properly.

"Where do you need this snack tray to go bro?" Anthony asks as he strides toward me holding a fruit and vegetable tray with cheese cubes.

"Put it on the table next to the sign in desk. That's also where I need the water pitchers to go," I tell him as I point him in the direction.

I recruited Ant, Saiyr, and my mom to help me with today as well as a couple people from the football team because I needed all hands-on deck.

Dad couldn't come because he had important meetings at the office all week, but I'm not even mad.

He was sad that he couldn't come but I told him not to even worry about it.

I follow Anthony over to the sign-in desk that my mom and Saiyr are sitting behind. He's making her laugh about something and she almost pushes him out of his chair from laughing so hard.

They were in charge of making sure everyone signed in properly and had a name tag on. Rummel, a guy from the football team, would then direct them to the waiting area where they were to wait to be called on by another guy from the team named Kendell.

"Okay everyone, everything's looking great, the actors should be here within the next 30 minutes."

They all nod and mumble in acknowledgement. "So, once we finish signing everyone in, we join you in the theater room to help judge?" My mom asks when her laughter dies down.

"Exactly." I say smiling back at her. She claps her hands in excitement and Saiyr looks excited to do his job too.

"You, Ant, Sai and I are all the judges," I lean against the sign-in table.

"Do we have the power to vote people in or out, or are we just there to give constructive criticism?" Anthony asks as he takes the plastic wrapping from the snack tray.

"I already have my Simon Cowell scowl ready to give hard my critic," Saiyr says in response to Ant's question.

"You're just here to give your opinion and put a different perspective on their auditions." Ant nods and goes out front to help direct the actors to the sign-up desk.

"When that girl went full blown opera and started belting out that one song, I died," Saiyr told my dad while we sat at the booth waiting to order our food.

We spent all morning going through audition after audition, and I was able to find actors to fit all the roles for my movie. As expected, there were some great actors, and a few not so great ones. We've been telling him all about the different auditions and when I planned on starting to film. I need it to be done by next Monday so I could start the editing process.

"If you need anyone to play the Sexy Cop number 3 in your film, you know I'm your guy," my Dad says as he winks at me across the table and I make a show of fake gagging.

My mom swats him on the chest while laughing, and Ant and Saiyr shake their heads looking horrified.

After dinner, we go back to my house and start planning out the rest of the week. I add the actors to a group chat and tell them we're going to start filming this Thursday.

I then email the script and continue to get the necessary planning done to finish this film. The last session with the contest team is this Wednesday night. That's when I'll pick up all the equipment.

It's now a couple days before Christmas, which is the due date for the competition. I'm finishing up the editing for my film and couldn't be any happier with the results.

The acting is astounding, production looks amazing, and this editing I'm doing is putting the cherry on top. I can't wait to submit it, but first I'm going to show it to my family at the Christmas party tomorrow.

All the three families that make up our complete family always spend Christmas eve together. We play games, eat a hell of a lot of food, and the parents force us all to go door to door caroling. Anthony and I are only child's, and Saiyr has 4 siblings.

I put the finishing touches onto the film and close my laptop. I lay in bed, so content with life, that I slip easily into a nice sleep. My insomnia hasn't made its appearance tonight, and hopefully since I'm done with the film, and got the big stress out of the way, it'll stay in hiding for the rest of my life.

"I want to sit next to Mal Mal!" McKenna whined, throwing a tantrum beside the couch.

This year, the Christmas party was at Ant's house and we were all gathered in his home theater.

"Kenna, Julian is sitting with Mal Mal sweetie, go sit with your sister McKayla," Saiyr's mom, Mrs. Jacobs told her daughter. McKayla was McKenna's identical twin but they both had two different personalities.

McKenna was more outgoing, whereas McKayla was more reserved. Julian was Saiyr's little brother and he was only two years old. He was sitting next to me on the plush red love seat that sat in the front row of their home theater. Saiyr's other brother, Jair, was eight, and took the seat next to Anthony. Saiyr sat next to Britney, the head cheerleader that he was "seeing" in the love seats behind me and Julian.

He didn't want to bring her, but when she accidentally met his mom last week by popping at his house for a quickie, she invited her to the party thinking her and Saiyr were in a serious relationship. Seeing as he's a nice guy, he didn't uninvite her and figured it'd be easier to have her over to have sex now.

Julian was showing Ant something on his Nintendo Switch he just got for Christmas. Behind them, my parents sat in their love seat and next to them were Ant's parents, then behind *them* were Saiyr's parents with a bickering pair of twins sitting between them.

Once everyone was in their respected seats, I stood up and decided to give an introductory speech before the movie started.

"First of all, I just wanted to thank everyone in this room for supporting me on this new journey I decided to take on in my life. It wasn't easy getting here, but it sure as he-..*heck* was worth it."

I hear some whoops and howls from the men in the family and laugh.

"I hope this film leaves you with a better understanding of not only my craft, but the type of film writer I want to be. With that being said, once I win this competition, I promise to mention you guys in my acceptance speech." Everyone applauds me and I go back and take my seat next to Julian.

Mr. Davidson, Ant's dad, hits a button on his remote and dims the lights. He then hits another button to start my film on the big projector in front of us.

As we watch the movie, so many emotions go through my mind, the most prominent one being pride. I can't believe I've made it to this point, all of this felt like a pipe dream only a few months ago. I'm so proud of myself, I want to shout it from the rooftops in every state.

After the movie, everyone congratulates me and pats me on the back, telling me I did an amazing job.

We all stay up late watching Christmas movies and enjoying the rest of the evening, and once midnight hits, the kids run to open the rest of the gifts they didn't get to open early, and I hit submit on my movie.

Now all that's left to do is to wait and see if my movie makes it to the final round, where they'll pick four movies to showcase, and vote live on which one they feel is the best and deserves to be crowned the winner.

Cross fingers that I am one of the four.

JORDAN

"French Vanilla latte with extra creamer, right?" Cam asks as she stands up from sitting next to me in the booth.

"You already know C," Rylie says in response, "Do you want anything babe?" She turns towards Zavier, whom she's nestled into on the inside of their booth seat. His arm is draped over the back in true guy fashion and they look like they should be on the cover of Vogue or something. They look so good together.

"No, I'm good sweetheart." He moves the arm that's draped behind Rylie so he's able to look at his watch. "I actually need to start heading out. My brother's plane lands in about an hour."

Ry gives him her puppy dog flirty eyes and I inwardly roll my eyes. He kisses the tip of her nose, then her lips, then her forehead. She scoots out of the booth to let him out then he kisses her again on the lips, but this time he gives her more than a peck. Their tongues dance together, and I swear I can hear the saliva being transferred between both mouths. I make a gagging motion towards Camille who's standing off to the side of them, and she hides her laugh with the dish tray in her hand.

They finally break free of their tongue tug-of-war and Zavier turns to me and Camille. "I'll see you guys later! Keep an eye on my Ry for me," He then winks at Rylie and walks out of the diner, making the bell over the door ding in response. Ry gives a longing sigh as she watches him leave, then plops back down into the booth that we're sharing.

"Oh Zavier, how I long to see your beautiful face once more," I tease trying to sound as close to Juliet as I can.

I grab Camille's hand into mine and stare deeply into her eyes.

"You make thy heart runneth over with thy love. Your beauty is unmatched by these horrid wenches of the lands," Camille says, trying to sound like Romeo and actually doing a surprisingly good job.

"Kiss me!" I gasp and pull Cam towards me but we both burst out laughing and I fall back into the booth, tears coming to my eyes.

"Shut up!" Rylie says laughing back at us and throwing her straw's wrapper at my face, "Romeo and Juliet have nothing on Zavier and I."

I cock an eyebrow at her and bust into a whole new stream of laughter.

"Let me get back to work before you guys get me fired," Cam says wiping the tears from her eyes. She stands up and goes to the back towards the kitchen so she can put in our regular orders, while tending to her regular customers that come in every day.

It was Christmas eve, so the place was booming a little bit more than usual. Ry and I were picking Cam up from work because she was going to spend the night at my house since her grandma was on a cruise for Christmas this year. Rylie was also spending the night because her family was coming over the next day anyway and we wanted to bring Christmas in together.

"How's you and Zavier?" I ask Ry as I take a sip of my water with lemon drink. Clearly, they looked as if they were doing good, but I really wanted to know if they had the official talk yet.

"We're doing amazing," she says but I could tell there was an underlying tone to her words.

"But?" I ask as I lean back into the booth.

"But we still haven't had the *talk* yet. I mean, he invited me over for Christmas dinner to meet his family, but I still want to know what we are before I embarrass myself by saying 'Hi I'm Zavier's girlfriend' and he chokes on his water at the table, ya know ?"

"That would be pretty embarrassing," I say laughing. She groans and puts her head down on the table. "Okay okay I'm sorry. You need to talk to him tonight. Hell, call him now while he's on the way to the airport."

"What do I say?" Her words sound muffled since her head is still down on the table. I flick the top of her head and she jerks up, holding the spot I flicked.

"Ow! Why'd you-"

"Listen," I cut her off mid-sentence, "This is not the confident self-assured Rylie I know. You need to take a few deep breaths. Now. Do it." I give her a stern look to show I'm not playing with her.

She does as she's told, and I can see her worry dissipate a little. "Now, clearly you and Zavier are crazy about each other. You guys have been going steady for a minute now and you're both exclusively involved with each other. You're going to call him tonight when we get back to my house and talking to him. It will be okay, me and Cam will be there to help you."

"She's right," Cam says as she walks up with Rylie's latte and some chocolate chip muffins.

"Did you hear the conversation?" I ask amused at her perfect timing.

"No, but you're always right," She responds shrugging her shoulders.

Rylie grabs a muffin and stuffs a huge chunk into her mouth. "I'm going to ask Zavier the question tonight," she says with her mouth still full.

"I'm going to need you to swallow and try again sweetie," Cam says chuckling at Rylie because she looks just like a chipmunk with nuts in its mouth. Rylie chews and gulps down the rest of her muffin. She repeats what she said to me to Cam.

"What time are you going to dinner tomorrow?" Cam asks.

"He says to be there by 6:00 pm." Rylie says taking a sip of her coffee.

"Are you ready to meet them?"

Rylie thinks about this question for a second then she nods slowly as she finds her answer in her head. "I think so, I mean I just met him a month or so ago. It feels like we're going a little fast but at the same time it seems right in a way. I don't know how to explain it."

"Well, like I said, we'll help you make that call tonight," I say to her and she leans back into the booth with her mug still in her hand.

One of Cam's customers waves her over and she stalks over to handle whatever it is they need. She has about thirty minutes left on her shift and we've been here for the past hour.

Zavier dropped Rylie off here so I could take both her and Cam back home with me.

"Are you going to call Cory?" Rylie asks me as she brings her mug up to her mouth for another sip. I lean forward and take a long sip of my water. Once I'm done, I lean back to the position I was in. I let out a sigh and nod.

"Yea, but I'm going to do it the day after Christmas."

"Why do you keep putting it off?" She tries not to sound irritated, but I know she's tired of me making myself suffer for longer than I need too. "I do not," I lie.

"First you said you were going to do it after your finals, but it's been a couple of weeks since then. Now it's the day after Christmas. Next, you're going to say after your birthday. Hell, you might even say after mine."

Rylie's birthday was April 12th, I wasn't going to prolong it that long. Was I?

"I'm going to do it the day after Christmas. I promise." I stretch my pinky across the booth table. Pinky promises were like blood oaths in this group and were taking extremely seriously.

She stretches her pinky across the table and intertwines it with mine. We both lean forward and kiss our hands at the same time then let go.

"Back to this Zavier thing," I say raising my eyebrow and laughing at her throwing her head back on her booth, tired of talking about confronting Zavier.

Cam stumbles as she walks back into my room after taking her third trip to the bathroom in the last hour.

"I almost fell down the stairs," she says wide eyed as she gets to the bed. Rylie falls over with laughter and I just shake my head at both of them. Or I feel like I'm shaking my head. I don't have full control over my body anymore.

"I think we had one too many spiked eggnog glasses," I say in response and Rylie keeps laughing. I shove her and she falls off the bed and now everyone in the room is laughing.

"I don't even want to hear the word eggnog right now," Cam slurs as she takes a seat on the floor by the bed, leaning her back against the side of it. Rylie lays next to her, face down in the carpet.

We were all drunk as hell from drinking the spiked eggnog Ben made and let us drink behind my mom's back while we watched Christmas movies and sang Christmas songs. It was now three am and we were trying to wind down. I should've known that wasn't going to happen.

"You know what?" Rylie says as she lifts her head from where she lays on the floor, "I'm going to call Zavier now." She slurs as she sits up and reaches for her phone that's charging on the nightstand above her.

"Are you sure that's the best idea?" Cam looks towards Rylie, but her eyes are closed, and she has a lazy smile on her face. We were so fucked up right now.

"Nope," is all Rylie says as she dials Zavier's number.

"I'm sure he's sleeping Ry," I say from the top of my bed where I'm laying down, making snow angels. Or rather, sheet angels?

"Hello?" she says, which tells me I'm wrong in my assumption.

"I was just calling to ask…what are we? This is something I need to know before I look your family in their eyes tomorrow. Also, I bought you a Christmas present already so if you tell me we aren't anything, I can just return it. Also, I miss you. But that's not important right now."

Cam grabs the phone and puts it on speaker to keep us from playing the guessing game to figure out what he's saying on the other end of the call.

"Whoa slow down," he says on the other side of the phone, sounding confused, "Where's this coming from?"

"Well, I've had a few drinks and I've been wondering this for a while but didn't have the balls to ask earlier but now I have some liquid courage in my system and my balls grew like three times bigger so now I'm asking."

She gives Cam and I a thumbs up and I give her my best attempt at a thumbs up. Cam's eyes are open now and she whispers, "You're doing great sweetie."

She sounds like a mom who's cheering on her kid at a dance recital who forgot all the choreography and is just flailing its arms around on stage.

There's silence on his end of the phone then I hear him let out a light laugh. "You're something else," is all he says and then there's more silence. He lets out a sigh and then continues.

"Listen Rylie, I like you, a lot, so much that I want you to meet my family which is something I'm always apprehensive about. There's just something about you that's different from the rest. You were already my girlfriend in my head, and I thought that was communicated through my actions, but I guess I should've said it upfront instead of assuming."

Looks like everyone can benefit from not assuming things.

"I would be honored if you would be my girlfriend. Officially. Also, don't return my present pretty please." I stifle my laugh with my pillow and Cam giggles next to Rylie.

"Who's that?" Zavier asks.

"Oh, Ry and Cam are here too. Say hi." She lifts her phone in the air for him to say hi to us even though we've heard him perfectly fine so far. "Hi," he says sounding embarrassed.

"But in response, I would love to be your official girlfriend. I won't return your gift," She smiles so hard that my cheeks started to hurt from matching her facial expression. "Okay babe, I'll talk to you tomorrow. Merry Christmas!"

"Merry Christmas!" Both Cam and I say right after Rylie.

"Merry Christmas you crazy weirdos," Zavier says laughing on the other side of the phone, "I'll call you tomorrow beautiful. Sleep tight." They share kisses across the phone, and I do the same gag I did earlier to Cam.

"Now that that's settled. More eggnog!" Rylie says, then bolts out the door before me and Cam have a chance to shout our protests.

An hour later, we're all so drunk, we can barely talk to each other. Well, let me change that, we can talk, we just can't talk in complete coherent sentences.

Ben cut off our supply of eggnog after Rylie grabbed up some more the last time. He said he didn't want us to die of Alcohol poisoning before Rylie and I were even legal enough to die. I told him anyone is legal enough to die, but he wasn't hearing me. He was awesome. I like Ben. A lot. He was the best dad a girl could ask for. Unlike Cory. Cory was the worst. Fuck him. I should tell him that.

I reach for my phone, but it falls off the nightstand. Rylie turns her head to where it fell next to her face. She was still on the floor, but Cam moved to lay down on the huge plush bear I had sitting in front of my huge floor mirror.

"What are you doing?" Ry asks me when I pick it up off the floor after struggling to figure out which phone on the floor was the right one.

There was like four of them. "Calling Cory," I state simply. Her eyes go wide and she scrambles to sit up. "You should wait until you know what you're doing. Right Cam?" We both look toward Cam and all we got in response were her soft snores.

I feel irritation start to spike out of nowhere. I knew exactly what I was doing. Besides, she wasn't one to talk since she just drunk dialed her boyfriend to see if he was *actually* her boyfriend.

"I know what I'm doing," I say to her and scroll to the thread of Cory sending me messages. I press the call button before I have a chance to change my mind. Rylie backs off and I'm thankful she's not going to argue with me about this.

"Hello?" a groggy voice answers after three rings. I must've woken him up.

"Cory?" I say trying to hide the drunkenness from my voice. There's a pause before he replies.

"Jordan?" he says surprised and I can hear him waking up slightly, his voice deep and gravely.

Rough.

"Are you drunk? Where are you?" The concern that laces his tone annoys the shit out of me and pisses me off. Who is he to be worried about me?

"That's none of your business," I spit out to him, "I was just calling to tell you I'm ready to meet. I'll text you the details later."

"Wait Jor, tell me where you ar-"

"Don't call me that," I bite back, cutting him off. "I'll see you later." Then I hang up. I didn't notice Rylie moved up onto the bed beside me until she pulled me into her arms and held me into her embrace.

I don't know why but I feel empowered or strong suddenly. "I'm proud of you," she says into my hair.

We fall asleep like this a few minutes later, me with the thoughts of why the hell Cory seemed like he was ready to come to my rescue as if I was in danger. I scoff at this thought as I drift off into my sleep.

Weighted.

Heavy.

Anxious.

I lift my head routinely from my hands. My favorite bench below me on the familiar white clouds that bring so much comfort. I feel her heated gaze to the left of me and turn to see her approaching.

The angel of my dreams.

The last time I saw her, I touched her without thinking and something between us sparked.

Literally.

I wonder if she felt it too. She had too though. It was so powerful that it shocked me out of my sleep. I'm sure it was the same for her.

Right?

"Hey there sunshine," I say smiling at her. She looks confused. And slightly intoxicated. "You okay?" I slide over, watching her plop down next to me.

"I'm fantastic, how about you Adonis?"

"Adonis?" I chuckle, Amused.

"Yea Adonis. Don't act like you don't know you're handsome." Her eyes go wide right after she says that, and she slams her hands over her mouth. "Oops," she says under her hands, her words sounding muffled. She lets out an airy giggle and it makes everything in my body twitch.

So, she thinks I'm handsome.

"I don't even know how it's possible that I'm here right now. I'm not even supposed to be having REM sleep while I'm drunk. Is this even REM sleep? Is this a real dream or is it some freaky realm or something we travel too?" She shrugs hard, swaying in her spot on the bench.

"Seems like you had fun on your Christmas night. Merry Christmas by the way."

"Merry Christmas! And yes, we had a lot of fun. This is my second night in a row being drunk. I called Cory yesterday and he pissed me off, but I told him I'd text him the details, but I haven't even thought of the details yet."

I put my hand up, surprised at the information she just casually slipped out of her mouth.

"Wait you called Cory yesterday? Good for you," she looks like she's about to fall over, but I don't reach out to help her because I don't want a fluke to happen and get kicked out

of the dream again. She ended up righting herself, and I let out a relieved breath.

"Yea, I called to tell him that I would text him the details of the place I would meet him at because I was drunk and started thinking about the situation, but I still don't know when and where I want to meet him." She turns to look at me and I try not to laugh at the lazy smile that's on her face.

"You should meet with him Saturday. Get it out the way so you don't go into the new year with your baggage blocking the door from being closed." She nods multiple times in understanding, and I wonder if she'll take my advice.

Hopefully she does though.

"Enough about my sperm donor, did you submit your film? How'd it look?" She lets herself fall to the floor in front of her and lets out a satisfied sigh as she relaxes onto the soft ground. I laugh and lay down next to her, my feet resting beneath the stone bench.

"It was amazing Jordan. Seeing everything come to life. Laughing, crying and getting angry with my family as we all watched it for the first time on screen. It was everything I could've hoped for and more. Now I just hope the film contest team feels the same way and I make it to the final round." I turn towards her to see her staring intently at me. I quickly turn my head back towards the sky, avoiding her intense gaze.

"I'm so proud of you," she whispers next to me, "You're going to win this whole competition and be the best film writer this world has ever seen." I feel her gaze move away from my profile and I take this opportunity to glance her way.

"Then you'll go on to have a beautiful family and your kids will continue on your legacy so that your name never dies."

"Are you and your kids going to be my number one fans?" I ask smiling up at the sky.

"I'm not having kids. I'm not ever getting married and I'm definitely not having kids with a random guy so," she trails off and we just lay in silence.

"I'm sure you'll change your mind. You'll fall in love and live the life you were meant to live."

She turns her body to where her back is facing me and she's in the fetal position. "Who are you to tell me? I don't want to love. I don't need love to live my life. I'll be perfectly fine on my own."

"What if someone were to love you?" I see her visibly tense up and inwardly curse myself for talking too much.

"Then I'd tell them they're stupid and wasting their time."

"I don't think they'd be stupid," I reply quietly, almost to myself. She doesn't respond so I guess she doesn't hear me. I turn back to look at the clouds in the sky and we lay down in this position for what feels like hours.

"I hope the next girl you date will make you want to do stupid things. You deserve it." Her words shock me, and I don't know what to say to them, so I just settle for a small but heartfelt thank you. I didn't think I'd be able to see her before her birthday, but I'm glad I did. She makes me feel grounded and safe. Hopefully I get to see her when I find out that I won the competition, so I can tell her it was all because of her.

Her friendship, her strength and courage to keep going. It rubbed off on me in real life, even though real life me doesn't even know she exists.

If only he did.

Our familiar rumbling sound comes to our ears and we still lay in silence as it comes bounding towards us. The sky turns dark and broody, mimicking the changed mood in our conversation.

"Good luck," I hear her say with what seems like sadness in her voice. I didn't mean to make her sad with what I said.

"Same to you even though you don't need it." I say back trying to lighten the mood a little.

As she turns her head towards me, there's a glimmer in her eye but before I could figure out what it is, I'm falling.

Deep.

Deep.

Deep.

JORDAN

Meet me at South City Kitchen in Atlanta at 6:00pm on Saturday.

I stare down at the text I sent Cory a few days ago. I woke up the day after Christmas wanting to get this meeting over with so I can hurry up and put it past me.

"You ready?" Cam asks me from where she sits in Rylie's backseat.

We were sitting in the parking lot of South City Kitchen waiting for the meeting between me and

Cory. I've honestly only been here once before and that was with my family when we were celebrating me getting accepted into Clark Atlanta. I don't know why it was the first restaurant to come to mind when I was planning this meeting.

"I think so," I reply to her, my stomach in complete knots. I was so nervous and anxious because I didn't know what to expect. I was seeing my father for the first time in 14 years.

14 years.

I had every right to feel all the emotions in the book.

"You're going to kick ass in there J," Rylie said from the driver's seat. "Besides, Cam and I will be out in the car for when you need to 'go to the bathroom' and escape out the back door." I swat her arm and give a nervous half smile.

I look at the time and it was 5:54 pm. I take deep slow breaths to calm my nerves, but they do nothing but increase them as I think about what is about to take place.

My cell phone buzzes and it's a message from Ben. It was a picture of him, my mom and Jamie all sitting on the couch with their thumbs up. Well, not Jamie, he was stretching for his toys off camera whining wanting to play. I smile warmly at the message that was sent along with it.

We're rooting for you Jor! Here if you need anything. X

P.S.: Jamie ate the last slice of pie, so we ran out of comfort food.

P.P.S: Good news! Your mom's making me go buy more pie! Love you.

My family was honestly the best. I shake my head laughing at them and move my gaze back to the entrance of the restaurant. We've been sitting in the parking lot for the past 30 minutes trying to see if we could see anyone who resembled Cory walking in.

"It's time kiddo," Cam says from the backseat and I look between them.

"Thank you," I say, and we have a group hug.

"Now go kill him...I mean *it*. Go kill *it*," Rylie jokes to help ease my nervousness and it works.

I walk up to the door of the restaurant and grasp the handle. I let out a defined huff before I pull it open.

I go up to the host and just tell her my name since I set the reservation over the phone.

"Right this way ma'am," the guy tells me as he grabs a menu and guides me towards the table. I swear it feels as though time is moving in slow motion. I hear my heart beating out of my chest as I look around trying to see if Cory is at any of the nearby tables.

"Here we are ma'am," he says to me. I'm standing directly behind him so when he turns to show me the table, the wind is knocked right out of me.

There he is.

Cory.

The man I haven't seen in 14 years.

My father.

He immediately stands up from where he's sitting when he sees me and rounds the table to stand in front of me. He bumps the table and almost causes it to topple over.

Looks like I'm not the only nervous wreck around here.

He still looks the same from what I remembered. Granted, there were a few age lines around his eyes to show that he wasn't still the same young, naïve boy, that left his family behind years ago.

He shared the same shade of light caramel skin as me and I could see that I got my freckles from him. His hair was a dark chestnut color and cut low with a wave all around it.

He had a muscular build and some tattoos flowing down his right arm. He was wearing a fitted black cashmere looking mock neck shirt, with nice grey slacks and a black Hermes belt to match.

So, he had a little money to his name.

Interesting.

His ears were pierced with medium sized diamond studs in both.

I didn't realize the host was long gone until Cory's gravelly voice crashed through my thoughts.

"Jordan, I-," he rubs the back of his neck, "It's so nice to see you. Can I… hug you?"

Against my own will, I give the smallest, barely visible nod, as I stare into his light brown eyes.

Astonished.

He pulls me to his body and crushes me. I'm unable to move my arms and I'm glad I can't because I don't know if I would've hugged him back. This situation is already weird and awkward, no need to let the awkwardness grow.

He breathes in my scent through my hair and squeezes me even tighter.

"I've missed you so bad. I thought I'd never see you again."

He eventually lets me go and pulls out a chair for me. I sit down, still shocked and unsure what to do with myself, then he goes back to his side of the table.

"Wow, you look so old. You're a woman now," he says smiling hard at me and I feel so weird sitting here with him.

"Thank you so much for agreeing to meet with me today. When I got your call I was surprise-"

"Why did you leave?" I cut him off, trying to keep him from making small talk. I just want the answers I came for so I can go.

His smile falls and he looks down at his hands that are on the table. He looks up and is about to talk when our waiter decides to make her appearance.

"Hi guys! Welcome to South City Kitchen, my name is Amber, and I'll be your server today. Can I get you started with some drinks? Or are you ready to order?"

"Water with lemon," Cory says but never breaking eye contact with me.

I usually always order water with lemon, but since Cory ordered it, I'll have to switch it up.

"Lemonade for me please. Thank you," I don't break eye contact either to show that I'm not fazed by his presence.

"Alright, I'll go grab those for you and be back to take your food order." She walks off leaving Cory and I alone once more.

"Let me start off by saying that is the biggest regret of my life. If I could go back in time and have things go differently, I would. I made a mistake and I am *so* sorry."

I scoff at his apology, not believing anything he's saying, "When did you realize it was a mistake?

Years after you moved on and completely forgot about us? What? Were you getting drunk at a bar reminiscing on your past and we just happened to pop up in your memory?" He physically winces at my words and I can't help but feel I guessed accurately.

When he recovers from my words, he shakes his head. I don't know if it's to tell me I'm wrong or if it's directed towards himself and he's ashamed.

"When I came in your room that night to say my final goodbye, I knew. I *knew* I was making the worst decision of my life."

"But you left anyway," I shake my head giving a menacing smile. I'm not usually vicious but this man thinks I'm so desperate for "daddy's love" that I'm going to take him back with that weak ass apology? Yeah, okay.

"So, why did you leave Cory? Why did you kick us to the curb? Kick *me* to the curb?" I'm so angry right now that I don't even realize there are tears streaming down my face. It isn't until I feel them hitting my hands that are clasped together in my lap that I notice.

Of course I had to show how weak I was at the moment I needed to be the strongest.

"I thought you guys were better off without me. I couldn't bare seeing your mom hurting, and knowing that I was hurting you too, killed me. I didn't intend on missing your birthday. I didn't intend on any of this happening." He tries to reach and wipe the tears off my face, but I jerk away, knowing his touch will burn.

"But it did happen," I spit at him, wiping my tears with the cloth napkin my utensils are wrapped in. I see the waiter coming towards us and I turn my head away, hiding the disastrous state I'm in.

"Alright, here we go."

She sets our drinks down on the table. "Are you guys ready to order yet?" I hear her click her pen so she can write down our order.

"Can we have more time please?" Cory asks her in a polite way.

"Absolutely, just flag me down whenever you're ready." She walks away leaving us to our conversation.

"I was immature. I was confused. I couldn't shake my old habits no matter how hard I tried. I was a slave to the temptation. And I know that that is in no way an excuse for my actions, but I thought about you every day. I wore a piece of you with me everywhere I went." I turn to look at him, confused at what he's talking about.

He lowers the neckline of his cashmere shirt and pulls out what looks like a silver chain. What's at the bottom of that chain causes my breath to hitch in my throat.

It was a heart padlock locket. One that matched the key that he left me that night in the gift box.

He kept it? All this time?

"This right here," he says holding out the locket towards me that's still secure around his neck, "This is what kept me going. This is what caused me to change and become a better man. I knew that if I didn't become a better version of myself, one that was worthy of being in your presence again, then I'll go on not being able to see you for the rest of my life. I just couldn't do that."

"Why couldn't me physically being there be that thing that kept you going? You literally had me already, why couldn't *I* be what caused you to change? Not some symbol of me."

He let out a heavy sigh and leaned back in his chair.

"It was hard to look at you. It was hard facing you. And I knew that if you were still actively in my life, then I wouldn't change for real. I've tried so many times and it didn't work. Distancing myself from you gave me that strength to fight for you. It was so hard Jordan. *So hard*. But now I think --- scratch that--- I know that I am able to say I can be the man I was meant to be for you. I can be your dad. Fully this time."

I shake my head violently, fighting off the words he's saying. Not trying to listen.

"For 14 years, I suffered. For 14 years I was stuck thinking it was my fault you left us. That because of me, mom was crying on her bathroom floor at random hours of the night. That you left because of something *I* did. No matter how many times mom tried to tell me that wasn't the case, I didn't believe her. I thought I was some super villain that scared my mom's superhero away and that I couldn't save her from her pain."

I give up trying to wipe the tears rolling down my face. I'm finally letting all my pent-up emotions from over the years out, and it feels damn good.

"I never allowed myself to love a boy. Never been on a date. Never even wanted to crush on a boy because I was afraid, I'd make them leave too. It wasn't until recently that I gave up the idea that Ben would leave us the same way you did, but I realized. He's *nothing* like you. He doesn't put the hurt on our faces, he erases it. He's been more of a dad to me than you've ever been."

He looks as though I punched him dead in his face, almost knocking him out of his seat. I wasn't done pounding blows on him though. I needed him to feel a fraction of the hurt I've been feeling for years.

"I say all of that to say, you left a void in my life causing me to miss out on experiences that girls my age experienced. First crush. First love. Prom date. High school romance. It's going to take a lot more than words for me to even begin to forgive you. You know, if I choose too that is."

"If you choose too?" He repeats the words I say but poses them as a question. When I just look at him, he just slowly nods in acknowledgment, a broken look on his face.

"I know that I can't erase the past. And I can't express to you enough how sorry I am that I put you through that. I can only hope that you allow me to show you how different I am and how I'll never leave your side again."

I realized that a huge weight was lifted off my shoulders after telling him the things I've been going through. This must be what closure feels like. I'm finally making steps towards closing this door.

I wave the waitress over, figuring we might as well start eating because my appetite came back to me and I can feel my stomach screaming for food.

We order our food and sit in silence for a bit. He looks unsure of what else to say, and what direction our relationship was going in. I'm nowhere near close to forgiving him, but there was a huge gap in time since that faithful day that needs to be filled.

"Where do you live?" I ask, wanting to know about his life after us. I want to know what he was up to these 14 years he wasn't in my life. He visibly relaxes, seeing this as a good sign.

"I actually live in Greensboro. North Carolina. About five hours away from here."

Wait, so he doesn't live in Atlanta anymore?

He can see the questions forming on my face, so he explains further.

"I took off work. Well, I took vacation but ended up having to take more time off. I wanted to be here whenever you were ready to talk."

"What if I never responded?" I take a drink of my water, not realizing how dehydrated I was from crying so much. He looked at me intently. I move my gaze so that I'm looking at the bottom of my glass.

"I would keep on trying. I wasn't going to give up. Ever." I look up at him and the severity in his eyes causes me to believe him a little bit. I give off a small smile and his expands, showing off the beautiful teeth I would always admire as a kid. "Wow, I missed that dimple."

I shake my head, hiding my smile.

Why the hell am I smiling?

Our food comes and he tells me about his job and what happened to him since he left. He says he's an electrician who, after hard work, made a name for himself and is somewhat well off. He has a nice sized house and is married. Even though my mom is re-married, that fact stung a little. He started a family with someone else before mending his old one.

"Actually, there was another reason for me finally being able to reach out to you." He looks almost guilty and scared to tell me this.

"Are you dying?" I ask, concerned. Even though I'm still mad at him, I don't think I'd be able to handle him dying. Not when he finally came back.

"No, actually, it's the opposite." He looks at me and I'm confused.

Huh? What is the opposite of dying? Wait...

"My wife and I are expecting a baby."

I don't fully hear his words. His voice fades into the background and my vision goes blurry. A baby?

"And when she told me she was pregnant, I was terrified. Ashamed. I felt like I was betraying you. As the pregnancy went on, I knew I couldn't fully accept this child without having you back in my life." His voice fades back into my ears and I shoot up from my seat.

"What?" is all I manage to say. He stops chewing on his food and I see the panic set in his face.

"So, you only met with me so you can feel good about yourself and be a loving father to another kid?" My voice raises a few octaves and people around us start to stare. I don't care though; they can stare all they want too.

"Wait no, that's not what I-"

Before he can finish his excuses, I'm bolting out the door. I run to Rylie's car and I see them inside laughing at whatever it is they're looking at on Camille's phone. I get up to the driver side door and knock on her window.

They both jump up scared, but when she realizes it's me, she unlocks her doors. I slide into the passenger seat and she starts the car. I look down at the floor and see that they ordered some food to go and it causes the damn to break loose inside of me.

I'm hunched over, sobbing uncontrollably and I feel Camille rubbing my back from behind.

"Oh honey," is all I hear Rylie say as she drives towards her house.

MALAKAI

CONGRATULATIONS FILMER! You're going to the final showdown where you'll compete against three other filmers! This is where we'll crown the winner and see who successfully embodied what we were looking for. It was so much fun seeing you all make magic with us this year! Let's do it again sometime ;). The information for the showdown is linked below.

See you then!

S.D.F.C.T

"I think I tied my tie wrong," Jerrod, one of the actors in my film, said as we got ready.

I invited everyone who was a part of the film to get ready at my house. Litya, the main actress, went over to help him not look like a total mess. I straighten my collar and turn to look at everyone in the spacious living room.

"Before we get this show on the road and head to the showcase, I just wanted to thank each and every one of you for being a part of this dream come true. Even if we don't take home the win, we're all still winners for chasing our dreams."

"We're definitely taking home this win bro, don't worry," Ant shouts from the other side of the room and everyone whoops and shouts in agreement.

"Yea, I already have my Oscar speech ready bro, remember?" Saiyr chimes in and everyone laughs. I shake my head smiling at the overwhelming support.

"Seriously, thank you." I grab a water bottle from the coffee table in front of me and raise it in the air. "To us!" I say and they all clap in unison. My phone pings and I look at the notification that popped up on the screen.

It was an Instagram DM.

TheMatthewWeiss: I look forward to watching your masterpiece today. Congrats on making it this far.

We all pull up in multiple different cars to the movie theater the showcase is being held. My parents wait for us outside of the theater and we all walk in together.

"Proud of you son," my dad whispers in my ear from where he stands next to me. We were out in the lobby of the theater a half hour later, grabbing some drinks for everyone.

"Malakai!" I hear someone call my name from across the room and I turn to see a crowd of paparazzi and fans clear a passage for Matthew Weiss to walk towards me.

"Hey Christian, good to see you again." He gives my father a handshake-hug that guys usually do with people they're familiar with.

"You guys know each other too?" I say quirking an eyebrow wondering why my dad didn't fess up when I confronted my mom on this matter.

"We went to college together for a little bit before I decided to give my all to this acting thing." Matt says as he clasps my shoulder and squeezes it. I turn to my dad and tell him with my eyes that we will talk later about this.

"I can't wait to see what you did with your movie Malakai," Matt says as he lets go of my shoulder.

Paparazzi takes pictures of us as we talk about the competition and its struggles. Soon, we hear the employees calling for everyone to make their way inside the theater. Matt follows us inside and gets stopped every few minutes by a few fans in the crowd. We get back to our seats where everyone we came with is sitting and wait for the production to start.

"Alright everyone, give yourselves a round of applause!" A girl who stands at the front of the theater yells out towards the crowd. The whole theater erupts into cheers and feet stomps as we clap to congratulate each other.

"You finally made it and tonight will be the moment of truth to see who will take home the victory. Just remember if your film isn't chosen, you are still a winner and we might have a little surprise for you guys." After a few more cheers, the crowd dies back down again.

"Time to bring on the first filmer! I would like to call Lexington to the stage to introduce her movie." A girl walks to the front of the theater and introduces the film she created.

After sitting through everyone else's movie, it was finally time for me to make my speech.

"I first off want to thank the film contest team for providing us with such an amazing opportunity and resources to work with. Can we give it up for them?" I start clapping and everyone else joins in. When it stops, I continue.

"If you would've asked me a few months ago if I thought I'd be able to pursue my passion of being a film writer, I would've told you hell no, I'm playing football." The crowd gives off light laughter.

"But football wasn't what I loved. I was finally able to fully realize this and gain the courage to take a leap of faith and put all my trust into God and the process. I am so blessed to be here tonight to share my first baby with you, and hope you take away whatever it is you need from this. Here's my film, *On a Cloudy Day*. Thank you."

I bow and the crowd erupts into cheers. I walk back to my seat and as I pass my friends, they all pat me on the back.

After the movie is over, I look around to see a few people wiping tears from their face. I receive a standing ovation and try hard to contain the emotions I feel at this moment. I'm so overwhelmed with joy that I can't believe this isn't a dream.

"Thank you filmers for putting your all into your movies. We will now take a brief intermission while our secret judges around the room vote on their favorite movie."

There are four secret judges sitting amongst the crowd. It could either be actors, producers, directors or just random citizens they picked at the door. I'm nervous but the standing ovation I received boosted my confidence.

"That reaction was crazy! I even got chills all over again from watching that movie," Saiyr says next to me. We're all still sitting in the theater as everyone around us mingles. Matt walks up to us and I hear the whole entourage I have around me gasp. (Mainly my actors who've just started out in the game and my project was their first ever gig).

"Wow, you guys were honestly amazing. Not many movies can hit me deeply like that, but you nailed it. All of you will make it big in this industry." He looks around at each one of us, giving us all eye contact to show his respect.

"You think I could get a spot in your new movie?" Saiyr asks jokingly. Matt gives a wide grin and scratches his beard.

"I think I can make a few arrangements." Saiyr laughs but I half think that Matt was being serious.

Litya and Jerrod fanboy from their seats as they ask Matt all their newbie actor questions. Once he satisfies their inquiries, they take pictures together then he waves goodbye to us as he goes to mingle with his fellow actor friends.

"Wow! You're friends with *the* Matthew Weiss," Litya says with huge heart eyes.

Jerrod, who seemed to have fallen in love with her literally the same day he met her, grumbled in jealousy next to her.

"I guess you could say Matt and I have a brotherly bond," I say jokingly but she takes me seriously.

"Oh my God! Why didn't you say this sooner?" She jumps up and down in her seat and I look to Anthony and Saiyr for help.

"Litya, let's take some deep breaths okay?" Anthony says to her and she immediately does just that. Litya also fell in love in one day but it wasn't with Jerrod.

"Sorry Ant, he's just one of the best actors out. Maybe you could come over and I could show you my favorite movie by him? We can analyze his acting skills together?"

"Actually," Jerrod buts in, "I was going to just ask you to do that with me Litya." She waves him off and turns back to Ant. My parents come back to their seats after talking with the friends they ran into and hand me a glass of champagne.

"Hurry up and gulp this down son before the feds see you and lock us up."

I grab the champagne glass and empty it in two gulps.

"Congratulations honey," my mom says as she leans over and kisses my cheek.

"I haven't even won yet mom," I say giving off a boyish grin.

"Yea but you're about too," she winks at me and the employees from earlier call to get everyone back in their seats.

"So, our judges have come to a decision and let me tell you folks, it was down to the wire!" Saiyr clasps my shoulder to my left and Anthony clasps the other to my right. I see my mom holding tightly to my Dad, and Litya trying to lean against Ant's arm.

"And the winner of the 2019 San Diego Film Contest is," I lean forward in my seat, anxious as fuck now.

"Lexington with her film *Chasing Nothing*!" The theater erupts into applause, but it all becomes white noise.

I lost.

My dream.

I'm a failure.

I wasn't meant for this.

I lost.

I fucking lost.

I feel the pity stares from all around me and see everyone's mouths moving in slow motion, apologizing to me. Saying it's okay, maybe next time.

I shake off Saiyr and Anthony as I stand up. I need to get the hell out of here. I check my pocket for my keys and bolt towards my car.

Once I get out to it, I slide into the driver's seat and lock the doors. Saiyr and Anthony are running out the building by the time I'm skirting off into the night.

Going somewhere.

Going nowhere.

Fuck.

I lost.

I poured my heart and soul into this.

And lost.

I scrub my hand over my face as I speed off down the road.

Hurt.

Pain.

Betrayal.

The bright light fades from my eyes, but my vision is still blurry. I can't stop crying, not even in a damn dream.

I walk towards the familiar bench, but before I could get there, I fall to my knees.

Uncontrollable sobs wrack through my body and I allow myself to succumb to them.

"Jordan!" I hear Malakai shout as he runs towards me. He kneels before me and tries to comfort me, but he can't do much without touching me. I look up to him with all the hurt and pain I feel etched on my face.

I want to silently communicate to him that my meeting with Cory was a disaster and that it was worse than I could've ever imagined.

How stupid of me to think he wouldn't move on with his life. It's been 14 years, of course he would have another kid Jordan. Of course.

Malakai reaches out to grab my hand but as soon as his fingertips brush my skin, an electric charge shoots up my body and he quickly pulls away. Just like when he hugged me that time before.

"Come sit down," he commands me, in a nice way but he still had an assertive tone lacing his words. I do as he says and take a seat in my spot on the bench. "Tell me what happened," he says as he sits as close to me as possible without touching.

I relay the events of the night and everything my father said to me.

"Shit," he dragged out and scrubbed his hand over his face. "I lost the competition," he said to me and for the first time, I was able to register the hurt on his face that mirrored mine. My sobs die down and I wipe my tears, sitting in comfortable silence with Mal.

I let out a wet chuckle, "Our lives suck." He chuckles next to me which causes me to smile.

"What are you going to do about your dad now?"

"I'm cutting him out of my life for good," I say already coming to my conclusion.

"But why?" he asks.

Why? What does he mean why?

"What do you mean why? He doesn't care about me for real. He only cares about clearing his conscious so he can move on with his new life, his new wife, and their perfect new baby."

He turns his head to the sky in deep thought. "I don't see it that way."

What?

"No offense, but it's not for you to see." He turns his body to me.

"No, hear me out. I don't think he just wanted to clear his conscious. I think he wanted to right his relationship with you because he loves you so much, that he can't live his new life without you in it. He'd feel like a fraud playing house to this family, knowing that you're out here thinking he doesn't care about you at all. Knowing that when he looks at this new kid, yea he'll love them, but he won't stop being able to think about you. He wants you apart of his family and his future. Besides, don't you want to know your sibling?"

I'm unable to respond to what he says because I'm too busy trying to figure out how to expose my father and his brand-new lies.

He doesn't love me. He doesn't.

But if he didn't love me, he wouldn't have bothered reaching out. He wouldn't have looked at me with so much love in his eyes. He wouldn't have told me about my new sibling. A sibling that deserves their big sister. A sibling that will have the chance to grow up with the new and improved dad. A sibling who will have what I never did growing up.

I turn to him and he turns the head he was hanging low to me at the same time. "I'm sorry you lost the competition. I know how much it meant to you." He shakes his head.

"It's just crazy putting your all into something, having the courage to take that something and knock on a new door with purpose, and then having that door slammed shut into your face." He puts his hands over his eyes momentarily, then scrubs them down his face.

His eyes are red, and it looks like he's been crying.

My poor Malakai.

My?

I scoot over and place my hand in the space I made between us. Offering him as much comfort as I could in my fucked-up state.

"Listen to me," I say trying to put confidence into my voice. I think I succeed because he looks at me like a lost little boy whose mom is giving them maternal advice. My heart breaks for him.

"I know it may seem like all of your hard work was for naught but trust me. It did more for you than you are even allowing yourself to see. It's opened doors for you, caused you to live in your purpose, and you befriended Matthew freakin' Weiss!"

He gives a shy smile and it fills me with warmth knowing that he's actually listening to what I'm saying.

"You are the most creative person I know. Don't let this one speedbump stop your whole road trip. Besides, you have

to break a few bones and tear a few muscles for them to get stronger," I shrug, and he laughs shaking his head at me.

"Look who's getting savvy with their words," he says looking at me.

"I learned from the best," I say back.

"You are amazing, you know that?" I feel the heat from his gaze and stand up, walking away from the bench. He follows behind me, and I lay down in our spot away from the bench.

"How do I do this Malakai?" I ask him, staring up at the sky.

"Do what?" he replies, sounding like he's still deep in thought.

"Live my life without shackles. Live my life without worrying or looking over my shoulder." He's silent for a moment before he responds.

"Just live."

I turn to him with the 'really?' face but he looks dead serious. I turn back and lay on my back.

Just live huh? Easier said than done.

"We should really start taking our own advice," I say to him and he just laughs.

"You're right Jordy Wordy."

"Don't ever say that again in your life. I mean ever," I say horrified at the nickname he just came up with. He laughs hard.

"What? It's not like I'll ever be able to embarrass you in public, so you'll be okay."

Something about his words stung me. Was it the fact they were true or the fact he sounded so nonchalant when he said them? Maybe it was both.

I wouldn't mind seeing Malakai in the real world. We could watch movies and critique them together while he did something dumb like stuff straws in his nose and make walrus sounds. I chuckle at the thought and he just looks at me curious. I shake him off and go back to looking at the sky.

It really was a beautiful sight.

Enchanting.

Mystical.

I wish I could stay here forever. I wouldn't mind if he stayed here with me. I wouldn't want to get lonely after all. I wonder if he feels the same way when he looks up at the sky or feels the softness of the ground below us.

I glance over at him to see his eyes closed as he lays on the ground. He was smiling. Wonder what he's thinking about. As long as he's happy and not sad over not winning the competition, I'm happy.

It's weird, a few months ago, I never would've cared if a guy was happy nor would I let it affect my happiness. Malakai has helped me to grow in many ways even if I didn't remember him after waking up. Hopefully someday something will spark my memory in the real world, and I can thank him in person for all the long talks and the non-biased shoulder I cried on.

Someday.

I hear the familiar rumbling of the distant wakeup call and rise to my feet. Malakai opens his eyes and looks at me towering over him.

"You okay?" I ask him, a little worried that his smile might be too fake. He nods and jumps up. I sometimes forget he's an athlete. I need to get back into the gym.

We walk back to the bench in silence, but the silence spoke many volumes. It gave off a sense of "you'll be okay, life is only just beginning". Maybe that's why Malakai was smiling. Because he felt the same sense in the air that I suddenly feel.

We sit on the bench and I can't help but feel like I should say something to him before we go.

"Are you," I blurt out loudly and immediately feel embarrassed.

"Am I what?" he says lightly laughing at me.

"Are you um…going to keep making movies." I switch up what I was originally going to ask.

"Are you going to keep breathing?" he asks me in a playful sarcastic way. "Of course, maybe one day you'll see my name in lights." He says waving his hands in front of his face like he's referencing Broadway.

The rumbling grows closer and I wish I could stay here just a little bit longer.

"Until next time Jordy Wordy." Malakai winks at me right before I fall deep into the blackness.

Falling.

Falling.

Falling.

Crashing.

JORDAN

My mom and Ben exchange a look on the couch across from where I'm standing.

"What?" I say irritated with their silent conversation.

"Well, I'm not saying you have to forgive him, but what exactly is it that's holding you back from doing that?" Ben asks me as he leans forward.

It's New Year's Eve and I'm mad at myself for bringing my demons into 2020 with me. I want to be in my sibling's life but I just can't bring it to myself to tell that to my father. I told my parents about the dinner I had with him, and now I'm trying to get their advice on what I should do.

I pinch the bridge of my nose, exasperated and exhausted with this conversation. It's not fair for me to take my frustration out on them, but I can't help it.

I walk over and plop down in the accent chair next to the couch.

"I don't know," I let out on a long breath.

My mom looks at Ben, then back at me.

"I think I know. You're afraid that if you let him back in, he'll just up and leave you again. Is that it?"

I don't look at her, I just sink down more into the chair. I grab the accent pillow from behind my back and throw it over my face.

"He claims he'll never leave, but how do I believe him? How do I even bring myself to trust him?" I say behind the pillow, slightly embarrassed. I hear some movement and a second later the pillow is taken off my face, being replaced with my mom's smile.

"Well sweetie, how about you just take baby steps. You don't have to jump in all at once."

Baby steps? I never thought of that. "You mean let him into my life little by little?"

"Exactly!" Ben says shooting up from the couch excited like it was his idea. Mom and I both look at him like he's crazy. She shakes her head then looks back at me.

"But remember, you don't have to do anything you don't want to do just because someone tells you that you should. It's just a thought."

I sit up in the accent chair, and my mom walks back over to sit on the couch next to where Ben is now standing. Just then a sleepy Jamie comes walking up to us from the stairs, rubbing his eyes with his favorite stuffed animal tucked under his arm.

"Look who's finally awake," Ben says as Jamie walks past his open arms and straight up to me. He looks betrayed and I laugh as I pick Jamie up and pull him into my lap.

"How'd you sleep Buu?" I ask poking his chubby belly causing him to giggle sleepily.

"Goo," he replied blinking up at me.

"Just Good?" I quirk up an eyebrow. He nods and I lightly push his head into my chest so he can lay comfortably.

"Wow, I see where your loyalty lies," Ben says holding his chest. My mom swats his arm laughing and stands up. "Rylie's family is on the way over now. We're meeting Camille and her Grandma downtown. I'm going to go start getting ready." I nod and she heads up the stairs.

Ben follows behind her and I look down to see Jamie fast asleep again.

"Come on Buu, let's go get ready." I carry him up the stairs to his bathroom.

"I see them over there!" Rylie points somewhere in front of us. I turn my head to where she's pointing. Camille and her Grandmother are sitting at the bar of the restaurant, talking to the bartender. They live alone at her grandma's house in southwest Atlanta. Her parents died in a boat crash a few years ago while on a cruise in a tragic series of events. To this day, she refuses to get on a boat.

We all walk over to them and I catch a glimpse of her Grandma's conversation with the bartender.

"So, you're saying you wouldn't dabble in this old lady's crockpot?"

"Grandma!" Cam says horrified and everyone, including the bartender, busts out laughing.

"What? I won't be here forever. I need to have as much fun as possible."

The bartender writes his name and number on a napkin, then slides it too her Grandma, laughing as he goes to tend to the other patrons at the bar. Part of me thinks he does it to humor her, but another part of me thinks he might actually be curious.

Since there's no peach drop this year, we figured we'd come out to one of the New Year's events downtown with the family. It was risky bringing a 2-year-old out to countdown but he had his nap so he should be okay.

I can't stop thinking about my father and how I still haven't settled anything with him. He text me saying that he had an emergency with his job and had to go back for the weekend but will be back in town on Monday.

I didn't reply.

I don't know why a part of me feels sad about the fact that he left. I mean, he's been gone for 14 years, it shouldn't make any difference to me. But it does. Also, when did I stop calling him Cory?

Another thing I can't stop thinking about is my future brother and sister.

Will they look like me? Or will they look more like their mom? Is their mom good enough for them? Will our father stay in their lives? Will they be lucky enough for that? All my answers to those questions are the same.

I hope so.

Hope.

I have hope that my brother or sister will get the best life possible. I have hope that they will persevere through any adversity. In order to ensure this happens, I need to be there with them every step of the way, no matter how I feel about our father.

I pull my phone out of my crossbody purse and send a text.

Me:

Let me know when you're back, we need to talk

The reply is instant.

Cory:

Absolutely. Happy New Year, I love you.

I tuck my phone back into my pocket and focus on the family in front of me. We all laugh, play games and give thanks that we all made it to a new year. The countdown begins and I don't feel an overwhelming sense of panic at the fact I still didn't fully close that door. It's getting there inch by inch and I'm okay with that.

As long as it's getting there, I'm okay.

I look at the people I love in front of me. Rylie is on FaceTime with Zavier when the countdown reaches 10 seconds. Cam is holding onto her grandmother, my parents are intertwined with Jamie between them, and Rylie's parents are cuddled up in their seats.

I grab onto the necklace that's around my neck. The same necklace that was left for me 14 years ago. I put it on today knowing my final decision about this whole situation after talking with my parents.

I just need to tell that decision to my dad.

Twisting the silver key in between my thumb and forefinger, I look up towards the night filled sky, silently saying my resolutions to myself.

To be a better me.

To conquer my demons.

To live life the way it's supposed to be lived.

To breathe.

The breeze in the air feels like a kiss on my skin as I look to the sky and feel a flicker of distant memories. I try to grab a hold of them, but they just float away.

What are they? Even though I can't grasp them, they feel so comforting.

3.

I tuck the key back into my jacket and look back at my family.

2.

2020 will be the best year I've ever had. I'll make sure of it.

1

Everyone around me shares a kiss. Rylie kisses her phone screen, and my parents kiss each other then both sides of Jamie's chubby cheeks. Mr. and Mrs. Evans share a slow intimate kiss. Cam kisses her grandma on the cheek, and she returns the gesture. A smile fills my face and the love I feel for my family is so intense, it almost chokes me.

A new Jordan is making her way through and I'm excited to let her shine. I'm shaken out of my thoughts as Rylie and Cam both run toward me and kiss my cheeks. We all engross each other in a hug.

Yea, 2020, look out for me.

Cory:

I'm back in town.

The message was sent to me at 3:00 am this morning. It was now 11:00am. I do my daily routine of taking a shower, taking down my twisted-up hair, and brushing my teeth.

I throw on a thick gray hoodie from Target, some black leggings, and my black old skool Vans. You can never go wrong with Vans.

Me:

What hotel are you staying at?

Cory:

The Westin Peachtree Plaza

Me:

I'll be there in 40.

Cory:

Great! I'll be here. I'll leave an extra key card at the front desk. Room 6118.

I go downstairs, grab my crossbody from off the island and go through the front door to get to my car. I honestly don't know how I made it to the hotel safely because the whole way there, I was too busy daydreaming.

Imagining how this conversation with my dad is about to play out and what my life would be like now that he's in it. My family is about to grow even more and I'm excited, scared, anxious and nervous all at the same time. I really hope I'm making the right decision.

I pull up to the entrance of the hotel and the valet immediately walks up and opens my door.

"Welcome to the Westin ma'am, do you have any bags you need help with?"

"No, thank you." I smile at him and give him my keys. I tell him to charge it to my dad's room and he gives me a ticket so I can come back and get my car. Even though I'm sure my dad can afford it, I still mentally remind myself to ask him if he has a cash app or uses Zelle so I can send him the cost of the valet.

I walk in and wait in line to talk to the front desk staff about the extra room key. I wonder why he didn't just meet me downstairs and take me up to his room that way.

The line progresses slowly. I guess this gives me more time to get my words together.

It's finally my turn and I get the room key. I walk over to where all the elevators are and find the elevator that will take me to the 61st floor. I walk in and press the key card to the little scanner and push the button.

The hotel is so packed that there's even a line to use the elevator. It must have cost him a ton to rent out the Westin for this long and during a busy holiday time.

I exit the elevator on the right floor and wave bye to the couple I met in there that was asking me about the Best places to eat in Atlanta. There were so many good places for different reasons that I just gave them my top 10.

I walk around the curve and stop in front of room 6118.

I take deep breaths. "Okay Jordan, you can do this," I say to myself. I knock on the door and wait patiently for him to open it. I hear some shuffling on the other side of the door.

He opens it, fully dressed in a black V-neck t-shirt with some black adidas joggers and some blue Adidas ZX Flux's. The matching necklace we share is dangling around his neck.

"Jordan! Hey!" He pulls me into a hug and at first, I'm shocked but eventually wrap my arms around him and pat awkwardly at his back. He releases me from the hug and lets out a nervous laugh as he rubs the back of his neck.

"Can I come in or..."

He's blocking the doorway, so I can't just walk into his room even if I felt comfortable enough to do that.

He hops to the side immediately. "Oh yes, sorry," he lets out another nervous laugh. "I'm a little nervous," he admits like it wasn't obvious.

I look around the hotel room. There's a dresser on the left wall, directly opposite from the king-sized bed on the right wall. On top of the dresser was a TV and a little tray of overpriced snacks and drinks. In the far-left corner of the room was a desk with a computer, and the wall directly in front of me was covered with floor to ceiling windows.

He had a beautiful view of the city and I wished I could see it when the sun was down, and the streetlights were all on. In the right-hand corner was a lamp with an accent chair sitting next to it and next to the lamp was a nightstand. There was another nightstand on the other side of the bed that was identical.

I walk in further and on the right wall was a closed door that more than likely led to the bathroom I take a seat in the accent chair in front of the windows and he took a seat in the office chair behind the desk. I look out at the view for a little then meet his eyes and let out a breath.

"I'm sorry for leaving abruptly the last time we met up." He waves his hands in the air, not accepting the apology.

"Please don't apologize, I'm the one who's sorry. I should've better articulated my words to you. I don't want you to feel like I'm only reconnecting with you out of guilt."

I subconsciously twirl the key on my necklace around in my fingers. I've been wearing it nonstop every day, it is becoming a part of me in a way. I'm trying to give it a new memory, a better one. He looks at the necklace and touches his locket.

"You're wearing it? Does that mean..."

I raise my hand to silence him so I can say the whole spiel I practiced.

"I gave what you said to me a lot of thought. And I mean a lot. You are in no means off the hook from your past actions but it's not healthy to hold grudges. It's also not fair for me to forgive you but still hold your past against you. With that being said, I forgive you, but I will not ever forget. I have made the decision to allow you back into my life, but I want us to take baby steps. Seeing as you live in a different state, maybe we can just talk on the phone for now and work our way up. I want to meet your wife and I want to be there for my baby sibling. No offense, but I don't want to be like you and abandon my brother or sister, I want to be an active role model."

He winces but tries to hide it. He leans back into the chair, silent for a long time. I play with the lint on my leggings and look up when I hear him give off a soft chuckle. "Role model huh? So, I'm not a good role model?"

I let out a snort and give him the "really?" look.

He laughs but then lets it die down to where there's just a small smile on his face. "Your mom did so good raising you. I never expected you to forget the past, in fact I'm glad you aren't, but you don't know how good it feels to hear that you forgive me. I haven't had a good night's sleep in years. Almost 21 years to be exact."

I remember the story my mom told about catching him cheating with his boss's wife.

"But it's not about me. I'm down for whatever baby steps are. Whether if it's me being limited to only talking to you 30 minutes a month, which is not enough for me to be satisfied but I'll suck it up, or 30 minutes a year. I'm down, as long as I'm in your life."

I nod and look back at the view next to me. Just then my stomach growls so loud, I'm sure the people on the first floor heard it. I throw my hand over my stomach and suppress a blush.

"Someone's hungry I see. You want to go to the Waffle House down the street?" He stands up and walks toward his closet by the front door.

"I could go for an all-star," I say nonchalantly like my stomach didn't just give a whole speech.

He laughs and opens the closet door, "Let me just grab a jacket and shoes and we'll be on our way."

I wait for him to do these things and stand up when he asks "Ready?"

Since the Waffle House is only about an 8-minute walk, we ditch taking my car. I noticed while we walked down the street, he made sure that he was walking on the side the street was on, keeping me walking on the right side of the sidewalk.

I wonder if he was a gentleman like this when he was with my mom.

We finally get up to the Waffle House and it's not that busy, but there are a few people in here you can tell are regulars. We wait for someone to clean off a booth and sit in one on the left wall in front of what used to be a second exit to this place. I don't even look at my menu because I already know what I want, and my dad doesn't either.

My dad.

Is it safe to call him that yet? I shake off my thoughts and look at him.

"Why did you move out of Atlanta?" I still had more questions that needed answers.

He rubs his chin in thought.

"Well, once I finished my electrician apprenticeship here, I decided to venture out, see if I could discover who I was outside of what I knew. It was either North Carolina or Florida, but I figured Florida was too easy."

"Too easy?" I quirk and eyebrow.

"Yea, too much fun stuff to do and the weather was too beautiful. I wanted something that was the opposite." He shrugged, "That was just my thought process at the time."

"Well what do you think now?"

He leans back in the booth and out the window. After a beat, he looks back at me.

"I think it's time to come home. That's another thing I wanted to talk to you about. Now that we've reconnected, I want to start the process of moving back here. I've already talked to my wife about it and she's all for it, thankfully."

My curiosity takes control of my mouth, "What if she wasn't all for it?"

He gives an amused look at my bluntness, "Then I'd reconsider my choice in a wife."

My breath hitches and he leans forward, reaching across the table to grasp my hand.

"Jordan, I mean it when I say I love you and will do anything for you. If my wife can't accept that, then she's not the one for us."

Us.

All I can do is nod and he squeezes my hand then lets it go. The severity in his tone and seriousness in his eyes tells me he's being completely honest. That goes along way for me.

Our waiter comes to take our order and once she leaves, we're back talking.

"Tell me about you," he says, "your school, family, friends, boyfriend." He emphasizes boyfriend like he's a gossiping teenager.

"I'm a junior at Clark. I'm still best friends with Rylie and I have another best friend named Camille. I have the cutest little brother ever; his name is Jamie and he's 2 turning three this year. No boyfriend, not too crazy on relationships. Remember?"

I can't tell if he catches the underlying message in my relationship statement because he doesn't give off any reaction. Once I'm done talking, he nods and then smiles.

"So, your mom remarried?" He didn't say it in a hurt or jealous way, he was just genuinely curious.

"Yep, to Ben. He's been amazing to us since he came into our lives. I'm so grateful for him. He gave me Jamie." He stills a little at my words but then relaxes.

"I need to thank him one day for stepping up when I couldn't."

I nod in agreement. He looks me over again.

"You really light up when you talk about your family. Hopefully one day I can put that same light in you when you talk about me."

"Baby steps," I reply, and he nods widening his smile.

We eat until we can't anymore and after, I walk him back to his hotel. We exchange goodbyes and he tells me he's going to go back home in a couple of days, but if I need anything, he'll be on the next flight.

I drive home smiling and happy. That old door is finally closed and a new one is starting to open.

MALAKAI

I toss the football, Ant and Saiyr battling to catch it as they run. We've been tossing the ball around for a couple of hours just like we did those months ago.

This is my first time out of the house since I found out I lost the competition. I'm only out here because Ant and Saiyr literally dragged me out of my bed and wouldn't take no for an answer. The night I found out I lost, I went straight for the liquor cabinet at the house and drunk my sorrows away until I was just numb in every aspect.

I put my life on the line for my new dream. I worked so hard during this competition and it all got flushed down the toilet.

I didn't answer any calls or texts and avoided seeing my parents while I was cooped up in the house. I didn't check my emails, my social media, or anything outside of the clock that was in my room.

I threw the ball again.

"The hell kind of throw was that?" Saiyr yelled, watching the ball flail in the air and land a few feet in front of him. I shrugged and walked over to sit by my bag in the grass. Ant and Sai glanced at each other before taking cautious steps towards me. They sit on either side of me, propping their arms on their bended knees.

"You have to move forward from this bro."

Anthony is the first one to start this conversation. I'm not in the mood to talk about this right now. I ignore him and continue staring straight ahead.

"This wallowing shit isn't healthy," Saiyr chimes in.

More silence.

Anthony stands up and dusts off his pants. "Fine, if you want to waste your life away sulking, go ahead. I'll just take your cash prize for myself."

"I didn't fucking win the competition," I yell at him, "There is no fucking cash prize."

"There she is," Saiyr says grinning widely, "I was beginning to think you lost the ability to talk, Mrs. Drama Queen."

"You think me being upset about my dream being stomped out in front of me is me just being a drama queen?" I scoff at him. "I literally gave up my life for this. I put my heart and soul into this." I stand up and realize that I'm yelling.

My yelling isn't directed towards anyone in particular though. I'm just mad at the world right now and I can't help it.

I grab my bag off the ground and start walking home. I don't feel like dealing with them on the ride back, so I'd rather walk. I'm almost to the sidewalk when I hear them yelling behind me.

"So is the money up for grabs then?"

Why do they keep mentioning money? There is no money. I didn't win the competition so it's annoying that he keeps bringing it up.

"That $25,000 dollars could go towards my bachelor pad."

$25,000? What $25,000?

I stop walking and whirl around, yelling back at him. "What the fuck are you talking about bro?"

They run up to me and Anthony picks up where Saiyr left off.

"The competition, you got second place. That's what we've been trying to tell your hardheaded ass these past few days."

I drop my bag to the ground. There is no second place, there's only one winner.

"What are you talking about, there is no second place. They've never had a second place."

Anthony shakes his head at me and Saiyr kicks the ball around, busying himself. "After you stormed off, we went back inside to get our stuff to chase after you but then they said they had a few surprise announcements. They crowned your movie as second place and said you won $25,000. They said the movies that made it to the top four, besides the grand prize and second place winner, got $10,000 in cash prizes and a deal with a producing company to help shoot a commercial campaign or something. They said they should be sending out an email with more information."

I can't get my phone out of my pocket fast enough. I quickly go to my mail app and search frantically through all the junk promotion mail.

Finally, an email the night off the showcase stares me dead in my face. I open it and skim the information, going into more detail about what Anthony said.

"You're also Instagram famous now too bro," Saiyr said.

I turned off my notifications for all my social media apps, even the badges that told me how many unread notifications I had. I look at him confused and he just laughs at me. I go to my Instagram app and see the little notification in the right-hand corner popping up saying I had over 999+ notifications.

What the fuck?

I click on it and it shows I have thousands of new followers and comments on my most recent post. It was the group picture I took with the cast of the short film right before we left for the showcase.

Multiple congratulations, heart eyes, and comments from accounts with blue check marks next to their names.

"How?" I asked no one in particular. I looked up from my phone to see Anthony shrugging.

"Your buddy Matthew Weiss posted a preview of your movie on his page, along with a picture paparazzi took with you guys together. People even started following me and Saiyr too." Saiyr kicks the football up like he was playing actual fútbol and walked back up to us.

"I got so many thirsty DMs from fans it's crazy. Or should I say, I'm about to go crazy." He winks at me and I shake my head at him, still shocked at the amount of love I got on my page.

"Yea you're about to go crazy with diseases," Anthony retorts back.

"Wait, how did Matt get a video of my movie?" I'm still trying to process everything one by one.

"Oh yea, turns out he was one of the secret judges who voted to have your movie win. It was actually tied amongst the judges and the tie breaking judge was a dog lover, so they ended up voting for the one that won."

"How do you know this?" I ask him, quirking an eyebrow. "Matthew came up to us looking for you after the announcement. He said he wanted to talk to you and to tell you when we see you to contact him."

"We tried telling you earlier, but you were being a drama queen," Saiyr says punching my arm. I punch him back harder and he just smiles hard like a crazy person. "Anyway, you should hit Matthew up ASAP, it seemed like he had something more to say than just a few encouraging words."

I go to Matt's Instagram and slide in his DMs, apologizing for contacting him so late and ask what it is he wanted to talk about.

As I wait for his response, I think about how I let my emotions get me out of character and kept me from being grateful about even having the opportunity to participate in such a well know film competition. And then to make it to the top four, it's so surreal.

I need to learn how to not let my emotions get the better of me and take it out on everyone around me. It's funny looking back, I told my team that no matter what happens, we were all winners, but I didn't even act that way when I found out I wasn't the first-place winner. In reality, I won in so many different ways, and my actions weren't for nothing.

I gained experience, connections, exposure, and most of all a stronger love for my passion. Yes, I doubted myself, hell I even doubted my ability to create, but it was because I ultimately believed in myself, that I was able to keep going.

I'll be damned if I stop moving now.

Now that I've experienced that competition, I'm ready to take my talents to new heights. I'm ready for my new journey being the real Malakai Woods. Just you wait, I'm about to make a name for myself that'll never die.

"Sorry for being such a dick," I finally say to them as we load up in Anthony's car.

"It's all good bro, I know you were hurting," Anthony said as he closed his car door, starting the engine.

"Yea it's all good bro," Saiyr pat my back from where he sat in the middle behind us.

"It's not okay. You guys were trying to help me open my eyes and I refused to see what it is you wanted to show me."

Their silent response tells me I'm right and we just let it go after that. We ride to my house blasting music and talking about the plans they're dragging me to next week.

That night, I drift off into an easy, deep sleep with a smile on my face. The future is looking so bright right now it's blinding me.

Blinding.

Blinding.

Blinding.

I lift my head up from my hands and look to my left. As soon as she approaches me, I jump up from the bench and walk up to her.

"Whoa, you okay?" She asks me, looking concerned.

"More than okay, I got $25,000 from the competition. And I'm making a commercial for a major company, I don't know which one yet, they're sounding out the list later this week."

She stands there, eyes wide, then she puts on an all-out grin.

Gorgeous.

"Wow Mal, that's so amazing! I'm so happy for you!" She jumps up squealing and claps her hands. She places her hand briefly on my shoulder and I feel a shock at the contact. It feels like if you were to rub a balloon against your hair and touch it, creating a static shock.

"I met up with my Dad again," she says still smiling. I cock up an eyebrow, surprised by her choice of words.

"Dad?" I say with a deeper question lacing my words. She nods and I think she isn't going to answer my question, but she finally speaks.

"I don't know when I started calling him that again, but it feels…. right."

Seeing the happiness on her face caused my happiness to grow even more. "That's a huge step J, I'm really proud of you. Looks like you were able to close those doors after all."

"It was stubborn, but it budged and eventually shut." She replied chuckling.

"No, you were stubborn," I joke walking back to the bench. She follows and we sit side by side, careful not to touch each other.

"You're the stubborn one. You wouldn't believe I wasn't a wet dream porno girl when we first met."

I bust out laughing so hard she joins in with me.

"Hey, you can't blame me, you were, are, beautiful. Of course, I'd think you were a wet dream. But then you started talking and I quickly realized it wasn't at all."

She makes a playful shocked face, "What do you mean?"

"I mean the models in my dreams, one, don't talk, and two, don't give sass or attitude like you did." I laugh at her and she pouts making me laugh even more.

"You still like me though," she teased shaking her head at me and smiling.

"Yeah I love you."

Silence.

Shit. What the hell did I just say? I sit there horrified at the statement that just left my lips, and I can only imagine the look that's on her face. We sit there for a long beat, and awkward tension fills the air.

"You can't," she eventually says.

I thought her rekindling her relationship with her dad would change her views on love, but I guess not. I didn't realize it until it just came out of my mouth, but I do love this girl.

I actually do.

"Why not?" I ask, challenging her.

"Because love isn't real, and it fades." She gets up from the bench and starts to walk away from me. I don't know where she's trying to escape too because there's literally nowhere to hide.

"Says who? Who says that love isn't real?"

I follow her, willing her to accept what I said. She whirls around to me, and her voice has risen two octaves.

"Experience says. Life says. Besides, even though I've forgiven my dad, doesn't mean I forgot what happened. My life was shit. My mind was shit. My emotions were shit. And even though I'm getting my life on track, everything else is still complete and utter shit."

She turns back around and picks up her pace. I run after her and can't help the rise in my voice.

"Both of our lives have been shitstorms Jordan. You're not the only gray cloud floating around in the sky."

She stops walking and turns around teary eyed at me. I take slow steps toward her and now I'm a couple feet away. She's about to say something else, but I finish talking before she has the chance.

"But guess what? Every gray cloud has a silver lining and you," I take another step toward her so now our toes are a breath away from touching, "you are my silver lining. I love you Jordan Jameson. Shit, I'm in love with you and I know you feel the same. No matter what you try to convince yourself or how hard you try to suppress those feelings, I know. They'll always shine through. And with you, I want to shine bright forever."

I grab the back of her neck and pull her in towards me, clasping my lips over hers.

After a moment, she gives in and I feel her wrap her arms around me. That powerful electric energy surges between us and the heat I felt before burns even hotter as our lips move in sync, intertwined with one another.

I don't pull away from her though. I want to bask in this moment. I move my hand to her hair and take the other one to cup her cheek. Our tongues are now dancing, and my *heart thumps loudly in my chest. A bright white light engulfs us, and we are lifted off the ground, floating in the air. I feel as though my whole body was set on fire but at the same time, never want this feeling, this moment to end.*

But you don't always get what you wished for do you?

JORDAN

FOUR MONTHS LATER

"Make sure you bring that matching swimsuit set we have," Rylie yells from my room down the hall.

I'm in the bathroom packing my toiletry bag, making sure I don't forget any of the necessities for my morning and night routines.

I walk back into my room and see Rylie stuffing my suitcase with some outfits I folded and laid out. Cam is painting her toenails by my floor mirror, trying her best to make it look perfect. Our junior year had just ended a week ago and it was now officially our summer vacation.

We were taking a girl's trip to Las Vegas for multiple reasons. It was a late celebration for my birthday in January, Rylie's birthday in April, and the fact that we were about to start our last year in college soon.

Since we were all 21 now, we could go out to bars and drink publicly, having fun and turning up. I didn't really do anything for my birthday this year, just like every other year before that, so it's nice to take a little vacation and let loose for once.

Camille's birthday wasn't until July, but we were already planning a mini road trip for her. Somewhere closer to Atlanta.

Once I finish packing up all my things, we bring all our suitcases down so Ben can put them in the car. Rylie's parents came to see her off and are sitting on the couch in our living room.

Her mom has been even more overprotective of her lately, but I just chalk it up to the pregnancy hormones. We found out she was pregnant right after my birthday when she announced it to the whole family at a family dinner they hosted. To say Rylie was shocked is the understatement of the century. Once her initial shock wore off, she became excited to be a big sister and is now obsessed with all things baby.

Her mom stands up from the couch with help from Rylie's dad, and waddles over to us. Her 6-month pregnant belly protrudes out in front of her and it's so funny to see. I hope she has a boy so Jamie can have someone to play with as he grows up. My dad and his wife, Sylvia, are going to give birth to my baby sister, Aurora, any day now.

Since I'm going to be in Rory's life (yes, I already gave her a nickname), I know her, and Jamie would end up being close.

"Be safe Ry, I'll need you for when the baby comes," her mom jokes as she kisses her cheek.

"Yea yea, you just make sure you rest and don't stress yourself out too much. Can't have you going into an early labor." She kisses her mom back then goes to hug her dad. "Please keep an eye on her," she says to him and I'm starting to second guess who's really the parent here.

Cam's grandmother is in Italy with her new boy toy, Paolo, the bartender we met New Year's Eve. Apparently, he wasn't joking, and they've been steadily seeing each other for a while now. I can only hope to be as carefree as her when I get older.

Rylie's mom hugs me and Cam next, telling us to make sure we sit next to each other on our flights because people try to act crazy out here and she won't hesitate to use her gun. I asked her how she planned on getting on our flight, mid-air, with a pistol, and she told me not to worry about it.

Well now I'm worried about it.

My mom approaches me after I finish talking to Aunt Stacy, and she pulls me into a tight hug.

"Be safe honey, I'm so proud of you." I return her hug and squeeze her just as tightly,

"Thanks mom."

She reluctantly lets me go when Ben clears his throat behind us.

"The car is ready girls." He's holding Jamie in his arms because Jamie insisted on riding to the airport with us. I guess he wanted to see his big sister off. I'm curious to see the type of man he'll grow up to be.

"I'm ready," Rylie tells him as she tucks her head rest under her arm.

"Me too," Cam says beside her.

"I'm ready," I say lastly and walk towards the garage.

We all pile into the car, me in the front passenger, Cam behind Ben, Rylie in the middle seat, and Jamie in his car seat behind me. The whole ride to the airport was Rylie and Cam talking about the places they want to go in Las Vegas, the celebs they hope to run into, and the money they're ready to spend.

I just stare out the window, my gaze fixated on the sky. It's extra cloudy today, and for some reason, when I stare up there, I feel a twinge of sadness deep within. I don't know why or where it stems from, but I can't shake it. It isn't until Ben pulls up to the curb that leads us to where we need to go at Hartsfield, that I focus on the here and now.

Ben rounds the car and opens our doors for us. I get out and open the side with Jamie's car seat so

I can say bye to him. I unbuckle his belt and pull him into a hug.

"Bye Buu," I whisper in his ear, "I promise to bring back a Spider-man toy from Hollywood. Special Collector's Edition."

Even though he doesn't fully understand the importance, he still gets excited for it all the same. I laugh at his huge bug eyes and lopsided grin. I buckle him back in the car seat and step back so I'm now on the curb.

Ben pulled all our suitcases out of the trunk, and I do a once over to make sure I'm not forgetting anything.

"All set kiddos?" Ben asks us and we all nod, excited to start this trip. We're only in Vegas for a little under a week, so we're trying to make the most out of this vacation.

"Alright, bring it in before I cry and have to get carried out of this airport."

We all laugh and pull into a group hug with Ben. He kisses our foreheads, mine a little longer than the rest, and lets us go.

"I'll call you when we land," I say waving to him and turn to walk into the airport.

After we go through the lengthy process of checking our bags in, going through security, and Cam having a bathroom emergency, we are now sitting outside of our gate, waiting for them to call our flight. We still have about 30 minutes until we have to board, and Rylie is asleep in the seat next to me, leaning against a dozing off Cam. It's 4:00 am so I don't blame them for being sleepy, but I'm wide awake.

I figure I'd call my dad, even though he probably won't be awake. He text me an hour ago telling me to call him when I got to the airport, and now is the perfect time.

It rings three times then I hear his groggily voice on the other end of the line.

"Jordan? Is everything okay? Did you make it?" I chuckle softly at the worry in his voice.

"I'm fine Dad, I was just calling to tell you we made it to the airport. Boarding in 30 minutes. How's Sylvia?" I hear him sitting up in what I assume his bed and curse myself for keeping him up longer with my questions.

"She's doing as good as she can be. She's getting all of her rest and has her overnight bag ready, thanks to your suggestions."

"Anytime. Anyway, I was just calling to tell you I'm here, I don't want to keep you up, I know you have to go to work. I'll text you when we land." I prepare my headphones so I can listen to music as soon as I get off the phone.

"Okay J be safe and observant. I love you."

"Yea, you too," I reply and hang up. We've been talking on the phone a lot more lately and I've even had a few conversations with Sylvia, his wife. I haven't met her in person yet, but they're moving to Atlanta in a couple of weeks, and we're hoping Rory stays in her belly until then.

From what I've witnessed, Sylvia is a chill lady and me and her get along well. Let's just hope it stays that way when she starts to see more and more of me. I'm still not at the point where I can tell my dad I love him, but I'm guessing that'll come with time.

I play games on my phone until it's time to board. I wake up the girls and we walk onto the plain with our carry-on bags hanging from our shoulders.

Vegas here we come!

MALAKAI

"I can't tell you how much I needed this weekend getaway," I say as we pull out of Saiyr's driveway.

"I bet. You've been working nonstop this whole year, it's time to relax a little," Ant replies behind the driver's seat.

Saiyr is starting off our road trip by driving the rental car we picked up earlier this morning.

"This is about to be the most fun you boys have ever had in life," Saiyr says flashing his megawatt grin. His eyes are hiding behind his Ray Bans, but I know mischief is swimming all in his irises.

Ant and Saiyr planned this long miniature road trip to Vegas a month or so ago and waited until the semester was over and I was done filming the commercial for Starbuck's summer campaign, to finalize it.

After I accepted my cash prize from winning the competition, I chose to work with Starbuck's among the list of companies willing to hire the film participants to give myself a challenge.

You can't grow without a little obstacles, right?

They ended up loving what I did and said they were going to contact me to help them work on a future project and that I should look out for an email from them soon.

I'm also working on something top secret and exciting as hell with Matthew Weiss. I'm somewhat Instagram and Tik Tok famous I guess because I am now verified on both and still don't know why.

My mom and I are also collaborating on a project that'll be released in two different parts. We're cowriting a book, and I'm producing a short film version that we will then release as a surprise to our amazing supporters.

I have so many things going on in my life right now, that this vacation is well needed. It's supposed to be a bro's only weekend, and even Saiyr swore off girls for this entire trip, no matter how good they look. He said he won't even try to get their numbers. Let's see how long that statement holds true.

Ant has never been girl crazy. Come to think of it, all the girls he's ever "been with" or "dated" have all approached him and he just complied, showing half interest. He's never pursued a girl in his life, and I never really noticed.

I should ask him about that later.

The drive is about two and a half hours with traffic, so it's a good little way away. They wouldn't tell me what hotel we're staying at, but knowing them, it was going to be nice. Probably crazy expensive too.

After an hour, Saiyr claims he has to pee, and we stop at a gas station. We use this time to pick up some snacks and switch drivers.

In the gas station, Saiyr hits on a girl at the fro-yo section and I just shake my head.

"What? The bro's trip didn't technically start yet, so I didn't break the rules," he says as we walk out the gas station together.

"The bro's trip started the second we all got in the car and started heading to the hotel," Ant shot back at him.

We drive an hour and sometime more before we are pulling up to our hotel.

JORDAN

"Wow! This place is huge!" Rylie says as she skydives into the huge plush king-sized bed in her room in the hotel.

We're staying at the Wynn Las Vegas resort and it's the most beautiful thing I've ever seen. Rylie's dad footed a hefty bill for this room.

Our suite isn't even a suite, it's a villa fit for a queen.

Literally.

We have two bedrooms, floor to ceiling windows with remote controlled curtains, a huge living room area, and a whole mini bar. I can't even describe the amount of jaw dropping things I see in this room.

Their exclusive nightclub was where Drake did his residency in Vegas. *The* Aubrey Graham. I was bound to run into a few celebrities on this trip.

"Who's sleeping with who?" I ask them as we finish our grand tour of the villa with the staff member. I wouldn't even mind sleeping on the couch the whole trip, just so I can wake up to the gorgeous view of downtown Las Vegas. And the living room too.

"Honestly, I can take the couch and you guys can get the bedrooms since it's your birthday celebrations," Cam says as she looks around the mini bar in the corner.

"But your birthday is in a couple months so it's your birthday celebration too," Rylie points out.

"How about we just rotate between who gets the bedrooms and who sleeps on the couch?" I suggest.

"So, we all three switch between the different options? I like it," Rylie says nodding her head.

"I'm down," Cam says, and we settle it that way. After a few seconds, she asks a new question.

"So, who gets the couch first?"

◌ ◌ ◌

After we get settled in our rooms and wake up from our naps, I go downstairs to the lobby to ask the hotel staff for more information about the things to do around here.

Once I develop an itinerary with help from the girl behind the help desk, I start to make my way back to the elevators.

Just as I'm walking off, I hear high-pitched squeals and see a crowd of people rushing to somewhere behind me. I turn my head to see what all the commotion was about, but I'm met with a wall of people blocking my path.

It must be some big shot celebrity or something coming to check in. I give an audible gasp out loud.

What if it's Drake?

I stretch my neck to try and see over the paparazzi that formed and the flashing lights to get a glimpse of the A-lister. I give up once my attempts are unsuccessful and continue my journey back to my room.

I'll have plenty more opportunities to see celebrities later during the trip.

"Bring on the grown men!" Rylie says as we exit the elevator to head to the XS Nightclub in the hotel. It was a Friday night and we were ready to party with the best of them.

The place is packed to the wall and we've already seen a celebrity over by the bar. Some actor from one of those crime shows I've never seen. Apparently, a lot of other people have seen it though by the way he had a crowd around him.

It must suck being a celebrity because there's no such thing as personal space.

We order a few drinks from the bar once it's our turn and throw them all back, prepared to get loose.

Maneuvering our way to the dance floor, we find an open space and just start shaking everything, letting ourselves surrender to the music.

My legs get tired after dancing for 45 minutes straight and I tell them I'm going to go find the bathroom. They come with me since we were still young women visiting a place we weren't sure of.

On my way to the bathroom, I stumble in my heels a little bit and bump into a guy next to me. He catches me before I fall even further and helps me right myself back up again.

"Sorry," I say shyly looking up at him, "I don't normally wear heels."

He gives me a reassuring smile and releases his hands from me, "Don't worry about it. You okay though?" I nod and start to walk past him.

"Thank you," I say, and I continue my walk to the bathroom.

He was really cute, and I know Rylie will give me a mouthful once I get into the bathroom.

I'm not here for her relationship advice though.

MALAKAI

"Are you sure this is the right place?" Ant asks as I pull into the parking lot of the Wynn Las Vegas hotel.

"Yea, according to the GPS. Why? What's wrong with it?" I pull into the closest parking spot I could find and turn the car off.

"It just seems…*too* nice."

I laugh and get out the car. "How is it *too* nice? Didn't you guys look at the pictures online for here?"

"Yea but you know how sometimes, if a price is too good and you look at the pictures, they look equally as good. But when you come to check-in in person, the place is a shit-sty." Saiyr butted in. Anthony nods and points at him, showing that that's exactly what he was going to say.

"I'm going to go check us in, you guys coming or are you going to stay in the car?"

They mumble trying to figure out what they wanted to do, and I just ended up walking off because clearly, they didn't want to come with me if they had to think it over.

I walk in and stand in line waiting to check in. I check my phone, and respond to a few messages from my parents, Matt, and my new manager.

A group of girls come up to me with shy expectant looks on their faces. I smile at them and go back to replying to messages. After a couple of minutes, I feel their gazes still on me and look up to see they are indeed, still staring at me. I look around, trying to figure out if they're looking for someone else because their staring was getting weird.

"Um, can I help you?" I finally say.

"Are you Malakai Woods?" One of the girls ask. They look about 14 years old and I look around their heads for their parents.

"How do you-," I start to ask but my question is interrupted with high-pitched squealing.

"OH MY GOSH! I TOLD YOU IT WAS HIM!" The girl with the blond ponytail said to her friends.

"Can I have your autograph!? And a selfie?" The shorter brunette asked me.

"Can you follow me on Instagram?" The third one asked and I put my hands up in protest, completely uncomfortable and unsure what to do in this situation.

They were causing a scene and other people were starting to recognize me as well. Soon enough, there was a small crowd of people around me, and paparazzi flashing their cameras all around. I take pictures with more people than I can count, and my hands cramp up from signing my name on so many things. Even the hotel staff were fans of me and ended up upgrading my room free of charge.

Once I found an opening, I made a beeline for the car.

As I approach, Ant and Saiyr stare wide-eyed at the group of girls running behind me and hurry up and hop back in the car as I slide into the passenger seat. We pull out of the parking lot fast as hell and decide to circle the block a few times to make sure the crowd of girls was gone by the time we came back.

We ended up having to call the hotel to have them get security to escort us to our room.

"Where are all the ladies at? Can I at least dance with some?" Saiyr asks in his seat next to me.

We're at XS Nightclub tonight kicking off our bro's weekend with a sloppy drunk, can't-remember-what-I-did hangover style night.

"It can still be a bros night if we all have fun with our own lady friend," he adds, thinking he could convince me to let up on the no girls rule.

"It's funny, I just ran into a group of girls on my way back from the bathroom that I know you'd like," Ant says as he approaches us at our seats.

"They were gorgeous too, and get this, they were a group of three," he wiggles three fingers in the air, taunting Saiyr.

He groans loudly next to me, trying not to listen to what Ant is saying.

"One of them literally fell into my lap."

Saiyr jumps up, picks his cup up from the table in front of him, and downs the rest of his drink. "I'm going to find them, fuck this."

He disappears into the crowd behind us, leaving Ant and I behind laughing. We down our drinks then go to find him.

When we finally do spot him, he's on the dance floor grinding on a 45-year old looking woman who was probably a soccer mom of 3 and had a faithful husband waiting back at home. This man worked fast when it came to females.

Ant and I glide across the dance floor and rescue him from possibly going back to her hotel room when we fall asleep.

He doesn't ever find the girls Ant was talking about earlier, and the rest of our night is a blur filled with bottomless shot glasses, and me eventually giving in and us all grinding on our own girl, careless and carefree about what the people around us are doing.

I needed this trip.

A moment of release and to forget all the stresses in my everyday life. If only I could have a moment like this every night, minus the alcohol and girls.

Just a moment where all the problems fade away and it's just a calm, peaceful, silence.

JORDAN

We wave bye to Cam as she rides off in her uber towards the airport. She's leaving Las Vegas a day earlier than us because she has to work and couldn't request off any more time until her vacation.

Doesn't make sense to me either, but we're going to let it slide.

"Where are you trying to eat breakfast Jor?" Rylie turns and asks me as we walk back into the hotel lobby.

"There was a little diner up the street that I saw when we were coming back from visiting the

Grand Canyon the other day." I point out and jerk my thumb in the direction the diner was located.

"Trying to go after we get ready? It's our last full day in Las Vegas and I want to make a few more memories before we have to get back to reality."

I hitch one shoulder up, not opposed to her thought process., "I'm down."

We walk into the diner and the staff behind the counter tells us to pick a seat anywhere. We choose a booth by the front windows, giving us a clear view of the street in front of us.

"We definitely have to come back here soon," Rylie says after we order our breakfast. "We should make this an annual thing," she adds, suddenly excited by her idea.

"I think coming here every year would ruin the beauty of this place. It'll just get boring," I state honestly.

Her face falls and I quickly try to put her back in her happy mood, "But I'm definitely down for this being our go to vacation splurge spot when we're in dire need of a getaway." She smiles again and I smile back.

We start eating our food and the bell chimes over the entrance of the door, telling us new people walked in searching for a hearty breakfast.

I glance up and recognize one of the three guys as the one that I fell on the other night at the club.

I start to feel this strange energy crackle in the air.

I quickly avert my eyes and they land on this beautiful man behind him whose eyes are already locked on me. I immediately look down at my food and keep eating so I don't end up staring at this guy.

Whoa, what was that? Why was he looking at me with familiarity? And why did he feel a little familiar to me too?

Rylie and I continue to eat and talk, but my eyes occasionally glance at the Adonis who took a booth with his friends on the opposite side of the diner. We were still in eye view of each other, and I'm starting to think he did that on purpose.

I need to get out of here before he thinks my glances are an invitation for him to talk to me.

MALAKAI

We wake up starving, stomach's the emptiest we've ever felt. My hangover causing me to act sluggish and a little off kilter as I walk to the bathroom to dry heave a little more.

We had too much fun at the club last night and it showed in how fucked up we looked this morning.

"I need food," Saiyr called from the floor by the bathroom door. He looked as though he tried to crawl to the toilet last night to throw-up, but he just couldn't make it.

"Food from where?" Ant asks, half of his body dangling off the bed, other half holding on for dear life.

"I can look one up," I suggest to them both and they wait patiently as I read out some options.

"Oh, there's a diner just up the street from here, and it's in walking distance," I say jerking my thumb towards the direction of the diner.

I eventually get them to get up and get ready so we can fill our stomachs and start to feel less shitty. Ant pushes the door of the diner open and we greet the hostess. Some weird warm energy pulls my gaze, and my eyes land on a beautiful girl sitting at a booth a couple of feet away. I can't stop staring at her and she eventually meets my eyes then looks down at her food just as fast.

I must look like a crazy person just staring at her like this, but I can't help it.

What was that comforting energy? And why did it cause some memories to try and pull to the forefront of my mind?

Memories I still can't grasp.

Even though the energy was inviting, I need to steer clear of this girl. The no girl rule was put in place for a reason. I don't need a girl I didn't know causing me to break that rule.

I choose a booth in the back so I can keep my eyes off her and keep my distance, so I don't seem like a total creeper.

It doesn't work because the booth that I choose gives me a perfect view of her and our eyes keep meeting each other by chance.

I need to talk to this girl before she leaves, not only because she gives me a vague sense of familiarity and I need to figure out why, but because my curiosity is peaked.

Plus, I need to stroke my subconscious so it can stop fantasizing about a relationship with her. I don't even know her, and I already want to see where it's going to go.

JORDAN

I don't know who this Adonis thinks he is, but I'm going to need him to stop staring at me.

"Helloooo, Earth to Jordan," Rylie says flapping her dry pancake in my face. I snap out of my thoughts and look back at Rylie. "What's gotten into you?" she asks me when we make eye contact.

"Sorry, that guy just looks very familiar to me," I say, "I can't pinpoint where I've seen him, but I've definitely seen him."

Rylie gives me a confused look and looks over her shoulder. She looks back at me with a devious smile on her lips.

"I don't know where you would know this man from, but if you did know him, why the hell have you never mentioned him. He's hot as fuck." She looks back at him again, probably trying to assess his features.

"By the looks of it, he seems to recognize you and wants to reacquaint himself by first, ripping off your panties and tying them around his head."

I almost choke on the water I'm sipping, and Rylie starts laughing at me.

"Why don't you just go up and talk to him? Neither of you can stop staring at each other so you might as well. Besides, we leave tomorrow morning so you can have a little fun with him to finish off your amazing vacation." She winks at me and I just roll my eyes at her.

"Yea right," I say, "Even if I *wanted* to entertain someone, I've never done it before, so I wouldn't even know how to start."

"Oh J.J., that's what I'm here for. To help you my sweet child."

I shake my head, "I'm okay. Besides, I've made amazing memories already with you guys. I don't need any more with some random beautiful man I don't even know. He could have some diseases or something else seriously wrong with him." I let out on a laugh.

"Suit yourself," she says shrugging and we continue to talk about something else. Me and Adonis make eye contact from time to time as we continuously glance at each other across the diner.

A couple hours later, we're packing up our food in to-go boxes and standing up to head out the door.

"Hey, wait, I have to pee really quickly, do you need to too?" Rylie says as she puts her bag on the table.

"No, I'm okay, I'll wait for you outside," I tell her and grab her bag. I head for the door while she heads for the bathroom.

Outside, I pace back and forth, trying to figure out where the hell I know the Adonis man-child from because it's really bothering me that I can't remember. I hear the bell over the door chime behind me, and I turn around expecting it to be Rylie, but it isn't.

Not in the slightest.

The Adonis man-child from inside stands before me with broad shoulders, a shy boy grin, and his hand rubbing on the back of his neck like he's nervous.

"Can I help you?" I ask him confused.

"Hey sorry, um…it's just," he takes his hand away from the back of his neck and cocks his head to the side, "do I know you from somewhere?"

I lift an eyebrow at him and mimic him by tilting my own head to the side.

"I'm not sure, do you?"

He chuckles and shakes his head. "I guess not. You just seem very familiar to me."

I nod my head slowly, confused as to what to say next.

"Do you live around here?" he finally asks.

"No, I'm only visiting. I'm from Atlanta."

"Oh cool, I've always wanted to visit there. They are considered the Hollywood of the south after all." I smile awkwardly and look around, willing Rylie to hurry the hell up so this man can stop talking to me.

I mean he is beyond gorgeous, but I just opened my heart to accept love from another human being who isn't my family. Meaning, I finally decided to give the relationship thing a try.

I'm not going to have my first relationship be an out of state one.

"Where are you from?" I ask to fill the awkwardness in the air.

"San Diego. I'm just here visiting too with my friends inside," he points his thumb towards the window of the diner. "I'm Malakai by the way," he extends his hand to me and I step forward to shake it.

"I'm Jo-," I start to say but my speech is immediately cut off once I place my hand inside of his. A strong warmness fills inside of me and my vision is suddenly filled with pictures flickering past like I was watching a long movie.

Memories start flooding back into my mind.

The clouds.

The never-ending sunset.

The bench.

The advice.

The friendship.

Him.

The love.

Love.

MALAKAI

My eyes go wide as the memories catch up to reality, and I'm looking the one person I never thought I'd see, in the face.

It was her.

She was here.

In front of me.

I was touching her.

"Jordan!?"

ACKNOWLEDGEMENTS

I want to start by saying writing a book is not easy in the slightest. It's probably one of the most challenging things I've ever done in my life. This book took over my life and was all I could think about for months. It's still all I can think about even as I type this. I was dedicating late nights and early days to finishing this and I'm so proud of the final product.

I want to thank my number one support system, which is my family. If I didn't have them in my corner, cheering me on during this whole process, this book probably would've never come about.

I want to first thank my fiancé for being by my side the whole way. Thank you for those times where you kept me on my toes and on top of my work with your "did you write today?" or "how many words do you have?" and your "did you hit your goal?". Your support doesn't go unnoticed and I hope you know how much I love and appreciate you.

I also would like to thank my amazing mother for believing in me and telling me I will go far with my work. I know I can always count on you to be in my corner and to do everything in your power to see me succeed.

To my brother, I want to say thank you for all of your plot suggestions and character scene suggestions. Thank you for asking me every day how my book is going and being impatient when it comes to wanting to read it. I hope it has met or even exceeded your expectations.

Finally, I want to thank all of you, the readers. Thank you for giving little ol' me a chance and taking a risk in buying a book that will forever mean the world to me. Thank you for your honest reviews, thoughts, and opinions, whether positive or negative. I take everything in stride and your words will help to improve my material, so my next story can be ten times better than my last.

Thank you, thank you, thank you!

ABOUT THE AUTHOR

Imani Lewis is a senior in college, currently pursuing a degree in Marketing. When she isn't writing unfinished first drafts, she is creating music and binge watching her favorite shows with her fiance. To learn more about Imani, follow her on Instagram, Twitter, and Facebook @ManiTheAuthor.

395

TITLES BY IMANI

On A Cloudy Day

Clear Skies (Coming Spring 2020)

Preview of

Clear Skies

Coming Spring 2020

jordan

"If you don't pick up the phone to call this man, I *promise* you I'll come back home, and that's something you don't want," Rylie says to me on the phone via FaceTime.

She sounds like my mom and I just groan as I throw myself back into my bed, staring at the ceiling. We both share a three-bedroom apartment together downtown, but she's barely home since she spends the night with Zavier 95 percent of the time. So really, I live alone, which believe it or not, gets extremely lonely.

After a minute, I finally lift myself back up and bring my phone to my face so I can look at her.

It's a shame that after being together for this long that I'm still scared to call my boyfriend.

"What if he thinks I'm being clingy?" I whine to her, looking for sympathy and comfort but she just shakes her head.

I mean this is my first ever boyfriend and I'm not trying to mess it up by throwing myself at him all the time. I've come to find out that relationships weren't as easy as the movies make them seem. I just wish they came with an instruction manual for dummies like me.

"Seriously, you guys have been dating for over a year and you're just now worried about being clingy?" She laughs at me and I just groan even louder repeating the same action as before.

I haven't been able to speak to him much lately because he's been so busy with work. When we do talk though, he apologizes and makes it up to me the best way he knows how.

By ordering us both a pizza and watching a movie with me via facetime.

He orders the same pizza as me every time so it could feel like we were sharing. It took me a while to accept what I feel for him and I'm so glad I did because I've been the happiest I've ever been since then.

"Seriously, if you need me to come over I will," Rylie says in a serious tone.

"No no, that's okay. Besides I don't want you to mess up your 'bonding time' with Cyn."

Cyn, short for Cynthia, was Rylie's one-year old little sister. Her mom gave birth last Halloween and ever since, Rylie has made it a point to be in her life. She was a firecracker just like her big sister and gave a hyper Jamie a run for his money.

At times, he would hide behind me when she came over because she played so rough. My little sister Rory, short for Aurora, is the same age as Rylie's but she was born in August. She is the opposite of Cyn in that she's more reserved. She's a little on the shy side and would rather play alone, with Jamie, or me, than anyone else.

My Dad and my stepmom moved back to Atlanta right before she was born and I visit every weekend with my little brother, Jamie, who was growing too fast for comfort. He's 3 years old now and is starting Pre-K next month. My mom was going to wait until the next school year started, but he's advancing fast and can talk in complete sentences now. I even taught him how to write his full name.

I like to take him to visit Rory because even though they aren't blood siblings, they're both my world and I want them to grow up close.

"Okay but if you need me, you know I'm here for you," Rylie emphasizes before I wave her off.

"I'm fine Ry, I love you. Kiss Cyn for me." She says her byes and we hang up.

Once the call ends, I go to my message threads and smile at the most recent message that prompted the call with Rylie.

It was a selfie of Malakai smiling on set in his director's chair, carefree and even more handsome than when I last saw him.

He was working with Matt (Matthew Weiss for those who don't know) on a secret film project that no one is supposed to know the details on, but he told me about it when he found out. The message under the picture says "Wish you were here, missing you terribly. I love you."

I smile at his words and a spark goes through me when I look at his face. We're in a long-distance relationship and that has been such a struggle. Wanting to be cuddled up with him and just to be in his presence every day is hard because I can't do those things. Him being three hours behind also caused difficulties, but I think we know how to handle that by now.

Going from never wanting a relationship, to being full on in love with someone is almost like a culture shock. I'm treading in unknown waters and my only lifeguard is my boyfriend.

The last time I flew to see him was in July and it is now December, almost Christmas time. We both graduated college this past May and he surprised me by flying over to see me graduate.

Due to the buzz his short film received from the movie competition, he's been in high demand, making films and writing commercials for big name brand companies.

I, on the other hand, didn't know what I wanted to do for the longest time. One day I realized, there's so much beauty in this world that has yet to be discovered and I wanted to be the one to discover it. Because of this realization, I now do freelance photography work that takes up majority of my time.

What I like about my job is that I can work on my own time and pick up jobs that I feel suit me. Malakai is busy 5 and sometimes 6 days out the week, whereas I'm usually busy only 3 unless I'm doing a big job that requires more shoots and longer editing periods.

During the week, I don't like to bother him while he's working so I usually wait for him to call me, but I'm missing him so much right now and I just want to hear his voice.

I glance at the time and it's almost 3:00pm, so that means he should be going on a lunch break soon. This thought gives me enough courage to pick up my phone and call.

I don't know why I'm so nervous because it's not like he never wants to talk. In fact, he always walks away from set to make time to talk to me. He said I was the most important person to him, and that no one can stop him from wanting to hear my "sexy rasp".

I smile and press the call button.

After a few rings, he picks up and I hear him shuffling to probably put his Airpods in.

"Hey baby," he says in his smooth, sweet, sugary voice. My insides melt at this sound and I squeeze my thighs together to calm down my excitement.

"Hey, how's filming going?" I say trying to not sound like an excited teenager.

"It's going," he says letting out a sigh, "It's just the actors are having a hard time relaying the message I need them too."

I hear him give an order to someone in the background before he gives his attention back to me.

"Hey, can I call you back later? Today's going to be a long day and I need to focus so we aren't filming at all hours of the night. Talk to you later. Love you."

Click.

I bring the phone away from my ear and just stare at it.

Did he just hang up on me?